Second Courses

A MIDLIFE SECOND CHANCE ROMANCE

ROBIN BLACKBURN

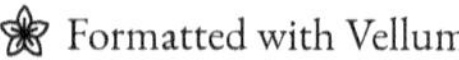 Formatted with Vellum

Chapter One

Burn it to the ground.

That's what I'd like to do.

Not metaphorically. Like taking down the patriarchy or dismantling those unattainable beauty standards for aging women.

I mean, *set actual fire to it*. With gasoline. Watch it go up in flames. Until there's only ashes and the remnants of memories.

I'm not going to do that, however. No matter how much I want to.

Because...prison.

But a girl can dream.

Shaking away those thoughts, I let out a laugh, one that glitches between maniacal and worrisome, and look at what lies before me.

David's. God, how I hate saying his name, even if only in reference to this restaurant.

Before David and I purchased it, before it became David's, an homage to the selfish prick, it had been a seafood place and then an Italian restaurant, neither of which was able to make a go of it. The restaurant business is not for the weak, even in Lake George, a town known for its tourists, who flock here each summer in their beat-up minivans and BMWs. Failure is more prevalent than success. (Like my marriage, one could say.) Due to someone else's misfortune, we bought this place for a steal. And David capitalized on his *Crown of the Kitchen* success to make this another culinary darling in his portfolio of trendy restaurants. Now, thanks to his dalliance with *Mindi,* a name that continues to pass my lips with equal parts disdain, disgust, and derision—and my stubborn streak—I'm holding the keys.

Like our—*my*—house here, it has a wraparound porch with outside seating, allowing you to look out over the lake and see the mountains to the east. There are docks for guests who come by boat to dine in the summertime. On the inside, because it is a house converted into a restaurant, there are several rooms, some big, some small, creating an intimate dining experience. In total, we can seat about 120 people.

It is utterly charming and loved by everyone who eats here.

Or it was, when David was at the helm.

Will guests feel the same way now that it's my restaurant? Someone with the culinary expertise of an eight-year-old? I mean, I know the difference between chives and onions, but a chiffonade versus a julienne? No, don't ask me to expound on those. Come on, my signature dish is reservations. But David didn't marry me for my cooking skills. Right now, I'm questioning why he married me at all.

Was it so that I could bankroll his restaurants after his *Crown of the Kitchen* win?

This is not the time to get caught up in the self-doubts that have ruled my life for the last few months.

Self-doubts about my worthiness. *If David didn't want me, why would anyone else?*

About my judgment. *How could I not have seen the signs?*

About my identity. *Who am I if I'm no longer David Montero's wife?*

Pushing those thoughts to the side, I glance around the parking lot. I can't help but roll my eyes as I see the big wooden sign emblazoned with *"David's"* on it. I'm unsure how heavy it is, but I make a mental note to see if I can take it down and drag it to the dumpster before leaving. *Ciao David's!*

I take the keys out of my purse and make my way to the main entrance. While the parking lot is cleared, nobody has shoveled the sidewalks, and I struggle to open the door with all the snow piled in front of it, but finally, I squeeze through.

I feel along the wall to flip on the lights. Click! Nothing happens. Still dark. I try several more times. Click! Click! Click! My frustration bubbles to the surface, as evidenced by my frantic flipping of the switch.

I take a deep breath.

Relax, Lynds. Maybe the breakers got tripped during one of the storms.

Using the flashlight on my phone, I make my way back to the utility room, proud of myself that I even remember where it is and that I thought to check. Score one for me!

I open the panel; everything appears to be on. But, to make sure, I flip all the breakers back and forth and make my way down the unilluminated hall to turn on the kitchen lights.

Once again...nothing.

What the hell is going on? Why is there no power?

Hmmm...could yesterday's snow have knocked out power here? No, the stoplights were working, and the lights were on at the convenience store next door when I pulled in.

All right, let's call the power company.

I do a quick Google search to find their number, and

I'm soon on the line with Rita. She has a voice that customer service managers dream of, and says she'll be happy to help.

"Can you provide me with the address of the business?"

"Sure, it's 4430 Lakeshore Drive, Bolton Landing." I'm consciously working to keep annoyance out of my voice, knowing how dependent I am on Rita.

"Thanks, gimme a sec, and I'll pull it up."

While Rita clacks away on her keyboard, I start pacing—partly because I'm anxious, partly because it's freezing inside.

"Um, could you provide me with your name?" Rita sounds all business now, unlike a minute ago when she seemed eager to help me.

"I'm Lyndsay Leach-Montero." For now. "I'm the owner of David's."

Restaurant name change. Must. Happen. Today.

"Ms. Montero, the power to David's was turned off two days ago. I can see in the notes that the request came from a David Montero." The last sentence comes out not quite a statement, not quite a question, and with more than a hint of curiosity.

That son of a bitch.

"That asshole is my soon-to-be ex-husband."

Annoyance is back, and Rita doesn't know what to say.

"Okay...He is listed as the current owner of David's," she says with extreme caution.

Letting out a deep breath, in hopes of exhaling my exasperation, I continue, "I apologize for my language, Rita. This has nothing to do with you. He and I have an agreement. I'm now the owner of David's due to our impending divorce. And now I'm standing in a freezing cold restaurant without any power, and I'm a little pissed off. If I don't get the power back on, I'm going to have busted pipes." Busted pipes will create a whole slew of new problems, from plumbing repairs to new tile and carpeting, which I need to avoid. I'm lucky they haven't frozen yet. Was this his plan all along? To sabotage me?

Inhaling a breath and a kinder, gentler voice, I ask, "How do we go about getting the power back on here?"

"Oh, honey, I've got one of those exes, too. Don't worry about your language." I feel the sincerity in her voice and an instant connection. I hope this means she can help me. She continues, "Do you have proof that the restaurant is yours? If you do, you can email it to me, and I can turn it on from here."

Proof? She needs proof. That's understandable. You don't want to turn the power on for just anyone. Of course, David should not have turned the power off. Dick move.

"Rita, I don't have any proof on me. Is there anything else that can be done to get power restored?"

"I'm sorry, but my hands are tied. You understand, don't you?"

Yes, I understand. I'm not happy, but I understand.

"Let me call my lawyer. If I can get you a copy of the agreement stating that I am the current owner, will that be enough proof?"

"More than enough. Send me that, and I can get it all turned back on lickety-split!"

She makes it sound so easy. Of course, on her end, it is. I, on the other hand, will have to call Rebecca and see if she can email it to Rita because, like an idiot, I don't have a saved copy of this agreement on my fucking phone, all so I can get the damn power turned back on.

I can do this. It's not like I'm opening the restaurant today. I ask Rita for her email address and thank her for her assistance, telling her someone will be in touch shortly. In her ever-so-chipper voice, she tells me she'll be there until five p.m. and hopes to hear back from me, casually adding that David is a jerk for doing this.

Couldn't agree more, Rita.

Then I call Rebecca.

Her secretary, hearing the anxiousness in my voice, puts me through immediately. Thank God for small favors. I explain what's happening and what I need, and Rebecca assures me that the restaurant will have power within the hour.

That's my tiger.

The day I walked into her office and hired her, I remarked to Chloe how Rebecca and I were polar opposites. She was all order and control, and I was all uncertainty and unraveling. I was a woman used to disappearing into the background while David let the spotlight shine upon him, never really wanting to share it with me. Rebecca claims attention innately, holding her place, claiming her presence. And the differences don't stop there. Our physical appearances might as well have made us yin and yang. I'm five eight and have dark brown eyes and shoulder-length black hair with streaks of gray throughout. I wear glasses, and while I'm what most would consider attractive, I'm not a stand-out-in-the-crowd attention grabber. Even at just five two, Rebecca is that and then some. She may look like an adorable calico kitten with her bright green eyes, her complexion like the Waterford China we received when we married, and copper hair that glimmers in the sunlight, but don't be fooled. She's fierce, and that fierceness radiates from her. And I'm glad she's my lawyer, not his.

I head back out to the Jeep, where I blast the heat, hoping to thaw my toes. Stupid Stuart Weitzman boots. I was dressed appropriately for the weather—except for my feet. I went for fashion there, a mistake I won't make again.

After a few moments, the feeling returns to my feet, and while I'm still angry at the power situation—or lack of power situation—I've released my fury singing to an angry Alanis Morissette anthem, and I'm ready to tackle another project.

Taking down the David's sign.

It's a large, two-sided wooden sign, about four feet by four feet, easily seen from the road. It was handmade by a local artisan and fits in perfectly with the outdoor aesthetic David created. In large script, it says "David's," and immediately below it, it says, "Fine Dining with Adirondack Charm" in shades of blue and green on knotty pine.

Two heavy-duty eye hooks hold it up, and while I'm sure it's got some weight to it, I assume it's more awkward than anything else. Like the eighty-eight-inch television I managed to bring into the house yesterday and then promptly placed in the basement because I don't actually need another TV. Just me being spiteful...again.

I drive the Jeep closer to the sign so I can stand on the running board to reach the eye hooks and unscrew them. I get one out and start to unscrew the other when the weight of the sign causes it to come crashing down, knocking me on my ass back into the Jeep and banging the sign into the driver's side rear door. I let out a string of four-letter words that would make a man blush and notice the huge scratch in the paint.

I check to make sure I'm not hurt. I'm not. Except for my pride. And the door can be repaired. It's a small price to pay to get the sign down. Entirely worth it.

I lean the sign against a shrub while I move my Jeep, hoping to avoid further damage, and then come back to drag it to the dumpster.

It's heavy, but I squat down, like I'm Sisyphus needing to roll a boulder up a hill and get it in the dumpster. The clang of wood hitting metal echoes in the cold, amplified by the emptiness, and it's so damn satisfying, like taking off your bra at the end of a horrendous day or fucking with a scam telemarketer who wants you to provide him with your social security number. *Au revoir, David's*!

I hop back into my Jeep, warming my hands, thankful that the remnant of David is gone.

Now, to come up with a new name.

But not here. I want to go home, where it's warm.

Just as I'm about to leave, the lights in the parking lot come on, and I can see, through the windows of the restaurant, that a few of the lights I attempted to flip on earlier are now shining brightly.

Rebecca—and Rita—to the rescue! In record time, too. Only forty-five minutes.

I should go back in and check everything out, but I'm tired—physically, mentally, and emotionally. Tomorrow is another day.

Chloe texted me as I was leaving the restaurant and invited me to her place for dinner...as long as I picked up dinner. No problem. Pizza and salads from The Harvest, it is. And there is no need to pick up a bottle of wine, as Chloe Bennett could be a sommelier if she weren't already killing it as the vice president of sales and marketing at one of the largest golf apparel companies in the northeast.

She owns the prettiest little Craftsman-style house in Queensbury, just south of Lake George. It's located on a cul-de-sac with a gorgeous white porch, wide eaves, and so many windows. While I wouldn't want to be responsible for cleaning the windows, they let in an incredible amount of light, perfect for showcasing all the natural materials and Chloe's impeccable sense of style.

I reach under the porch to grab her spare key and let myself in. Chloe should be home from work in a few minutes, and Tyler, her eldest son, is with her ex tonight, so it's just us girls.

The house feels a little cool, probably because Chloe turns the heat down during the day while she's at work, so I start a fire. With a quick flip of the switch, her electric fireplace instantly adds warmth and ambiance to the living room.

Settling in on her cushy sofa, I reflect on...all of it.

The lake house is mine.

David's is mine.

I have moved out of our Manhattan apartment and permanently relocated to Lake George.

My divorce is expected to be finalized within the next two to three months.

That's a whole lot of change. A whole lot.

However, I need to keep pumping myself up and telling myself, *You've got this!*

There's no way but through, right?

As I wipe away a tear that has fallen without my permission, Chloe's car pulls into the driveway, and she enters the house like a hurricane. Winter scarf trailing behind her like a shooting star, blonde hair cascading from under her red beanie, and cheeks the perfect shade of pink from the below-freezing temps.

"You are an angel! I didn't even have to ask you to start a fire!"

I get up from the couch and grab the pizza and salad, placing them on the coffee table. There is no kitchen table for girls' nights; it's the couch and cozy blankets for us.

Chloe grabs a bottle of red, plates, forks, parmesan cheese, and red pepper flakes, gently placing them on the coffee table as she flings herself on the couch.

"So...fill me in."

As I pour two glasses of Pinot Noir and return to my spot on the couch, I brace myself for her reaction.

"I am the proud owner of David's. The keys are in my purse. However, the asshole did cut the power to the place, so that took a bit to work out. I also got the lake house and have officially moved in, and David has signed the NDA…" but before I can continue, she's bouncing up and down on the couch, à la Tom Cruise on Oprah, in celebration.

"What a prick, but yes! Yes! Yes!" Her next question quickly overtakes her excitement. "What did he say about the NDA?"

Ah, yes…the NDA. "Well, he accused me of lying to him all these years, which, while true, was not done with malicious intent. And when he learned the full scope of what he had to gain by signing, he quickly shut the fuck up."

"No big surprise there. He's always been driven by money and his narcissistic tendencies."

I don't correct her and refrain from saying, "He hasn't always been a narcissist." Mostly because I'm not sure that's true. You don't win *Crown of the Kitchen*, become a celebrity chef, and open several successful restaurants without some ego. But narcissist? Perhaps Chloe's right. Maybe that's precisely what he is. He exhibits all the telltale signs. The need for constant validation. The inability to handle criticism. Transactional relationships. Charm that comes with an expiration date. And yet I failed to see it during the twenty years of our marriage.

"My big question is, why did he give up David's so easily? It's an homage to…*him*. You'd think he'd want to hold on to it." This is the question that's been nagging at me ever since Rebecca handed me the keys.

"Yeah, it's a bit suspicious, isn't it? I wonder what he's got up his sleeve." I don't honestly know, and I've been racking my brain to figure it out—but I can't. I can't see what his angle is.

Chloe continues, "What else did Rebecca say?"

"The divorce should be finalized in the next eight to twelve weeks."

"Whoa! That's fast. I take it you're not contesting it?"

"What's to contest? He wants a divorce, and we're splitting everything fifty-fifty."

"Yeah…it still seems fast."

"It's fast. But he's ready to move on. So, I need to move on as well." This last sentence is the line I've been feeding myself for weeks now, as if it will be enough to nourish my destroyed sense of self.

"I know I shouldn't be happy about this—because of the divorce and all—but I am thrilled that you will be so close."

She reaches over and gives me a hug that feels so good. I don't want to let go.

"I know. And knowing you are here is making it all a bit easier."

As I'm about to take another bite of pizza, Chloe's glacier-blue eyes lock on mine and she asks, "So, really? What are you going to do with the restaurant? I'm thrilled you're taking the lake house because that means you'll be just a few minutes away, but *the restaurant*??"

I watch as her lips come together, forming a thin, tight line, which I'm sure is holding back a wince I saw flash across her face. She has finally said the words I know she's been thinking. "Do you think I can't run a restaurant?" It feels a little confrontational when I say it, and I know Chloe isn't asking me about the restaurant to be mean, but…

"I did not say that. I just think going through a divorce is a LOT. And then to add to it the managing of a restaurant… well, it would be overwhelming for a chef or restaurateur, let alone someone with limited experience in the business."

Limited experience is being kind. She's right. What the hell was I thinking?

"I'm a quick study, and I've listened to David prattle on about his restaurants a lot these last twenty years. No, I'm not a chef. No, I'm not a restaurateur. But I'm smart. I can learn. I just need the right people to support me." Who am I saying this for? Me? Or Chloe?

"You are one of the smartest women I know, no doubt about that. But restaurant life is not for the faint of heart. It's lots of long hours and temperamental chefs..." She says no more, knowing she's preaching to the choir.

It was those long hours that had covered up David's affair for the past year.

And while he would never admit he was temperamental, he was. So temperamental, some might even call him volatile at times. But it was only when he was in the kitchen.

Are all chefs like David? I have a hard time believing Eric Ripert is constantly yelling at his kitchen staff to pick up the fucking pace. In a sexy French accent, no less. But maybe.

While I'm thinking about Eric Ripert, Chloe continues to ask questions. "Do you know who the current chef is at David's? Is there staff? With them being closed for renovations since October, is there anybody left?"

I don't know the answer to these questions. I vaguely remember David saying he had moved the chef who was in charge there to one of his other restaurants. As for everyone else, I have no clue.

"Well, this is not going to allay your fears, but I don't think there is any staff at all."

Chloe looks gobsmacked.

"No one?" Incredulity drips from those two little words as mozzarella drips from her mouth.

"Yeah, I believe he moved the chef who was there to Marabella in Philadelphia, and many of the others were locals and had no choice but to find other jobs with the restaurant being closed for so many months."

Chloe grabs another slice, taking a hot minute to think before she speaks—which is probably a good thing—because I can tell she's not thrilled with my responses. Not thrilled at all.

"So, you have a restaurant but no chef. No staff. And let me be brutally honest here, no clue how to run it."

The pizza pause certainly didn't change what she had to say, but I love her anyway. I love Chloe because she doesn't hold back with me. It's not the type of friendship we have. We're tough and can take the truth—even when we don't want to hear it. We've seen each other through it all. High school boyfriends. Her near-fatal car accident during our senior year of college. Receiving representation for my first book and subsequently selling it to my publisher. Her being named vice president of sales and marketing at Pine & Par Golf Apparel. Some crazy fun vacations when each of us was happily married. Then her divorce. Now mine.

A smirk forms, and I reply, "Yes, that's exactly what I have." I need to bring the focus onto something that will bring me joy, and continue, "Let's not dwell on what I don't have or know. Let's get to the important stuff. We need to come up with a new name for this place because I'm sure as hell not going to run a restaurant named David's."

Chloe reaches over and grabs my hand. "No, you are not. We *will* come up with a new name."

I smile at my best friend, feeling thankful for our decades of friendship.

"Lynds, I have to ask, with you moving up to the lake house full-time, are you worried about running into..."

Before she can finish that thought, I cut her off. "No, Chloe. I haven't spoken to him in thirty-five years. There's no need to worry about something that most likely will *never* happen." But even Chloe intimating that I might run into him makes a bolt of electricity race through my body, a bolt that I need to shut down before I explode like an overloaded circuit. Adding him to the mix of things right now is just too much.

After all, I don't even know if he lives in the area, so there's no use imagining a reunion.

Chloe raises her glass of wine and says, "Okay, if you say so! Cheers to new beginnings and saying goodbye to David the slick-dicked asshole."

I'll drink to both of those things.

Chapter Two

After helping Chloe clean up, I head back to the Lake George house. There's a fresh dusting of snow covering the driveway, but my Jeep has no trouble. In Manhattan, my Jeep looked out of place among the Porsches, Audis, and other luxury vehicles in our Upper West Side neighborhood, but as a teenager, this was the vehicle I always wanted. I dreamed of Chloe and me driving around Lake George with the top off in the summer, waving at cute boys. Now, it makes sense here in the Southern Adirondacks. I'm glad I never gave it up, even when David tried to convince me to purchase something else, something he thought more befitting of *us*. Something more befitting of *him*.

I get out and quickly head inside to turn on the heat, looking around our—*my*—home.

How long will it take me to break that habit?

It was built to mimic the traditional grand Adirondack camps, like Great Camp Pine Knot and Great Camp Uncas. And, while many people give their lake homes and cabins names, like Loon Landing or Hemlock Hideaway, David was pretentious enough to name ours like it was of the same stature as one of those great camps. Ours—*mine*—is named Great Camp Lake Georgia, a play on Lake George and Georgia O'Keeffe, who spent many summers painting in the area. I hate the name. Another thing I'll need to change.

But one thing I won't be changing is this home. I adore this house. It's such a departure from our apartment in the city. The apartment was austere, clinical even. Filled with marble and tile and stainless steel. The color palette was black and white and shades of gray. No pops of color to be found. But here, things are so different. There are natural materials everywhere. Massive logs adorn the facade, and a rock chimney climbs up the left side of the house. Giant boulders have been placed strategically throughout the landscaping, and there are pine, birch, and hemlock trees that I would swear have been here for centuries, standing guard over the property.

A porch wraps around almost the entire home, providing great views of the mountains and the lake. I've spent many summer days sitting in the Adirondack chairs, reading or napping in one of the three daybed porch swings. When that cool breeze, tasting of black-eyed Susans and wild lupine, comes in off the lake, there is nothing better.

While the house's exterior is rustic, its interior is much more modern. Yet, unlike our apartment in the city, this home has touches of me everywhere. Yes, stainless steel appliances, marble countertops, and a butcher block island fill the kitchen, similar to the apartment and all David's choices, but the sameness stops there. The open kitchen cabinets are filled with pottery picked up from travels to Bolesławiec and Talavera. Oversized serving platters in different hues of blue and gold, a kaleidoscope of colorful bowls, and floral pitchers for the perfect sangria make the kitchen feel more like an art studio. While David always appreciated the pieces for utilitarian reasons, I love the parts of me that they bring to the space, and I love that I chose each and every piece. In a marriage that so heavily focused on David and his career and his doings, this was one small corner of our life where I had a say. My choices, my colors, my memories, quietly claiming space of their own.

Standing here now, the moonlight spilling across the island and catching the curve of a cobalt bowl, I realize how much I've missed having something that feels like mine.

The bedrooms and living room pay tribute to the area with traditional Adirondack furnishings purchased from a local craftsman and bedding that is comfy and cozy, no matter the season. In the spring and summer, pristine white chenille bedspreads envelop you, and in the fall and winter, it's weighty Black Watch plaid to keep you toasty warm.

There is more pottery from local artisans on the tables, and landscapes of the area, painted in the softest of watercolors, cover the walls. I pick up an oversized bowl that is sitting on the sofa table and remember the craft fair in Lake George where we purchased it. The artisan was so thrilled to meet David that she had marked the piece down considerably—even though I told her it wasn't necessary. David had shushed me and happily taken the discount. I should've insisted we pay full price.

Without hesitation, I hurl the vessel against the wall, watching it shatter into a million shards just below a photo from our wedding day. I look so happy in that picture. But David...

That smile I thought was because of his complete and utter adoration for me looks more like a practiced expression, like a smug chef with a secret recipe. Was marrying me, an up-and-coming author with a couple of bestsellers, all part of some plan? Considering his big ask of me several years into our marriage, I'm beginning to believe it was.

Once again, the heartsickness returns. How could I have been so wrong all this time?

It's not only the bowl that's broken; it's everything. My marriage. My sense of self-worth. The life I thought I had.

I slump against the counter and feel hot tears rolling down my cheeks. I want to stop them, but I can't. I need to clean up this mess. Unable to stop my blubbering, I grab the broom and dustpan from the pantry and begin sweeping up the shattered pieces.

If only I could pick up my own life as easily.

I wonder how I had not noticed how infrequent the "I love yous" had become.

Was I blind, or was I consciously ignoring the signs?

I know the answer.

I was trying to hold on to us.

Not really us, more the idea of us that I, and the media, had cobbled together. And in doing so, I had ignored all the breadcrumbs that David had been leaving on the trail to the end of our marriage. Breadcrumbs? Christ, they were entire baguettes.

I drop the final fragments into the trash can, crank up the heat a little more, and open the sliding doors, stepping onto the back porch. This portion of the wraparound is enclosed, and while cold, it's currently free from snow. I wipe away my tears, close my eyes, and inhale the cold, fresh air, like a newborn baby taking in its first breath after leaving its mother's womb. No more crying. For now. I've cried too much lately.

This is a fresh start for me.

When I open my eyes, I can see that the lake is not frozen over, but is as smooth as glass as the snowflakes hit the surface, not creating a ripple or a sound.

I think about the last time I was here in the fall. David and I came up to hand the keys to the restaurant to the contractors. We spent the weekend here, admiring the fall foliage and sitting by the lake with the firepit going, drinking mulled wine. It was a perfect weekend.

I clear the fog from that memory and tell myself, no, it wasn't perfect. Perfect was what I told Chloe it was. What I persuaded myself it was. But it was a weekend of us drinking mulled wine by the firepit as we scrolled our phones, barely conversing. It was me going to bed early, hoping we could reconnect, while David stayed up late watching football. At least, that's what he told me he was doing.

The cold wind hits me like the truth of my recollections from last fall, and I find myself wondering if I am going to be able to live in this house and not constantly be reminded of the memories we made here. That remains to be seen, but I have to try. I currently have no other choice, no other place to go.

I head back inside and can feel the living room warming up. That's good. Soon, it will be warm and cozy, and I can spend some time settling in. But before I get too comfortable, I grab my starter from the fridge. She needs to be fed. I need to make bread.

I'm not a very good cook, and I can't make fancy desserts like *Mindi*, but I can make bread.

About seven years ago, a neighbor gave me some sourdough starter. I remember politely nodding as she handed it to me and told me how I needed to nurture it, feed it, and how, in return, it would reward me with the most delicious, crusty, holey bread. I thought she was crazy. David was the chef. Not me. But I did what she said. Eventually, after some trial and error, baking bread became "my thing."

In good times and bad. When stressed. When happy. Whenever. I bake bread.

I love the entire process: feeding and waiting, stretching and folding, rolling and shaping, flouring and scoring, buttering and eating.

Thank God I'm not gluten-free or carb-avoidant.

As I take out the 50 grams of starter that I'll use, add my water, flour, and salt, I can't help but think about the meme Chloe sent me last week. It was a video of Steve Perry of Journey singing "Don't Stop Believin'" with the words, "If you can sing every lyric of this song, it's time to feed your starter." I had laughed at the time and sent Chloe back the laughing/crying emoji, but as I put my starter back in the refrigerator, I can't help but ask myself, *Have I become so pathetic that I'm a meme?*

Perhaps I have.

But come on! *Everyone* can sing all the lyrics to that song.

In any case, this loaf of bread will bring a little comfort to my soul this evening—meme or no meme.

Making some bread will help. Help me feel settled. Help me feel anchored.

I leave her on the counter to work her magic and head to the bedroom to put away the clothes that I dropped here earlier this morning.

Opening the closet, I notice that all of David's stuff is gone. No navy-blue sport coats. None of his French cuff dress shirts. Not even the flannel shirts I bought him to help him fit in a bit more here in the North Country. Not sure when or how this happened, but I'm grateful I don't have to make a trip to Goodwill to get rid of his belongings. Although, burning his Gucci loafers and cashmere sweaters would have brought me immense pleasure.

I put away all my stuff, making a point to flow into his former spaces.

His part of the closet is now mine.

His dresser is now mine.

His nightstand is now mine.

I don't have enough stuff to fill any of these things up, but that doesn't matter. I need to do it to make this place my own. Erase the images and memories of David.

Slowly.

DAVID MONTERO TAKES IN THE LONDON SITES WITH NEW SWEETIE PIE, PASTRY CHEF, MINDI PATTON

Not what I wanted to wake up to this morning. He's jetted off to London. With *Mindi*.

For the last few weeks, I've only been reading the headlines on *The Pulse* when it mentioned David or me, trying not to go down the rabbit hole and read all the sordid details they were sharing. But today, I click the link, unable to help myself.

Celebrity Chef David Montero was spotted around London with his new girlfriend, Mindi Patton. Our sources say Patton is the pastry chef at Lindo, Montero's uber-popular New York City restaurant.

Chef Montero is in London filming guest appearances on the British edition of *Crown of the Kitchen*, a show that propelled him to popularity over twenty years ago in the United States.

Montero and Patton looked quite cozy as they rode the London Eye, visited Buckingham Palace, and dined at Heddon Street Kitchen, where they were seen talking and laughing with one of Britain's most famous celebrity chefs, Gordon Ramsay.

Montero is in the process of divorcing his wife, author Lyndsay Leach-Montero. Leach-Montero published three bestsellers in the early 2000s and currently resides in New York City.

Well, I do NOT currently reside in New York City, and it's over fifteen bestsellers—not that *The Pulse* knows that—but those are things I probably can't sue them over. Although I wish I could. When David asked me to give up writing and to be his "full partner in love and life"—his words, not mine—I didn't do it entirely.

But I did do it enough that I can see, with humiliating clarity, just how quickly my own dreams slid to the back burner. One "supportive" choice here, one "sacrifice" there, and suddenly, I was gone. Or at least muted.

I supported his rise, while he made me shrink so he could take up more space.

And, while I'd like to email the editor at *The Pulse* and confirm that, yes, I am divorcing that no-good, cheating sack of shit, I won't give them the satisfaction.

Once again, I only wish this would all disappear, and the spotlight would fall on someone else. *Come on, Melanie! Confirm that you're filing for divorce!*

I shoot Chloe a quick text to make sure she's seen the latest. She responds in a flash with "Saw it." Followed by the eggplant emoji, the angry face emoji, and fire. I can't help but chuckle and respond with a laughing-crying emoji and a thumbs up. Ninety-nine percent of my communication with Chloe is done via emojis and memes. It works for us.

I get up and make my way to my now very well-stocked kitchen, thanks to a late-night grocery delivery, which includes not one, but two different caramel creamers, to make some coffee.

I was unsuccessful last night in my attempts to come up with a new name for the restaurant, although I was successful in coming up with a concept that I think will work. Provided I can find a chef who shares my vision.

I want Unnamed Restaurant—which is how I'm referring to it for the time being, so I don't have to say its former name

—to focus on farm-to-table. I want us to source as much as possible from the surrounding areas. I want us to showcase as many foods and drinks from New York, New Jersey, Vermont, and Massachusetts as possible. I want it to be upscale but not pretentious. David tends to lean toward pretentiousness, to the point where his restaurants feel exclusionary and haughty. I want the opposite of that.

But I need a name.

And I need a chef.

I head to my office and spend about an hour placing ads on all the local job boards, the hiring websites, and the local paper. I'll start there, although I may have to expand my reach if I don't get any qualified applicants.

To avoid constantly refreshing my email in hopes that the most perfect résumé will arrive in my inbox, I head to the shower to get ready for the day. I'm off to Unnamed Restaurant to get a look at her with the lights on.

Chapter Three

It's warm inside, and when I flip the light switch at the main entrance, the lights actually come on. *Hallelujah!* Now, to see what I'm working with.

Last year, when David broached the subject of renovating this location, I didn't think it was necessary. The restaurant had an Adirondack vibe with hardwood floors, rustic tables and chairs, and walls painted in hues of green and blue, just like the former sign outside. It was still upscale, but diners knew they were in the Adirondacks. Of course, then David wanted to elevate it a bit more. While he had left the hardwood floors, the entire restaurant had been painted tan. Warmed Putty, I believe, is the shade. It should've been called Boring Beige. It's completely void of any visual appeal.

Don't get caught up in the paint color. It's just paint. Some art on the walls can bring these rooms to life.

Looking around, I see he has removed all the doors between rooms. I'm not sure why. Not a choice I would have made. In the past, we could close those doors for private parties. I'll need to think about that. Maybe the doors are in the basement, and I can have a handyman put them back on their hinges.

He has also replaced all the tables and chairs—much more modern and industrial-looking—along with the light fixtures. I don't hate it. In fact, I think I can make it work with the farm-to-table concept. They can stay.

Then I walk into the kitchen and find myself mesmerized by the entire space.

While I never spent much time here in the past, even a complete restaurant rookie would know that everything is state-of-the-art, from the industrial gas stoves to the convection ovens to the sous vide machines to the high-powered blenders. I glance down at the Wolf nameplate on the stove in front of me and remember when David told me he was swapping all our current models for these. My eyes had glazed over, and the only thing I clearly remember was the amount it was going to cost, an investment he assured me would be worth it. After all, he couldn't cook on "anything so inferior." David went all out when it came to equipping a kitchen. It was easy for him to do when it was my money he was spending.

The workstations for prep, salads, cooking, plating, and baking/desserts were made of shiny stainless steel—so shiny you could apply your lipstick when looking at them. David instilled in his kitchen staff the need for an immaculate work area—even if he had to yell at them to make it happen—and all his chefs polished their workstations to a showroom shine before heading home each evening.

To my right is the walk-in cooler that is as big as most people's primary bedroom. While I know he and Mindi weren't here when they got caught *in flagrante*, I'm going to avoid the walk-in for a while. No need to be reminded.

So far, so good. I can make this work. Just a few minor tweaks.

I don't find the doors in the basement, which is a

bummer, but I do find the wine cellar. I know he moved a bunch of his prized collection to Philadelphia when renovations started, but there appears to be a decent selection to get me started. I'll need to do a complete inventory to see what we have and, most likely, enlist a sommelier to help me. I know a good Pinot Grigio, but not much else. Before heading upstairs, I grab a bottle of Trimbach Pinot Gris Personelle 2015, the lesser-known cousin of Pinot Grigio, and equally delicious. It will be the perfect accompaniment to the very gourmet grilled cheese on sourdough I have planned for this evening's dinner—if I can get my bread baked in time.

Once I make my way back to the kitchen, I take a hard right so I can take stock of the silverware and glassware. I will need to replenish a few things to get through the busy summer season, but we have enough to get started. I also check the selection of dinner plates, salad plates, side plates, dessert plates, appetizer plates, and others I can't even name—so many damn plates—all stacked in meticulous towers, awaiting their moment to grace the table of future guests. They are simple and white and will do just fine. David always said, "The food should be the star of the show, not the china on which it is served."

I take a peek at the wraparound porch. All the outdoor dining furniture has been covered with heavy tarps for the winter. I know the porch furniture was replaced just two years ago, so most, if not all, should be okay. It will just need to be uncovered and power-washed to remove the winter grime.

Finally, I head to the bar area. While there is no liquor, it appears to have everything else a bartender needs. When I get one hired, I will have them double-check.

Standing behind the long pine bar, I look out over the biggest of our dining areas, still finding it hard to believe that this is all mine. Unnamed Restaurant is mine.

And I'm determined to make it a success.

~

IT'S ALMOST FIVE P.M. WHEN I GET HOME. FINDING my dough right where I left it, I do a few quick stretches and folds, shape it into a ball, and let her rest in a banneton. I turn the light on in the bottom oven, a cheat which will help my bread rise quicker, and turn the top oven heat to 450 degrees. I will have bread for dinner.

I plunk myself down on the sectional and take a few minutes to check my emails. So far, I have a couple of résumés from a few locals with kitchen experience. Not precisely the standout résumés I was hoping for, but I'll interview them. I may need them if push comes to shove. I reply to each of them and ask them to come to the restaurant early Monday morning to speak with me. Maybe by then, a few more candidates will have applied.

By the time I'm finished replying to emails, my oven is hot, and I put my bread in. No fancy design tonight, just a simple slash to allow the gas to escape while it rises in the oven.

I pour a glass of wine, crank up the fireplace, and turn on the television. I don't want to watch anything; I just need something to cut through the silence. You forget how quiet it can be when you live alone. Deafening. You think I would be used to it after David being gone for so much of the last eighteen months. I'm not.

Last night, Chloe suggested I get a dog, but a dog is a lot of work. More work than I want while trying to get Unnamed Restaurant off the ground. Then she jokingly suggested a fish. Fish? They're not pets. Although she did throw out the idea of getting a piranha, which I didn't even know was possible until I googled it. She said I could imagine I was feeding it David every time I dropped a live goldfish into the tank. She's hilarious, but I'll hold off on the pet thing.

Twenty minutes pass, and I remove the lid from my bread

oven so it can brown. I can tell from looking at it that it's slightly underproofed—which is what happens when you rush the process like I did today. Whatevs. Even underproofed, it will still taste better than any mass-produced loaf I could buy at the grocery store.

Only thirty minutes to go until it's ready.

Back on the couch, I text Susan to let her know that all is well in Upstate New York. She replies, *Well enough to start writing again?* I don't respond. I can't avoid writing forever. But I'm going to avoid it for now. I have nothing to write about—so the choice is relatively easy.

Then "You're My Best Friend" starts playing, and I look down to see Chloe's familiar name and number.

"Hey, Chlo, what's up?"

"Nothing much. Everything good at the restaurant?"

"Yup, as good as can be expected when you don't have a name, don't have a chef, and really don't have a clue as to what you're doing. One day at a time, right?"

Chloe laughs and reassures me that everything will be okay. After today's walk-through, I kind of believe her. I can do this.

We continue talking for a few more minutes when Chloe says she has to jump off to fix dinner for her youngest. Like me, she's not much of a cook, so I know it's a euphemism for her need to order DoorDash.

As I hang up, a new name for Unnamed Restaurant pops into my mind like an unexpected firecracker, and it's perfect—thanks to Chloe and her phone number. More specifically, the area code of her phone number—518—right here in Upstate New York.

Going forward, Unnamed Restaurant shall be known as 518 Farm-to-Table.

Now to find a chef!

I CHECK MY EMAIL ONE LAST TIME BEFORE I WALK into 518 Farm-to-Table. God, it feels so good to no longer be referring to it as, well, that name we shall no longer mention, or Unnamed Restaurant. This reminds me that I need to call the sign maker today to see if he can craft a new one. Add that to the to-do list.

Unfortunately, there are no new résumés in my inbox. I'm disappointed. I knew this might be the case, and I'd have to broaden my search, but I was hoping for a diamond in the rough. I do have one potential candidate for desserts and pastry who looks promising. The others...well, I'll find out soon enough.

I turn on all the lights and head to the kitchen, where I drop off my laptop and a tote bag with a few groceries to get me through the morning. I've also got a couple of notebooks (because one is never enough) and my sparkly pens. Always sparkly pens.

Interviews are scheduled for the first half of the day, and I decide to hold the conversations in the kitchen so potential candidates can see what they're working with—which is A-M-A-Z-I-N-G! Not that I'm sure we've got the quality of candidates to truly appreciate this fact.

I grab a couple of dining room chairs and drag in a small bistro table and call it good.

Last night, I spent a significant amount of time searching "Questions to ask a potential chef" and came up with a list that should help me weed out the applicants who aren't a fit for the restaurant. After all, there's more to being a chef than impeccable knife skills. You need leadership, adaptability, and the capacity to create an environment where the kitchen can thrive.

As the front door opens, I take one last glance at my questions, paste on a smile, and welcome my first potential hire.

"Okay, thank you for stopping by. I'll be in touch if I have any additional questions," I say as I walk the last candidate out the front door.

OH MY GOD! I'm so glad that's over.

While it wasn't a complete disaster, I'm not entirely sure farm-to-table will happen if I have to hire today's batch of interviewees. I think we could pull off freezer-to-fryer. Maybe.

I sit down to review my notes on each of the candidates.

Anthony Morelli: Mid-20s, specialty dish—peach cobbler, which he learned to make in prison with canned peaches and boxed cake mix. PASS.

Matt Plimpton: 18, just graduated high school, fry cook at a burger joint, eager to learn, thinks he wants to be a chef. MAYBE?

Candace Jacobs: Early 20s, just graduated from Johnson & Wales with her culinary degree, wants to be a pastry chef. BROUGHT ME FLOURLESS CHOCOLATE CAKE AND HOMEMADE CROISSANTS. HIRED.

Blake Ferguson: Mid-40s, former sous chef at David's, talented but temperamental (like David), was not keen on my farm-to-table concept, do I want to hire someone who worked here before? MAYBE?

Helena Markham: Early 60s, grandmotherly, has spent many years working in kitchens in the area, no fine-dining experience, but not afraid of hard work, says she's a quick study, needs someone to give her a chance at her age. MAYBE?

Todd Belcher: Mid-30s, sous chef at local hotel, signature dish—Clams Casino—old school dish for such a young guy, but I like Clams Casino. Looking for a long-term position with room to grow. HIRED—but not promised a specific position.

That's a pretty ragtag group right there. I won't be pulling my ads down from the job boards and newspapers quite yet.

But I can't dwell on this right now. The wine cellar needs my attention. I need to take inventory.

As I grab one of my notebooks and a pen and head to the basement door, I hear the front door open. I'm not expecting anyone else. All my culinary inquisitions are done for the day.

Then I hear a deep baritone voice yell, "Hello? Anyone here? Um, I saw the lights were on, and the sign was down...is this place for sale? I know the owner is getting divorced..." I stop dead in my tracks.

I stop breathing.

It can't be.

But it is.

Even after thirty-five years, I'd know that voice anywhere.

Chapter Four

I inhale through my nose, wondering what my hair looks like. Did I run a brush through this black-and-gray mane this morning? Did I put on any makeup? I think I did both. I hope I did both. I certainly don't want to run into him looking like the wreck I've been for the last several months. I push my glasses up above the bridge of my nose, force a smile for what seems like the millionth time today, and turn around to head to the dining room, where I can hear him moving tables and chairs. Why is he doing that?

Projecting my most confident, self-assured voice, I reply to my unwanted guest, "I'm the owner of this restaurant, and it is currently not for sale, Marcus." The stress I place on his name makes him whip around like a tornado, looking for the woman whose voice he just heard, or more likely, looking for the eighteen-year-old girl he remembers, surely recognizing the cadence and timbre of my words.

He stares at me for a split second, and then he breaks out in uncontrollable laughter. He's practically doubled over, he's laughing so hard.

Meanwhile, I'm giving him a death stare in hopes that he

will scurry away like a rat—which this restaurant does not have, by the way.

But he doesn't.

After what seems like an eternity, he composes himself and says, "Lyndsay, it's been a while. I wasn't expecting you. I had no idea you were taking this over. I assumed it was being sold. Because of the divorce."

"I *am* taking it over, so as I said before, it's not for sale. Thanks for stopping by, but I need to get back to work."

My eyes direct him to the door, but he doesn't move.

And he doesn't break eye contact. It's a little unsettling.

Those same sea glass blue eyes, still magnetic, still framed by those long, dark lashes. Still impossibly familiar. I never could say no to them. He'd bat them at me, knowing exactly what he was doing. They were my weakness.

The years have added a few lines around them, but the effect is the same. One look and I'm a teenager again. The sight of them now stirs something in me that I thought I had long since packed away.

"So, you're taking over, huh? Interesting..." His *interesting* is filled with skepticism. Before I can once again direct him to the door, he continues, "What does a writer know about running a restaurant?" Once again, what's with the skepticism? So annoying. But he does know I'm an author. He's one up on me; I have no clue what he does for a living.

"Well, you can't be married to David Montero for twenty years and not learn a thing or two," I reply, once again trying to sound confident, even though my insides are wobbly like Jell-O from seeing him after all these years.

"Sure, sure, but according to *The Pulse*, you didn't seem to have much to do with the restaurants over the years, other than finances and helping Montero get his empire off the ground." His voice denotes some irritation, as if he believes David has been using me all these years, which is strangely curious after all this time, yet I'm here for it.

But *The Pulse?*! Fuck *The Pulse*! Why is he reading such trash?

"You'd be surprised how much you can pick up." Aggravation is creeping into my voice. I can hear it. *Get it together, Lynds.*

"Yeah, I'm sure. So, what are you doing here today? I've driven by several times in the last few weeks, but there hasn't been a soul around. And then I noticed the sign was down. Today, the lights were on, so I thought I'd stop in and see if maybe a real estate agent was here getting it ready for sale."

Okay…I'll bite. "Why would you want to buy this place, Marcus? Looking for an investment?"

"Perhaps." He says it with a shit-eating grin on his face, as if I should be in on the joke, but I'm not.

"Oh, well, it's not for sale." This is the third time I've said it. Why can't he take the hint?

"Who's going to be your chef here? I assume it's not going to be David," he says with a slight snicker in his voice. If you didn't know him, you wouldn't pick up on it, but I've heard it before. I know exactly what it sounds like.

"No, it will not be David. I spent most of the morning interviewing candidates. I'm very excited by the excellent quality of chefs in the area." I say it with a straight face, even though inside, I'm thinking: *You can't hire the felon, or the fry cook, to be your head chef.*

I can see the doubt in his eyes at my words, and then his lips curve into that familiar, knowing half-smile. His lips. The lips I kissed almost nonstop for two years when we were attached at the hip in high school.

"Really? Some good ones, huh? How about you interview me?"

"For the head chef position?" The dubiousness in my

voice is heavy, and now it's my turn to laugh. I quickly add, "Do you have a résumé?"

"Yes, let me go grab it. No, I don't have a résumé, but you can ask me whatever you want. I'm an open book."

"You're kidding, right?"

Then he grabs a seat and pulls another one out for me.

"Nope. Let's do this!"

Okay. I'll call his bluff. This should be entertaining if nothing else.

I still have my notebook and glittery pen in my hand, and I take a seat across from him at the table. I will treat this like a legitimate interview. I will ask him all the questions I posed to the morning's applicants. After all, I'm a professional. I'm a restaurant owner.

"Can you tell me about your culinary training and background?" I ask with my brightest, most professional smile— the kind that conceals the fact that I've already written him off before he opens his mouth.

"Sure, I graduated from the CIA? Have you heard of it?" There's that damn smugness again.

And...FUCK!

He graduated from the *Culinary Institute of America*? You've got to be kidding me.

"Yes, Marcus, I know of the CIA. I'm assuming, due to your age, that you went to the Hyde Park location since the Napa location didn't open until the mid-1990s." See, I do know a little bit about the culinary world. I, too, can be smug. Although I picked up this factoid from a celebrity chef episode of *Jeopardy!* that David insisted on watching, bitching the entire time that he hadn't been chosen as a contestant, but Marcus doesn't need to know that.

The self-satisfied curl of his mouth is still on his face, but he gives me a slight nod, acknowledging that I'm not a complete idiot about the culinary world.

"Yup, I took a couple of years off after high school to figure out what I wanted to do. Worked in some local kitchens, mainly as a dishwasher, but I loved being in that atmosphere, and I didn't want to be a dishwasher all my life. So, I applied to the CIA."

I think back to when he broke up with me right before high school graduation. He really didn't have a plan for his life. While I knew I wanted to be a writer and was heading off to college, he was still figuring things out, unsure of his future. It wasn't a bad thing; lots of kids don't know what they want to do after graduating high school. But then we were over, and I never did hear what he ended up doing. Erasing Marcus from my life was the only way I knew to get over him.

He continues, "Then I came back to the area and worked in several local restaurants, slowly working my way up. Started as a line cook, then moved to junior chef and to line chef. Then the chef I was working for took a job as executive chef at The Sagamore, so I followed him there as a sous chef."

I hate to admit it, but I'm impressed. Not that I'm showing any indication of this as he explains the upward trajectory of his career. But come on, The Sagamore is THE TOP resort in the area. If even half of what he's saying is true, he's a hundred times more qualified than anyone I interviewed earlier today.

I gently nod, like any good interviewer would do, as he then explains that after a couple of years, when his mentor retired, he was named executive chef at The Sagamore, where he stayed until about two years ago, when he quit. How did I not know he was a chef at The Sagamore? I'll tell you how. The Sagamore was just one of many places David never wanted to go to when we were up this direction. He always said you were paying for the location, not the food, and didn't want to spend his time or money there. But I know it's because they wouldn't hire him as a line cook fresh out of culinary school. He holds grudges—forever.

"You quit? Why did you quit? The Sagamore had to be quite the culinary feather in your chef's toque?" I may have gone a little overboard with the chef lingo on that one, but hey...

He doesn't even react to my poor play on words.

"Oh, I went through a divorce and needed a change. I spent eighteen months doing pop-up restaurants in the South, from the Carolinas to Texas." His voice seems to have a touch of melancholy. Divorce can certainly bring that on.

I am about to say that I'm sorry to hear about his divorce when he rebounds back to his old self and shares that he just got back to the area a few weeks ago.

"Which is why I stopped by to see if this place was for sale —because I need to get back in the kitchen."

Of course, he does, but does it have to be *my* kitchen?

No. No it doesn't. Keep going with the interview, then thank him for his time, and send him on his way.

But do not sound impressed by his credentials.

At all.

I wish I had my list of questions in front of me, but I remember another one and ask, "Do you have a signature dish, and was there some sort of inspiration behind it?"

"Hmm...signature dish? Well, it's not a dish I've ever shared with guests in any of the restaurants I've worked at— only with staff—at family meals. It's a rustic stew, like my mom used to make. Super simple ingredients, slow cooked for hours to bring out the best flavors. My mom always made it when I was growing up. She could make something from nothing, and it always tasted delicious." The heaviness is back in his voice. "Maybe you remember it? I think she made it for you a couple of times."

I do remember it. It was the epitome of comfort food in a

bowl. His mom would make it during the dead of winter, on Sunday afternoons. Rich, hearty, and made with the kind of care you could taste. The smell alone could thaw you from the inside out.

My mom called me at college when his mom passed away. His dad had never been in the picture. I can only imagine how crushing her death was for him based on my memories of them both. I probably should have called him when his mom died, but I was still hurting and not willing to look past my own anger to at least offer him my condolences. Young and selfish, for sure.

I think of my own mother, who is still alive and well. I love her, but our relationship has not always been smooth. It's never been Joan and Christina Crawford level by any means; it's more like Debbie Reynolds and Carrie Fisher. We've had our ups and downs, but everyone who knows us knows we love one another. And even though my mom can be annoying and overbearing, I am glad she's around. I can't imagine what I would do if I lost her. And I imagine how much worse it must have been for Marcus to lose his mom at such a young age.

"I was sorry to hear about your mom. She was always so nice to me when we hung out at your place. And I remember that stew she made. I remember a snowy Sunday our senior year, when we got back from ice skating, and she had it all ready for us for dinner." My mouth waters thinking about the dish, and my eyes water looking at his heavy-hearted expression.

"Yeah, she was a good mom."

In order to avoid the uncomfortable silence that could easily sit between us after the mention of his mom, I ask, "Do you have any experience developing and creating a menu?" Although I know the answer is going to be yes. I can ask every question on my stupid list, and he's going to check every box. Every. Damn. Box.

"Oh, yeah. Lots. When I was at The Sagamore, we developed our menus seasonally—which was great. In the main restaurant, we kept our menu relatively small so we could lean into the ingredients at their peak during whatever season it was. Plus, I loved to source stuff from local farmers and producers as much as possible. Same for the pop-ups. I would hit the local farmers' markets when I'd get to a new city and see what was available. It was a fantastic way to connect with the local food scene."

Seriously? He's perfect. He's just what I want.

Let me qualify that statement.

He's just what I want *in a chef.*

Of course, I can't help but see that he's still incredibly handsome. His once dark hair is now more gray than anything else, with little flecks of black and silver that go so well with his blue eyes. He's still very fit, not like a lot of chefs who pack on more than a few pounds after so many years in the kitchen. He's dressed in the uniform of men here in Upstate New York, and he makes that uniform look mighty nice. Levi's, flannel shirt, North Face vest, and Timberland boots—Timberland boots that look like they belong on him, not like he's posing as someone from Upstate. While David would wear these things to try to fit in when we were up here, he always looked uncomfortable in them, as if they might cause him to break out in hives. David was better suited for his short, tight Euro pants, which allowed his bare ankles to show with his Italian leather loafers. Marcus makes his attire look better than most custom-made suits.

"Can I ask what you were thinking for a menu here? Are you keeping David's menu? If I recall, he went for the fine dining, white tablecloth thing."

"Yes, he did—and, while I want upscale, I don't want pretentious." Why am I sharing this with him? I'm not hiring him. I'm not.

But I can't seem to control my mouth, and it all comes spilling out.

"I want to do farm-to-table. In fact, the new name of this place is 518 Farm-to-Table."

Now he's doing the nodding thing, listening intently to what I have to say. The sincerity in this gesture hits harder than it should. When was the last time a man listened to what I had to say?

"I want it to be locally sourced ingredients—as much as possible—from here and the surrounding states. I want local beers, local wines, local spirits. I want to showcase all that this area has to offer. And I want the food to be fabulous and fun. I want it to be exceptional and accessible. I want it to be memorable and mouthwatering." My mouth keeps spitting out words like a garden spits out tomatoes in the month of August. I need to stop. But I also need to remember this for the website—which is another thing I must put on my to-do list.

"That sounds amazing, Lynds…" I don't like the way he so casually uses *Lynds* in the sentence. *Lynds* is reserved for my family and friends, and after our breakup, I would not consider us friends. But I don't correct him.

"Yeah, I'm really excited. It's going to be a push to get it all together, but I'd like to open in the spring, before the summer rush, so we have a few months under our belt before all the tourists arrive and things get crazy."

"Oh, definitely. You want time to work out the kinks and get buy-in from the locals. They'll be your harshest critics. Are you going to try and keep it open year-round?"

"Yes, that's the plan. I'm living here now, and I think the year-round residents would love a place like this during the quieter months." *Stop! Just stop talking.* But I can't. "I would certainly cut back on the hours—maybe Wednesday through Sunday—during the winter. But fall is gorgeous here with the foliage, and spring is lovely with the flowers in bloom and the green coming back to the mountains." I probably sound like someone who has never run a restaurant before, seeing restaurant life through a soft-focus lens, but I do know it will take a lot of work.

Before I can share that I know all the work that will be involved, Marcus says, "I know I probably don't have to tell you, but it won't be easy. You're following in big footsteps, and David certainly made his mark around here with this place. Locals loved it, as well as the tourists—even if it was highfalutin and haughty."

Haughty? That's the word I used to describe David's—and it makes me laugh out loud. He has described the old restaurant—and its founder—perfectly.

"Yeah...change is hard for everyone, but if people will give me a chance, I know I can make this place a success. I know it." I say that last *I know it* more for me than Marcus.

"It sounds like you've got an excellent plan. I can tell by the way you talk about it that you really have a vision...and a passion."

If passion stems from spite, then yes, I have it in spades.

His eyes never leave mine as he speaks, and I feel a pink flush making its way to my cheeks.

I murmur, "Thank you," caught off guard by his nice words. Why I'm surprised, I do not know. He was always my biggest supporter, always believed I would achieve my goals.

"Well, I'll let you get back to whatever you were doing. I'm sorry for taking up so much of your time. Good luck, Lynds."

But before he can even get up out of his chair, the words I told myself I would not say blurt out of my mouth.

"Marcus, would you be interested in being the head chef here at 518 Farm-to-Table?"

Chapter Five

What the hell am I saying?

I just asked my former high school boyfriend, who broke my heart a million years ago, to be the head chef at the restaurant I'm opening, which was formerly run by my soon-to-be celebrity chef ex-husband, who also broke my heart.

This has the makings of a disaster. Titanic level.

Yet, I said it. And I can't take it back.

Marcus's face breaks into a huge smile, and, uncontrollably, so does mine.

It feels right. He's the right person for the position, I know it. What happened in the past can stay in the past. We're adults. I'm a restaurant owner, and he's a chef. Nothing more, nothing less.

But he still hasn't said yes.

"Well, I was wondering how long it would take you to ask me. I was trying to think of a way to give you my phone number—in case you were going to give me the ol' *Thanks for coming in...I have a few more candidates to interview*—and then decide that I was the right person to be the chef here and wanted to call me."

That part about *Thanks for coming in* was exactly what I was going to say…until I accepted that he was perfect.

For the chef's position.

"So…your other candidates, they just weren't exactly what you were looking for?"

I let my guard down and break into a genuine laugh. "That may just be the understatement of the year. Although if you say yes, I'll let you take a look at their résumés. I actually did hire two of them. One as the pastry chef—and she has the potential to be fantastic—but she's young. The other has worked as a sous chef before. He had a vibe I liked, and I wanted to have *someone* if push came to shove. I didn't promise him the head chef position—just that he had a job in the kitchen."

"Hmmm…I'll admit that pastry and desserts are not my strong suit—so if your gut says she has potential, then that's good enough for me. As for the other one, I guess it will be a wait-and-see type of thing." I rein in my surprise that Marcus trusts my *gut* on this. David would've chosen someone entirely different, even if I had hired a world-renowned pastry chef, just to prove to me the kitchen is his domain.

I can see him mulling things over, and I really just want to hear that three-letter word from his mouth—which he still hasn't said yet.

"Before I answer, can I ask a question?" he says, his look full of gravitas.

"Of course."

"How do you know I can cook?"

At this, I laugh—an honest, startled sound that bursts out before I can stop it. Not because it's funny, but because it's true. How do I know he can do what he says? I'm standing here considering him for a job based on his words and my nostalgia.

"Ummm...I guess I need to trust you," I manage.

"I'm sure that's not easy after the way we ended things." He pauses, holding my gaze a moment longer than necessary. "So why don't I prove it to you? Do you have any food here?"

I think about the meager rations I brought with me this morning. Some sourdough, a half-stick of butter, and various cheeses that I pulled from my refrigerator.

"Well, I have some bread and cheese, which I'm sure is not what you had in mind."

"Okay...hold on a minute, and I'll be right back," he says, as he makes his way to the front door and back outside.

I watch him go and can't help but chastise myself for what could be a bad decision of monumental proportions. Bringing Marcus back into my life after all these years is not what I had planned. At all.

A few moments later, he returns with a pear, what appears to be some sort of luncheon meat based on the packaging, and a squeeze bottle of mayonnaise.

"You're in luck! I picked up a few groceries this morning —so let's go see what we can make."

I appreciate his positive outlook, but I don't think lunch is looking too promising at this point in time. Not exactly gourmet or upscale. Nevertheless, I follow him into the kitchen to see what he can pull off.

As I lick my lips of the remaining crumbs from my grilled turkey, pear, and assorted cheeses on sourdough sandwich, I ask, "Why did you use mayo to coat the bread for grilling versus butter? I always use butter."

"Old chef's trick. Mayo has a higher smoke point than

butter, so it's less likely to burn. This gives you a more evenly browned crust on the bread and allows the cheese to melt inside."

"Which is why I always end up throwing my grilled cheese sandwiches into the microwave to get the cheese melted. All I can say is that yours is delicious—and I will be stealing this chef's trick for all of my future grilled cheese needs."

Pretending to stab a knife in his heart, he says, "The microwave? That's sacrilege for a chef." He's looking at me and laughing, a relaxed chuckle, like so many we shared when we were dating.

"Can I ask a question, Lynds?"

"Sure," I say hesitantly.

"Is David a screamer?"

My eyes go big at the question, and now I'm bent over cackling—again. We spent so much of our two years together laughing that it feels as natural as slipping on a favorite sweater you forgot you owned but fits just right. I manage to spit out, "I don't think that's any of your business, Marcus," my tone teasing and softer than I mean it to be, sounding almost like an invitation back into the space we once shared.

He turns beet red and says, "No, no, no...I didn't mean it like *that*. I meant, does he have a tendency to yell a lot in the kitchen?"

I knew what he meant, or at least I assumed that's what he meant, but it's still nice to see a little embarrassment manifest itself on his face and in his voice.

With a big sigh, I reply, "Yes, he is a screamer, as you put it. He yells a lot at the restaurant staff. He yells at the cooks. He yells at the waitstaff. He yells at everyone. But *never* when the cameras are around. He would never want it to get out that this is how he runs his restaurants—with fear."

As I say the words, I can't help but think about Mindi. Does he yell at her? And if he does, why does she take it? I wouldn't put up with that, that's for sure. Then I scold myself, acknowledging that I put up with a lot more from him.

But he's her problem now, not mine.

"If I say yes, I want you to know, I don't yell. I may occasionally raise my voice if we are slammed or if things aren't going as smoothly as I think they should, but it's more of a tone thing—not yelling. I treat all of my crew with courtesy and respect—from the dishwasher to the owner. I'm also not afraid to apologize if I'm wrong or out of line, and I'm generous with compliments for a job well done."

This is music to my ears. I've only ever been in David's kitchens, and then only briefly, so all I know is yelling, but Marcus appears earnest with his words. It's all almost too good to be true.

"And I apologize if I came across as cocky or arrogant when I first walked in. I wasn't really expecting to run into you. To say I was caught off guard would be an understatement. Then you said you were conducting interviews, and I'd be lying if I didn't say how much I *need* to be back in a kitchen. I've enjoyed my time away, but cooking is like breathing for a good chef, and I need to breathe."

His passion for cooking is evident in his eyes. At the mere mention of cooking and the kitchen, you can see a glint like the shine of a perfectly polished chef's knife. It's not just a job to him—it's an art form, a calling, maybe even his true love. It's who he is.

"No worries. I think we were both surprised," I say, not wanting him to feel bad for telling me about his talents. After all, I'm used to cocky chefs. "But I have a very important question."

He looks up from the pan he is cleaning and says, "Ask me anything."

His face looks serious, stoic. Maybe he's expecting a question about our breakup or something from our past, but I'm not going there today. There's only one thing on my mind.

"Are you saying yes? Do you want to be our head chef?"

"Yes, I'm saying yes. I very much would like to work here with you, Lyndsay."

The way he says it, with a smile and lilt that would make women of any age swoon, brings a slight flush to my cheeks and a grin that I can't control. I stand and walk over to him, extending my hand, and say, "Then you are hired, Marcus Bremerton. Welcome to the team."

I have a head chef.

~

"YOU HIRED *MARCUS BREMERTON* TO BE YOUR HEAD chef? Are you freakin' kidding me? What's that phrase...out of the frying pan, into the fire?"

Chloe is on my couch, glass of wine in hand, looking at me like I've lost my ever-loving mind. I'm ready to begin justifying why I hired him, when she adds, "But tell me...how does he look?"

Marcus was always handsome in high school. No doubt about it. One of those guys who never seemed to have an awkward phase. No acne. No need for braces. No dorky haircuts. No uncool clothes. He just seemed always to be... Marcus.

And, while all the girls thought he was good-looking, with dark hair, the bluest of blue eyes, and a body that was muscular but not overkill, he never let it go to his head. He was friends with everyone, always using his kindness and killer sense of humor to befriend all—jocks and geeks, preppies and punks, goths and metalheads. They all liked Marcus. I can most assuredly say that while he was easy on the eyes, it was his personality that attracted you to him. Everyone wanted to be around him. I was just the lucky one who got to call him my boyfriend.

"Um, he looks like Marcus." Which isn't a lie.

He looked like an older, still extremely handsome, Marcus Bremerton. Okay, beyond handsome.

"Um, yeah...I'm gonna need more than that."

"What do you want me to say? He's got the same short hair with more gray than black, but don't we all? His eyes are still that captivating blue, like the color of the lake in the spring after the ice has melted." Shit! I didn't mean to say that last part aloud. Chloe's giving me a knowing look, but I just dig myself in deeper. "And damn if he doesn't still have those dark, ultra-long lashes..."

"Dang! I would've sworn he wore mascara in high school. I mean, I know he didn't, but, man, those lashes were to die for!"

"Yeah...they didn't go anywhere."

"Did he put on a few pounds? Tell me he's fat!"

"Chloe! That's not nice, and he's not fat. He's really fit. I mean, it was hard to see under his flannel shirt, but he looked good." The tone of *he looked good* denotes a more than slight objectification, and while I would scold any man who spoke about a woman this way, it's Chloe. She's my bestie, and we've talked about boys, and then men, since we were twelve years old. However, I do regret the words as soon as I say them, as I know what Chloe is going to say next.

"You don't think it's a big mistake hiring your *ex-boyfriend* to be the head chef at your *new restaurant*?"

"I think there weren't a lot of great candidates, and he certainly has all the skills—and more—that I was hoping to find. I really don't see that I had a choice."

Chloe wants to believe me, but her doubt is visible in the way she raises her eyebrows at me.

I continue, "We'll need to establish some boundaries, of course. This is a business relationship."

"Uh-huh. Keep telling yourself that. Is he married?"

"Umm, he mentioned that he divorced a couple of years ago, which is why he left The Sagamore and went on that pop-up tour down South. I didn't see a ring."

"But you looked!"

Busted! I did look.

But he could have a girlfriend...or a boyfriend. I don't know his relationship status. And I haven't had time to do a proper social media stalking to see what I can find out.

"Yeah, I looked. I looked because I was wondering if he'd need family health insurance." I'm not sure why that popped into my brain, but score one for me! Quick! Very quick!

"Yeah...I don't believe you."

"Chloe, health insurance is a very important benefit—and it's also very expensive. I need to account for everything in my budget." I say it with a straight face, but neither of us is picking up what I'm putting down, and we both dissolve into laughter, loud and unrestrained.

"All I'm saying, Lyndsay, is that this has the potential to be complicated. You were devastated when he broke up with you in high school. I don't want to see you rebound into a relationship because it seems easy or convenient."

"Wait! Didn't you just tell me the other night that I need to go out and sleep with someone and just get it over with? That I needed a hookup to help me get over David?"

"I did, and I still believe that. But sleeping with your first is not some random hookup. No matter what you may try to tell yourself. It would be an emotional train wreck—and you know it."

She's not wrong. And I don't need a train wreck. I don't even need a bump in the tracks.

"Okay, okay…you're right. Like I said, we'll establish some boundaries. We're adults. It will be fine."

"Might want to put those boundaries in writing, jus' sayin'."

"Haha. Very funny."

But she's not wrong. I'm not sure what that would look like in a contract.

NON-ROMANTIC AGREEMENT CONTRACT

This Agreement ("Agreement") is entered into on this ___ day of _______________, 2023, by and between:

Lyndsay Leach, hereinafter referred to as "First Party", and

Marcus Bremerton, hereinafter referred to as "Second Party."

WHEREAS, the First Party and Second Party agree to engage in a strictly professional and non-romantic relationship; and

WHEREAS, the Second Party acknowledges that they may be considered enticing by some standards;

NOW, THEREFORE, in consideration of the mutual promises and covenants contained herein, the parties hereto agree as follows:

1. Non-Engagement Clause

The First Party hereby agrees that under no circumstances shall she engage in any romantic, intimate, or sexual relationship with the Second Party. This includes, but is not limited to, any form of sleeping together, flirtation, or general cavorting.

2. Temptation Clause

The Second Party acknowledges that they may possess certain enticing or alluring qualities, but the First Party commits to resisting all such temptations, no matter how compelling the circumstances may seem.

3. Affirmation of Professionalism

Both parties affirm that this agreement serves to maintain a strictly platonic and professional dynamic, ensuring that neither party will cross any boundaries of intimacy or temptation.

4. Duration

This Agreement shall remain in full force and effect indefinitely or until such time as both parties mutually agree to amend or dissolve this contract in writing.

5. Breach of Contract

In the event of a breach of this Agreement, the offending party agrees to provide an acceptable form of restitution, such as an apology, public acknowledgement of the breach, or a lifetime supply of awkward, avoidant glances.

IN WITNESS WHEREOF, the parties hereto have executed this Agreement on the date first above written.

____

Lyndsay Leach
First Party

____

Marcus Bremerton
Second Party

"My next question—did you tell your mom?"

Oof. *Way to bring down the mood, Chloe.*

"No, I came home and told you. You were the first person. But I will need to tell her, and soon. She's volunteered to come help me with a few things at the restaurant, and there will be no avoiding Marcus."

While I was dating Marcus, my mom loved him. Loved him like her own son. He had dinner with us on Friday nights. He spent holidays with us. I think he was at our house more than his own because his mom was always working to make ends meet, and my mom and dad, well, they welcomed anyone and everyone who wanted to hang out at our place. We were the house where all my friends spent time; it's just that Marcus spent a little more time than most.

But when he broke up with me before graduation—without a reason—my mom was done with Marcus. I can't say that the breakup was more brutal on her than it was on me, because that's not true, but my mom was crushed. I think we spent five days together, eating pint after pint of Ben and Jerry's Cherry Garcia for breakfast, lunch, and dinner. After five days, she declared that I could no longer mention his name and, in mom-like fashion, told me there were other fish in the sea.

She would not be thrilled by this *business decision* I have made.

But that's all it is. A business decision.

"Please, please call her now and put her on speakerphone and tell her. I want to be here for it." She's laughing wildly, practically hyperventilating, as she says it, knowing that my mom's reaction is going to be nothing short of WTF.

"Yeah...not happening. I'll give you the recap *after* I speak with her, but you don't get to be here for the live-action version."

"Party pooper!" she says with her best faux-pouty face.

"That's me! Spoiler of all fun!"

I get up and grab the bottle of wine off the counter, refill both of our glasses, and throw some chips and dip on the coffee table. Once again, dinner is served! Chloe cooks less than me, so this is practically a gourmet meal.

She reaches for the bag and digs into the French onion dip, getting a big ol' scoop before she asks me how Marcus and I left things.

"We traded phone numbers, and he's supposed to meet me at the restaurant tomorrow so we can talk about the menu.

We really need to get that all squared away before we can do much else."

"Can I see your phone?" Chloe asks.

I'm not sure why she wants my phone, but I grab it from the end table and hand it to her.

I can see her scrolling through my contacts until she finds his name.

"Does he have a ringtone?"

"No," I reply, knowing that in just a few seconds he will have his own *special* ringtone. All the important people in my life have their own ringtone—an '80s song I have chosen for them. Dare I say an '80s song that I've specially curated for that person? Yes, I'll say it because a lot of thought and effort go into making sure that the song fits that person at that particular moment in time. And the songs are wide and varied, from Def Leppard to Duran Duran to Queen and everything in between.

With a look of extreme satisfaction on her face, she says, "He does now!"

And when she hits play, all I can do is fling myself back on the sofa and giggle like a burst pipe, unstoppable.

The unmistakable voice of Marvin Gaye is singing "Sexual Healing."

I manage to curtail my laughter and say, "Didn't you just tell me to put the boundaries in writing? *That* would be more than crossing boundaries. *That* would practically be an invasion. Plus, you know the rule. All special ringtones must be from the '80s."

"1981. I checked. But you're right. Marvin Gaye is not appropriate based on my admonishment."

Then she's back at it, changing the ringtone once again.

"How about this?" Chloe asks, doing very little to hide the mischievous look on her face as she hits play once again.

This time, Joan Jett and the Blackhearts' "I Hate Myself for Loving You" blasts from the tinny phone speaker.

I can't help but laugh out loud again—and it feels so good after weeks of wallowing in my own misery. Chloe's love of the '80s runs as deep as mine, and if I say no to this one, she's just going to pull another song out of the jukebox that plays in her head.

"I can live with that," I reply. "As long as we're clear on the fact that I do *not* love him now, nor do I plan on loving him in the future."

Chloe grins at me, placing my cell phone back down on the coffee table, and says, "Whatever you have to tell yourself, Lynds."

After seeing how fantastic he looked and knowing that we're going to have to work together in such close proximity, this is most assuredly what I need to tell myself. In fact, I may need to get it discreetly tattooed somewhere that I can look at when I need a reminder.

Because...damn! He is still as fine and charming as ever.

Chapter Six

"I've got coffee!" he yells.

"Coming!" Coffee is just what I need.

Marcus hands me a large caramel latte—did he remember this is my fave?—and asks, "What were you doing in the basement?"

Taking a large gulp while reaching into the cabinet where I stashed the croissants that Candace, our new pastry chef, dropped off, I reply, "I was doing inventory in the wine cellar. We're definitely going to need to replenish the selection. There's not as much down there as I thought." I shove a buttery croissant into my mouth and, with flaky pastry tumbling down the front of my shirt, add, "Here, try one of these. I think you'll approve."

With his mouth full of croissant, he vocalizes his approval of Candace's skills with a teeny moan that is quite sexy. "I know we have no need for croissants on the menu, but these are incredible."

"Wait until you try her flourless chocolate cake. It's orgasmic." Whoops! Could have used a better adjective there. But he doesn't seem to notice.

"Looking forward to it!" He takes another swig of his coffee, which smells distinctly black, unlike my sweet concoction, and continues, "So, are you ready to discuss the menu?"

"Yup. Let's get after it." I'm excited to hear his thoughts and suggestions. I have a big-picture idea, but I know that Marcus and his team will have to execute it, so it's critical that he's involved in the process.

We make our way to the dining room and sit at one of the tables for six, giving us plenty of room to spread out. I have my notebooks and sparkly pens, of course, plus my laptop, and I can see that Marcus has brought his computer as well.

"I was wondering..." He looks at me with some trepidation. "If you'd be interested in doing farm-to-table with a Southern flair?"

He's watching my reaction, trying to gauge my feelings about his suggestion.

The Northeast is not exactly crawling with Southern restaurants, a few fried chicken joints, and a couple of good barbecue spots, but around here, Southern cuisine isn't prevalent. This could be the perfect concept to set us apart. I wanted farm-to-table, and he's just done an eighteen-month sweep of the south—it's the unique meld we need.

"I LOVE it!"

"You do? I didn't want to steal your thunder, but the two things really mesh well."

"I'm in. I love the idea. I think farm-to-table with a subtle Southern component could be a hit. Make us stand out. Southern cuisine always seems so welcoming, and I know with the right ingredients, we can make sure it's elevated yet comforting."

He responds quickly, his apprehension gone, his face pure enthusiasm. "YES. Those are my thoughts exactly. I was nervous last night about bringing this idea to you—nothing like stepping on your new boss's toes on the first day—but I couldn't seem to let it go."

"Marcus, there's no need for you to be nervous about bringing ideas to me. We need to work together, more as partners, okay? And please don't ever refer to me as your boss again."

A deep laugh comes from him, a sound that brings me immediately back to our high school days, making my head swim with memories and a hint of giddiness that I can still elicit such a response. "Okay, yes...you're right—which means you won't mind me sharing the sample menu I put together last night. It's just a sample, just ideas. We can change or delete anything you don't think vibes with your big picture."

He has a sample menu? Wow! I'm impressed.

Starting up his laptop, he slides his chair closer to me, our elbows touching, and I find myself staring at his forearm. A tattoo of a sleek chef's knife runs lengthwise, the blade angled so the point aims directly toward his wrist—sharp, deliberate, and impossible to miss. The design is bold black ink with subtle shading, giving the steel a realistic, almost reflective edge.

From the hilt of the knife, instead of a plain handle, tongues of flame burst upward, licking along his forearm in stylized arcs of red and orange. The fire looks alive, curling and twisting as if it's feeding off the heat of Marcus himself. The contrast between the cold steel and the hot blaze makes it unforgettable. It's the kind of tattoo that tells you everything about him in one glance: dangerous with a knife, consumed by his craft.

"Lynds, what do you think?"

I snap myself out of whatever that fixation was and bring my eyes back to the screen.

What he has put together is so impressive and amazing that I'm sure there is drool running down my face. Duck confit sliders with apple chutney? Yum! Southern fried chicken and waffles? My stomach is grumbling just thinking about it. And the desserts? My sweet tooth would be here night after night to taste any of these. This menu is incredible. I don't want to change a thing—and I need to tell him this because he's staring at me, and I think he's holding his breath, waiting for my thoughts.

"It's...it's freaking amazing!"

He lets out a big sigh of relief, and I can see the tension leave his shoulders as they drop down from his ears.

His eagerness for me to love what he's put together is as evident as a neon sign blinking in the night. "You like it? Really? What do you want to change? We can change anything. I was really just brainstorming last night...the Southern influence is subtle, but people will taste it, for sure."

His voice trails off, and he's staring right at me. Wanting to reassure him that I love it, I place my hand on top of his and say, "I wouldn't change a thing."

Then, I quickly pull my hand away, as if I've been burned by the flames of his tattoo. I don't think he noticed my sudden retraction, but I need to remind myself: *Boundaries. We need boundaries.*

"I didn't have time to put together thoughts for the bar, but a full bar, of course, and we could do local beer, wine, and hard cider flights, and maybe some Southern-inspired cocktails to tie it all together."

"Marcus, you have put together an incredible menu—right down to the descriptions." The writer in me is impressed that he took the time to think about how to represent each dish, and I know our guests will be salivating as they read.

But I do have questions.

"Do you think we can source all these ingredients? Do you think we can find kitchen staff to support you? You can't do all this alone. This menu is not a one-person show."

"I already started reaching out to farmers and purveyors last night, and everyone I talked to was eager to work with us. Once it warms up, there's room out back for a rather good-sized garden. I can plant the herbs and tomatoes we need there. You hired a pastry chef, so we'll need to share the dessert menu with her and make sure she can also handle the breads and rolls—which, if her croissants are any indication of her skills, will be a walk in the park for her. If you could take charge of the bar and beverages, that would help immensely. Do you remember Heather, who graduated with us? She owns a large wine and liquor store; I'm sure if you call her, she can get you pointed in the right direction for everything we need on that end."

His voice is effervescent, like a newly opened bottle of champagne. He has a plan. And right now, I'm just along for the ride—and I'm relieved.

This is a huge weight off my shoulders, having a chef and a menu. I could never have come up with something this good. Plus, Marcus's contacts and connections are things I could never bring to the table. David handled all of that, and I'm not sure how much he really worked with true local farmers and vendors.

"Now for the big question...how soon do you think we can be ready to open?" I ask, hoping we can do this by June first, at the very latest.

"How hard are you willing to work?"

I need this distraction. I need to forget about David. Forget about the fact that I'm fifty-three years old and soon to be a divorcée. Forget that my career is at a standstill. Maybe getting this restaurant off the ground will be what I need to get my creative juices flowing once again, so I can come up with something for my next book.

"I'm in. All in. I've got nothing on my calendar, and I'm

ready to roll up my sleeves." I mean, I have a book to write, but...

"Then, what do you think about an April first soft opening?"

Whoa. Six weeks. I was originally thinking May first, giving us ten weeks, but if Marcus thinks we can do this in six...who am I to argue? I'm going to cling to his enthusiasm and go for it.

"Okay. April first opening it is." I can't believe I'm saying those words. "April Fool's Day. Let's just hope the joke isn't on us."

Marcus grins. "Yes! I'm glad you're on board. And don't worry. The only joke will be how fast we blow people's minds. Now grab your notebook and those glittery pens of yours, and let's start divvying up the tasks that need to get done because the list is long, and time is short."

I nod, trying to swallow the flutter of panic under my ribs. Six weeks. Six. Weeks. But this is what I need. A deadline. A deadline that scares me as much as it excites me.

As we're wrapping up our division of duties, I hear the front door open, and my mother's voice calls out, "Lyndsay...whose truck is that parked outside?"

No, she didn't tell me she was stopping by.

No, I didn't call her last night to tell her I had hired Marcus as my head chef.

No, I'm not prepared for her reaction when she sees him.

She makes her way into the dining room, where Marcus's back is to her, but not for long.

"Hello, Mrs. Leach! It's so good to see you again."

My mother's mouth hangs agape, but no words are coming out. This might be a first for her.

"Mom, you remember Marcus Bremerton from high school, don't you?" I'm standing behind Marcus, giving my mom a look that clearly conveys: *Don't say anything stupid, Mom.*

Marcus's hand is outstretched to my mom, in an attempt to shake hers, but before he can do so, my mom says, "Lynd-say, can I see you in the kitchen?"

I feel like a child again, one who's about to get in trouble after doing something she shouldn't have.

"Sure, Mom. We'll be right back, Marcus." I attempt to make my voice light and breezy, but it comes out strained and stilted, the tension creeping into my words despite my best efforts.

My mom grabs me by the elbow and ushers me back to the kitchen. I have the same feeling I did that one time, when I was eleven years old, and my mom washed my mouth out with soap after I used some of my newly acquired middle school vocabulary on her.

The door to the kitchen swings closed behind us, and in a more than miffed but less than angry tone, my mother says, "What the hell is he doing here?"

Deep breath, Lynds.

"Yesterday, I hired Marcus to be the head chef here at 518 Farm-to-Table." I offer no explanation and no apology. I say it in a matter-of-fact manner, hoping she will let it drop. Knowing that's not going to be the case.

"You did *what*? Are you insane? Has the divorce made you daft? You really think hiring the boy you loved so madly when you were younger is the best move as you divorce David now?"

I never told my mom that I loved Marcus when I was growing up, although I did. It must have been readily apparent from the way we acted around each other. What started as young love at sixteen grew into true love by the time we were eighteen. Or at least, I thought it was true love—until he ended things.

I know she's looking out for me, but I need her to know that I've got this all under control. "Mom. I have not lost my mind. Marcus is an incredible chef with a résumé that rivals David's—just without all the celebrity bullshit. He's the best person for the job, and it was strictly a business decision."

Her face conveys everything I need to know. She doesn't believe a word I said.

"Lyndsay, you can tell yourself that, but that boy broke your heart, and I don't want to see that man do it again. You can say you're not vulnerable now, but you are. Divorce isn't easy, and you've had no time to process what's happening. You've just jumped into this restaurant project with both feet as a way to dull the pain. I don't blame you for doing it; it's what I would do in your situation. But hiring Marcus?"

My mother knows about dulling the pain. When my father died five years ago, she jumped into *everything* with both feet. Volunteering at the food pantry, animal shelter, and nursing home. Serving as a board member on both a local women's philanthropic group and our community theater. Nothing as drastic as starting a new business that she knew very little about, but let's say the proverbial apple has not fallen too far.

I cut her off. "Mom, we're not discussing this anymore. I made a business decision. That's all. I expect you to be polite to him and make him feel welcome. Remember, at one time, he was like a son to you."

I can tell she's reminiscing...probably back to the days of him sitting at our kitchen counter, sharing bits and pieces of his school day with her, eating her warm chocolate chip cookies, and swigging down a glass of ice-cold milk. It was practically a daily ritual for two years. She grabs my cheeks with both of her hands, locking her eyes with mine, and says, "He was, but you're my flesh and blood. You always come first. Don't ever forget that." And then, like I'm seven again, she kisses my forehead and makes her way to the dining room, with me following behind her, silently kicking myself for not having told her about Marcus before now.

But my mom is class all the way, always has been, and always will be, and enters with a big smile on her face, extending her hand to Marcus, who in turn wraps her up in an awkward hug.

"From the look of things, Lyndsay didn't have time to tell you that she hired me to work here. I can imagine how shocked you must have been to see me when you walked in. I know when Lyndsay and I broke up, I probably didn't leave you with the best impression, but I hope you can forgive me for the past. I was young and dumb and didn't always make the best decisions."

I can see my mom's face soften at his words, and I admire him for owning up to his "mistake" in breaking up with me, although I still have no idea why he did so all those years ago. This is probably an elephant we will need to remove from the room before our working relationship goes much further, but for now, this apology to my mom is enough.

"That was many, many years ago, Marcus, and yes, you were dumb and broke my daughter's heart, but I can forgive."

I roll my eyes, wishing she had not thrown in the part about him breaking my heart, but she did. Marcus catches my eye roll.

"Thank you, I appreciate that," he says, with a smile that could melt an ice queen's heart—so it takes nothing for my mom to melt. I watch her step towards him once again, and she embraces him, in a much less awkward hug than the one a few minutes ago.

And then, without missing a beat, she's back to her old self. "Lyndsay, what are you doing with these naked walls?

This beige paint is boooooring!" "Boring" comes out like a child stuck reading a book on the very first day of summer vacation.

"Well, Mom, I was thinking of reaching out to some local artists to display their works here. We could make it an art gallery of sorts and sell their paintings and sculptures here. What do you think about that?"

I know she will love the idea. One of her many volunteer positions has her working at the Lower Adirondack Regional Arts Center, and she's befriended many talented local artisans over the years.

"Leave it to me, darling." She says "darling" with a mix of affection and mock exasperation, like she's Bette Davis. "I'll reach out to my artist friends, and we will create some gorgeous gallery walls to cover this dreadful greige."

Perfect. She took the bait. That's one thing I can check off my to-do list that is as long as a CVS receipt.

THE NEXT FEW HOURS PASS BY AT LIGHT SPEED WITH him and me each making nonstop phone calls. Local farmers and producers. The sign maker. The printer for new menus. I call Heather to see if she has time to talk about the restaurant's bar. Marcus gets us set up with one of the big local food supply companies for all the basic ingredients the restaurant needs. I call and place additional ads for servers, bussers, and dishwashers. He calls Candace to ask if she can come by tomorrow to discuss the dessert menu.

With each phone call, we take a gigantic step forward.

I feel a sense of relief...and accomplishment. The niggling doubts that had crept into my mind over the last few weeks— not just about the restaurant, but about my own self-worth and value—are starting to dissipate.

Then I see him thumbing through the résumés from yesterday's round of interviews.

"What do you think? Is there anyone that you think can work in the kitchen?"

"You are not going to believe this, but I'm going to hire all of them."

It's my turn to look at him with disbelief.

"All of them? Even the felon?"

"Did you ask him why he went to prison?"

I did not ask, and from the tone in Marcus's voice, I'm going to get schooled on this one. But I'll bite. "No. Did you?"

"Yes, I called him this morning when you were in the wine cellar talking to Heather. I was straight up with him and asked him what he did. He went to prison because he broke into a pharmacy to get insulin for his dad. His dad couldn't afford the medicine that was necessary to keep him alive—which is completely fucking ridiculous, people should be able to afford the medications they need—and Anthony did what he thought was necessary to save his dad's life. I can't fault him for that. If breaking into a pharmacy would've saved my mom's life, I would've done it. No doubt. Consequences be damned."

I see that wistful look again on his face as he mentions his mom. I let him sit with it for a moment, knowing I can't take away the grief he feels, even after all these years, and then say, "I'm glad you called him and asked. And I'm glad you're giving him a chance." Once again, that Marcus magic appears like it so often did in high school. His ability to befriend anyone, give anyone a chance. It's good to see that his heart is still so big.

"They're all going to need some training, even Blake. I'm sure David trained him well, but every kitchen is just a little different. I told them to give me the rest of the week to get things settled here, get the kitchen stocked, and then we would start training on the new menu, probably the middle of next week."

"You talked to Blake?"

"I did. I think he thought he had a chance at the head chef position and was not thrilled to hear you hired me. We haven't worked together in the past, but I know of him—the restaurant community is pretty tight-knit in this area. He's talented, but we'll have to see if he can get past not being the big dog in the kitchen."

"Oh, is that what you are? The big dog?" I laugh, and he does, too.

"Yup. Bowwow. That's me!"

I start to pack up my laptop and notebook and say, "Well, it's been a long day, and I'm exhausted. I think I'm going to head home. Are you just about finished?"

"I have a few things I want to wrap up, so I think I'll stick around if that's cool with you. Oh, wait. Scratch that. I don't have keys to lock up. I'll just leave with you and finish up tomorrow."

I reach into my purse and pull out the extra set of keys I had made on my way in this morning. "Now you have keys." I smile at him and place them gently in the palm of his hand. For a moment, neither of us moves.

He closes his fingers around them and softly says, "Thank you, Lynds. I know it took a huge leap of faith for you to hire me, but we're going to do great things. I know it."

I nod in agreement, unable to find the right words, and head for the front door.

"Lynds..."

I stop, my hand on the knob. "Yes, Marcus."

"I know you tasted my grilled cheese, but you haven't really tried my food yet. You have no idea if I'm a good chef or not—even if the grilled cheese was perfection," he says with an impish grin.

He's right about that.

Jokingly, I say, "You didn't lie to me about your skills, did you? You are capable of more than grilled cheese?"

"No, not at all. But you should taste my food, really see what I can do. How about I cook for you on Friday night? I can whip up a few of the recipes that we're putting on the menu, and you can try them—see what you think? My place? Say seven p.m.? I can give you directions."

Dinner with Marcus. At his place.

Remember the boundaries.

"I'd like that."

Yet here I am—crossing the boundaries.

Just this once.

For the sake of the restaurant.

I need to taste his food, don't I?

"Great. It's a date."

I know he just casually said those words, but I remind myself: *This is not a date. This is two coworkers having dinner. This is a restaurant owner and her chef tasting the new menu. This is far from a date.*

And I will keep saying those words to myself until I believe them.

Chapter Seven

5 18 FARM-TO-TABLE TO BE RUN BY FORMER AUTHOR, LYNDSAY LEACH, AND LOCAL CHEF, MARCUS BREMERTON

For once, I'm thankful to see my name in the headlines—even if it is just in the local newspaper. I'm also grateful that I haven't been the subject of *The Pulse*'s headlines for over a week now.

Thank you, Melanie, for FINALLY announcing that you're going through with the divorce. You deserve better, girl!

The newspaper reached out to me yesterday to ask for some specifics on when we plan to open, what the menu looks like, etc., and said they'd be sharing them soon. I guess soon meant today. Must've been a slow news day.

And yes, the "former author" stings a little. With the divorce happening, I wish I could scream it from the rooftops that I am STILL an author, and a very successful one at that. But the anonymity has served me well, and there are NDAs galore in place, so I'll let this headline go.

I'm not heading to the restaurant today as I can make calls

from here and sort through the candidates for waitstaff, bussers, and dishwashers. A lot of apps from high school and college kids. The college kids won't be home until mid-May, which may leave us a bit short-staffed to start, but I think with the number of applications we've received, we'll be able to limp through.

I finish sending a few emails to some of the applicants and head to the kitchen to grab another cup of coffee, making a mental note to follow up with the printer about the menus. Seems there is a question about the font choice. As long as they don't use Comic Sans or Arial, I'm pretty flexible.

I also check my sourdough. It's in the bulk fermentation stage, and I do a few quick stretches and folds to help build the gluten structure. My timing should be good to have a loaf to bring to Marcus's house tonight for dinner.

As I put the cloth cover on my dough and set her back on the counter, Joan Jett's voice fills the kitchen, belting out "I Hate Myself for Loving You."

I can't help but smile as I answer.

Working with him this past week has been—surprisingly—easy. We've fallen into a rhythm without trying. We see things in a similar manner. We bounce ideas off each other, not always agreeing with what the other has thrown out, but challenging each other just enough to make things better. We don't always agree, but we always listen. There's an ease between us that feels both new and achingly familiar. We just get along.

It's a lot like when we dated in high school. We were never a couple that had massive fights and broke up just to make up. Our relationship was without drama, uncomplicated. Maybe it was because we were young, and life wasn't complicated at that age. Whatever it was, I sometimes still long for those easy days.

"Hi Marcus," I say, trying to erase the smile from my face as if he could see it over the phone and know how happy I am to hear from him.

"Did you see the paper? They published the article today. That should help create a little buzz for our opening on April first."

"I did see it. And you're right—they really seemed to like the new menu." And I was thrilled that there was only the tiniest mention of David's, just saying that we would be taking over the location in Bolton Landing.

"Okay...just wanted to make sure you saw it. We're still on for tonight, right? Seven p.m.?"

"Yup. Looking forward to it! Wanna give me a hint at what dishes you're making tonight?"

"Nope. It's a surprise! See you tonight."

I JUMP OUT OF THE SHOWER AND THROW ON A ROBE so I can put my bread in the oven.

My ball of jalapeño cheddar sourdough looks picture perfect. Earlier, I scored a series of small cuts that look like wheat stalks, and she will be gorgeous after she comes out of the oven.

I finish blowing dry my hair and put on some foundation, then run back out to the kitchen to take the lid off my bread oven.

She's doing fabulous.

Now, what am I going to wear tonight?

It should not be such a big deal. He's seen me almost every day this week, so jeans and a sweater would be fine. But I don't want fine. But I also don't want to look like I'm trying too hard. What says you're trying just enough?

I mean, no. Boundaries.

In the back of my closet, I find my gray sweater dress—the one that makes me feel both comfortable and confident—and slip it on with some black tights and my favorite pair of boots. From my jewelry case, I grab my go-to chunky silver necklace and a pair of hoop earrings that catch the light. I brush my black-and-gray hair and decide against pulling it up in a ponytail, instead letting it frame my face naturally. A touch of mascara, a hint of blush, and a mist of Jo Malone on my wrists.

Not bad, if I do say so myself.

As I stare at myself in the mirror, my reflection blurs beneath the weight of too many questions about the end of my marriage that I've been holding onto for weeks. Why wasn't I enough for him? Was I more to blame than I let myself believe? Could I have done more to keep our marriage intact? Should I have insisted on marriage counseling? Did I give up on us too easily?

I don't come up with any clear answers. Just innumerable what-ifs.

Maybe I was more distant as I tried to figure out the next step in my secret writing career. The words had stopped flowing for me like they once did, and I did not—nor do I now—have a strong hook for my next book. Eighteen months of stalled pages and mounting doubt. And because David never knew about my books, I had not confided in him. Just internalized it all.

Maybe it had been showing more than I thought. Maybe he mistook my silence as indifference, my withheld career woes as something more personal. Maybe while I was struggling to find my voice on the page, I lost it in our marriage, too.

Perhaps this secret I'd been keeping for so long did more harm than good. I had let us drift apart, even if I didn't recognize I was doing it at the time.

It still did not excuse his cheating on me, but I could almost understand it more.

Almost.

The anger I feel toward him is slowly disappearing. Not gone but going. And it's not for his sake, but for mine. Being angry all the time is no way to live.

It's not the way I want to live, that's for sure.

I'M ABOUT TEN MINUTES EARLY—NO BIG SURPRISE— so I drive around Bolton Landing. The town is quiet at this hour, the kind of calm that settles in after sunset. A few locals linger on the sidewalks, heading to dinner or, perhaps, home after an early supper.

Soon, I hope these same people will be walking through the doors at 518 Farm-to-Table. I want the locals to love it, to feel like it's theirs as much as mine. Their approval matters more than I care to admit. I want them to embrace this venture like they did when it belonged to David. Without them, the restaurant cannot be what I want it to be. Need it to be. Because it is a second chance for me. I'm not sure if it's a second chance at a career or trusting myself or reclaiming my confidence, but whatever it is, I need it to be successful, and I crave their affirmation.

I take a left and find Marcus's house. Located about three blocks back from Lake Shore Drive, it's a small ranch with a porch and a stone and cedar exterior, lending it a rustic charm despite its relatively new construction. The door is navy blue, and soft white light cascades from the windows. It's the kind of house that looks both grounded and welcoming, much like him.

I walk up on his porch and ring the bell, only to hear him yell, "Come in! My hands are full, but the door is unlocked."

He's at the stove, and every burner is in use—and the house smells of savory herbs, roasting meats, maple syrup, and a hint of bourbon. It smells like our menu reads.

He still has his back to me but tells me to throw my coat on the chair and to pour myself a glass of wine.

I will. I need to calm my nerves.

Why am I so nervous?

"I brought you something."

"You did? You didn't have to do that."

"It's just some sourdough bread...jalapeño cheddar."

"Did you pick it up from The Bolton Bakery? I didn't think she was open this week. Ski trip, I thought."

"No, I made it." A flush comes to my cheeks as I say it, embarrassment taking over. Who am I to bring bread to a chef?

"What? You made it? I thought you said you didn't cook." He's now turned from the stove and staring at me, a playful look of suspicion overtaking his face, bringing those distinct crinkles to the corners of his eyes as his smile forms.

"I see that look on your face—you're not quite sure if you should believe me or not—but I *did* make this bread, Marcus Bremerton." My tone is playful. "Sourdough is the one thing I can do, and I do it pretty damn well."

His grin is now as wide as a Cheshire cat's smile, and he says, "Wait. So that bread for the grilled cheese...you made it? Why didn't you tell me? That bread was amazing! I would've sworn it came from The Bolton Bakery."

I love that I have managed to surprise him with my one culinary talent and say, "Yup, that was all me."

"Impressive! I can't wait to try this one. There's a bread knife in that drawer to the right of me. It will be perfect with all twenty-two cheeses I picked up for us to try. Oh, and pour yourself a glass of wine. Red's on the counter. White is in the fridge."

"And the red Solo cups and Boone's Farm are where?" I joke, knowing this will bring him back to our high school days in an instant. "And please tell me you are kidding about twenty-two different cheeses?"

"Sorry, no Solo cups or Boone's tonight." He lets out a laugh at my reference to my favorite high school drink and vessel for consuming it. "And yes, I'm kidding about the cheese, but only slightly. I think I have at least eight. Meredith just kept saying, 'You've got to try this one. Oh, and this one!' and I finally had to stop her and tell her to pick her absolute favorites so we could at least narrow a few things down. I think she wants to impress you. She mentioned that she tried to get David to buy from her in the past, but he refused."

My heart drops at the mention of David. I know it won't be the last time he comes up in conversation, although I wish it would be. Shaking away the memories that want to return, I break off a piece of the aged cheddar she has sent, bringing my focus to the here and now. To the wine and cheese. To Marcus and me.

"Can you slice me a piece of the smoked Gouda and put it on top of your bread?"

He's busy stirring a pot of clam chowder and what I assume is the bourbon apple compote for the pork tenderloin. It all smells incredible. The rich aroma of the chowder, creamy and savory, fills the air, mingling with the sweet and tangy scent of the compote. My stomach growls in anticipation as I watch him work, his movements confident and precise. The kitchen is warm, cozy, and full of life, a stark contrast to the cold, quiet night outside.

I bring the bread and cheese over to him, but he has no free hands. He says, "Hey, just pop that in my mouth so I can keep stirring," and opens wide.

I do it.

I'm so close that I can't help but inhale his cologne, a

mixture of salt and cedar and a hint of sandalwood, which smells just as intoxicating as the meal he is preparing, and when my fingers brush his lips, a chill runs up my spine.

"Lynds...your bread is incredible. You should've told me about this secret skill of yours the other day."

"Thanks, I really just make it for me or family and friends."

"Well, I think we should discuss you making bread for the restaurant. Small loaves of sourdough that we put on each table? What do you think?"

"I think that's a discussion for another day."

He takes a step closer to me and drops his head, almost like he's leaning in for a kiss, but then he pauses and gently squeezes my arm, saying, "That's a discussion I'm going to hold you to."

Why am I disappointed that he didn't kiss me?

I smile at him, wanting to change the subject, and make a not-so-smooth transition by sharing that I love his house. It's relaxed and comfortable, just like Marcus has always been. A brown leather sofa and a black leather lounge chair take up most of the space in the living room, but he also has a small industrial coffee table, and there's an end table with numerous cooking magazines on it, plus a pine-scented candle that he's lit. His kitchen is state-of-the-art, to be expected, with a Bosch stove and a collection of high-end cookware hanging from a pot rack over a gleaming slab of marble that catches the light, reflecting it in soft ripples. Music plays softly in the background. Steely Dan. Not what we listened to together in high school, but I remember "Reelin' In the Years" being one of his mom's favorites. I can't help but smile at the memory of the two of them belting out this song into a ladle and a whisk when I showed up unannounced one Sunday. Neither of them had a care in the world and continued on, as if they were going to be inducted into the Rock & Roll Hall of Fame.

"Thanks. It's only two years old. I had it built while I was away doing the pop-ups."

"You built a house when you weren't even in the same state? Brave man! I can't imagine doing that."

"You certainly do place a lot of trust in your contractor when you do something like that, but it all worked out."

We're both quiet for a moment, and it feels slightly awkward. I know I'm thinking about the trust I gave so freely to David, only to have it broken. But what is Marcus thinking about? I don't want this to get weird. It's been easy all week. Nonstop talking as we work through to-do lists and make choices and decisions to keep forward momentum. There's no need for it to be weird tonight.

Finally, he breaks the silence with, "I hope you're hungry."

"Famished. I don't think I've had anything since a container of yogurt this morning."

"Then keep trying some of Meredith's cheeses and pay attention to the ones that you really like so we can decide where to use them on the menu. Obviously, on the artisan cheeseboard, but there may be other places we can incorporate them. I just need to add a little more cream to the clam chowder, and we can start with that. Things will be slightly out of order tonight—hope that's okay?"

"I'm just excited to try your food, make sure you're a real chef and all...not some impostor who bamboozled his way into my restaurant." The good-natured ribbing feels unnaturally natural. I could never tease David about his cooking skills. One night, early in our marriage, he tried his hand at a French dish—I can't even remember what it was— and when he placed it in front of me, he asked for my honest opinion. In my honest opinion, it could have used more salt, but it was still delicious. And while I don't remember the meal he prepared, I remember he didn't speak to me for three days. All over the fact that I wanted a touch more salt.

"Phew! Pressure! Well, if I'm a charlatan, you'll know it pretty quickly. My cheese selection skills are not going to be enough to hide a lack of culinary abilities."

"Not too worried about you being a fraud if the smells coming from this kitchen are any indication."

I see the look of pride on his face, and he gestures to me to take a seat at his kitchen table, which, while large enough to seat four, only has two chairs positioned rather close to one another. He brings over a cup of clam chowder for each of us. It smells of the ocean, but also like the kitchen of a Southern nana. I take a large spoonful to find that it is chock-full of clams and potatoes and celery, and spices that provide a little heat on the back end, spices that aren't typical for this classic New England dish.

"So, what spices did you add to this to give it a Southern flair?

"Is it too hot? If it is, just tell me. I can tame it down. I added Creole seasoning and hot sauce. Creole seasoning has oregano in it, which I like. But when I make this again, I may try Cajun seasoning, which has some thyme."

"Well, this is fantastic, and I think it will be a hit with our guests. David never used Creole seasoning in his chowder." The minute that last sentence comes out, I want to snatch it back, but I can't. I clear my throat, trying to recover. "I'm sorry. I should not have compared your chowder to David's." I set my spoon down and drop my gaze to the table to avoid his.

"Don't worry about it, Lynds. He was a big part of your life, and he's a chef. Comparison is natural."

He's so gracious, and I force a smile, trying to brush it off, but inside I'm kicking myself. I raise my head, look at him, and say, "Anyway, let's focus on *your* food this evening."

"Fair enough. But seriously, Lynds...if there is something

you don't like, speak up. I can take it. And don't worry about finishing every bite—if you do, you'll be bursting at the seams. I've got a lot of dishes lined up for us."

He clears our soup cups and grabs two salads from the refrigerator—the apple and arugula salad and Berkshire bacon and blueberry salad.

"Try both of these, while I finish up the duck confit sliders and the bacon-wrapped scallops."

He glides back to the stove, where a sizzling pan welcomes the scallops with open arms, while I sample both salads. I'm impressed by how such simple ingredients can deliver colossally big flavors. Knowing what ingredients to put together to create a dish is truly an art, and Marcus is the sculptor.

He continues to move around the kitchen, grabbing things from the pantry and the fridge, heading back to the stove, adding a few herbs and some salt, then tasting, only to add a dash of something else and taste again. It's a bit like watching a dance, and I find myself observing his every step. I can't take my eyes off him.

Soon he brings over the two appetizers and joins me—but just for a minute—so he can put the final touches on the entrées.

There's not a bite I've tasted that I would change.

Finally, he puts down a plate with Vermont maple-glazed pork tenderloin and one with pan-seared trout with lemon-herb butter and joins me at the table.

"I only made one plate of each. I thought we could share."

Sharing plates seems so...intimate, but I don't say anything except, "These look gorgeous. The plating is incredible."

"I'm glad you like it. Dining out really is a culinary experience that should involve all your senses."

I look up from getting a piece of the tenderloin, and Marcus is staring at me. And it's not the first time I've caught him looking at me for just a moment too long this evening.

"What? Do I have something in my teeth?" His expression suggests otherwise. I won't go as far as to say it's a look of longing. More a look of wonder.

"No, it's not that. I can't believe you're sitting here after all these years. I was just thinking about what a fool David was. You are a gorgeous, smart, vibrant woman, and David must be an idiot." He pauses, his eyes never leaving mine. "But I was probably the bigger idiot thirty-five years ago."

I feel my face flush.

Boundaries.

But I need to know.

"That was a long time ago, but since you brought it up, why did you break up with me? Without a reason. I thought things were good, better than good, and then, out of the blue, you tell me that we're over—and without telling me why." My voice is calm and quiet as I work overtime not to let it reflect how much the breakup devastated me.

He drops his head and, for what seems like an eternity, does not speak, until he finally says, "You were too good for me, Lyndsay. You came from a great family that not only welcomed me, but all your friends, with open arms. You knew exactly what you wanted from your life—to go to college, study English, write the next great novel—and look at you. You did all of that and more. I, on the other hand, had no idea what I was going to do with my life, if I could even afford college. And then, in June of that year, right before graduation, my mom was diagnosed with cancer. Since it was only her and me, I knew what I needed to do. I had to stay and help her. She needed me. I had a lot to figure out, and the last thing you needed was to be dragged down by my life."

My chest aches that he ever thought that to be the case. "I wish you had told me what was going on, about your mom...I could've helped." Although at eighteen, I'm not sure what I could've done.

"You needed to go off and do the whole college thing, enjoy everything college had to offer," he says, his voice soft. "I couldn't tell you that my mom was dying and that we were broke."

The frankness of his words slices through the air like a knife, sharp and unavoidable.

"I don't know what to say…I was crushed when we broke up, but it sounds like you were dealing with just so much…" My heartache was nothing, nothing, compared to what he went through.

"I was. It was a lot. I was working multiple jobs to keep my mom and me afloat. Taking her to doctor's appointments and for chemo…missing you, second-guessing my decision to end things."

The look on his face pulls him somewhere far away, back to 1988. For me, those years shimmer in memory, a time that was simpler and easier for me. For him, they're shadowed by loss, by dreams that never had a chance to grow.

He continues, "Then when she passed away, I found out that she had been putting money into a life insurance policy while I was growing up. We may not have been able to afford name-brand cereal, but Mom was putting money away for something she knew would one day help me. That's what allowed me to attend the CIA. That and a great scholarship." He shrugs slightly, as if trying to shake off the weight of the memories.

I reach over and place my hand on top of his.

"It doesn't change things, but all I can say to you is that you were always good enough for me." My voice is low, only wanting to ease the doubt that I might've created, even unintentionally, all those years ago.

"I'm sorry for how I handled things between us. At eighteen, you think you know it all. That you've got all the answers. But you don't. I'm not sure I've got all the answers now, and I'm fifty-three years old."

He's certainly right about that. At what age do we have all the answers?

"Can I ask you something, Lynds?"

Who am I to say no when he's opened up like this? "Of course."

"What really happened with you and David?"

I think back to that night, the night David told me he wanted a divorce, and it replays like a video at five times speed. Am I really prepared to talk about this? Does he really want to hear the details, or is this the type of polite conversation that divorced—or soon-to-be-divorced—people make?

"Do you really want to know?" I ask.

"I wouldn't have asked if I didn't."

He's looking at me, blue eyes locked on mine, and I know that his question was asked with the utmost sincerity. Maybe I'm caught off guard because David asked so few questions that went deeper than surface level during our final years together. *What did you do today? Did you happen to stop by the dry cleaners?* There was so little substance to our conversations. And after such a profound drought of depth, it's unnerving to have someone ask questions that make me share my emotions.

I take a slow inhale and a gulp of wine, hoping that both will keep my voice steady and any residual tears locked away, and say, "He invited me to one of our favorite restaurants, the place where we met, and told me he wanted a divorce."

I stop talking. Not wanting to give any more details. Hoping this answer will be enough, although I know it will not. Even as a teen, Marcus always wanted more. *Why do you love writing so much? What's a dream you've never said aloud? What makes you feel closest to me?* I can remember him asking me these questions so vividly, it's like I'm seventeen again. I know this sentence that I've spit out is not going to satisfy him.

He says nothing. Letting us both sit in the silence until I start speaking again.

"Can I tell you something?" I don't wait for his reply. I just keep going. "That night when I walked in, he barely acknowledged me. He sat at the bar entertaining those around him, regaling them with his stories, giving me this cursory nod like I was one of his waitstaff showing up for work. By the time he graced me with his presence at our table, I'd been there twenty-five minutes. Waiting. Just waiting.

"Then, when he finally did sit down with me, he could barely look at me. He stayed hidden behind his menu. Providing me with curt answers to my questions. Like I was an interruption or an intrusion."

I remember wondering what the hell was going on. At the time, we had been like parallel lines that never met as he poured everything into the new restaurant. And I was accustomed to it. Every time a new venture or opportunity came his way, he went at it like a man possessed, as if the current project were his magnum opus. Like no other opportunities would come his way. But it was never the case. Opportunities were abundant when you were David Montero.

I continue. "He asked me a couple of banal questions about my day." I remember I lied to him about how I'd spent the afternoon, saying I'd been at some library meeting, instead of what I had been really doing, which was writing, or attempting to write. "And then I watched as he drummed the fingers of his left hand on the table."

That detail, that one tell, told me something was up.

"Things got really quiet at the table for a few moments, you know, like might happen on a first date, when you don't know exactly what to talk about. Eventually, I couldn't take it any longer and asked him, 'Is everything okay?' Which was a huge mistake. He's always hated that damn question."

I pause and notice that I'm looking down at the table...in shame? Regret? Both? I raise my chin to see if Marcus is still looking at me. He is.

"What did he say?"

"After what felt like an eternity, he let out a big breath, drained his martini glass, and said, 'Lynds, I want a divorce.'"

In the restaurant, I had laughed nervously, thinking he must be joking, but who jokes about wanting a divorce? It wasn't like I had reached over to his plate and stolen some of his French fries, and he was poking fun at me, saying, *If you don't stop stealing my fries, I'm filing for divorce.*

"I thought it was a joke. I even asked him that. To which he flatly replied, 'No.'"

It's like I'm back in the restaurant reliving that night. My throat tightens, and I clutch the edge of Marcus's table, suddenly aware of how uneven the surface feels beneath my palms. I'm here with Marcus, and while the circumstances are different, my actions mimic those from that evening.

I let out an audible exhale, wanting to stop talking, but I feel like a child who's been given permission to tattle on a sibling, and I can't stop.

"He told me he had been thinking about this for a while and that he just couldn't do *this* anymore. *THIS.* You know, be married. Share his life with me. The person who had stood beside him for twenty years."

More like stood behind him.

"I snapped and asked, 'What exactly can't you do anymore?' And that's when I saw a flicker of something on his face. I wasn't sure if it was regret or guilt, but I eventually got my answer."

Marcus does not interrupt. While Chloe knows the story, I

have not told anyone else the details of that night. It's as if he knows I need to say this, speak my truth.

That night, I wanted to scream at David that this *was* us, that marriages ebb and flow, that twenty years doesn't stay picture-perfect. But the words stayed stuck in my throat, tangled up with a lump of panic and disbelief, a lump so big it threatened to choke me. I feel that same lump this evening.

"Do you know what he said next?"

Marcus shakes his head.

"He said, 'I'm not blaming you. I'm just saying that somewhere along the way, we stopped being...partners. And I can't pretend anymore.' Partners? We were never fucking partners. From the moment he asked me to give up something I loved, to give up a part of me, the partnership was over."

Marcus doesn't ask what David made me give up. Maybe he knows. I choose not to explain. That's a conversation for another day.

"And then he pushed his martini glass aside, asked for the check, and told me he had to leave."

The tension at the table that night had sent the waitress scurrying to get our check. I can see her dropping it on the table and retreating as if she were involved in the skirmish that was unfolding in front of her and didn't want to get hit by the shrapnel. "As I threw a fifty on the table to cover the tab, I asked him, 'Do. You. Love. Her?' I enunciated each word as if the clarity might soften the blow to his reply. But he lied to me. Said there was no one else."

Now I'm angry. My nervous system is in overdrive. My face is flushed, and sweat drips down my neck. I'm right back in that restaurant, and the tears start to come. I feel like fleeing, just like I did that night.

But I don't. I brush the tears away, and Marcus places his right hand on top of mine. He doesn't offer advice or platitudes. We sit in the quiet, both of us soaking up what has been shared.

Finally, he says, "Thank you for telling me. I know that was extremely difficult for you."

I snap myself out of the past, wanting the movie playing inside my brain to stop, and look Marcus in the eyes. His words are genuine, and while I know I needed to get this off my chest, out of my brain, away from my heart, I'm also angry with myself for spilling so much of my personal life. "So, what you've seen in the tabloids is pretty accurate. He was cheating on me. He initially denied it, but the truth always comes out." I want to tell Marcus that I wasn't entirely truthful with David, but I can't bring myself to do it. I don't want him to think less of me, like I was leading a duplicitous life, even if I was. It would cross the boundaries I'm trying to put in place. Plus, there are legal implications, and it's not a secret I'm emotionally prepared to share with him.

Instead, I say, "I guess we each had our secrets. Just mine weren't meant to hurt him, only to help. While his practically destroyed me."

Marcus remains silent. We let the moment breathe, and when I can take it no longer, wanting to guide things back to the present, I say, "Now that we've cleared the air on our big breakup and the oh-so-public end of my marriage, what's for dessert?" My weak attempt to bring some levity back to the evening.

He attempts to push aside the concern that is on his face, smiling feebly, and asks in a voice trying to be funny, "Dessert? You want dessert, too?"

"Um...I'm joking. Just trying to lighten the mood. I know you said you're not much of a pastry guy or baker..."

But he's already up and out of his chair, grabbing for a pie that I did not see on top of his refrigerator.

"It's not your mom's chocolate chip cookies...God, those

were good...but Candace has been practicing her portion of the menu and brought in this maple pecan pie today. I told her I was cooking for you tonight, and she insisted that I bring it home. Will this satisfy your sweet tooth?"

"It certainly will!"

MARCUS HANDS ME THE LAST DISH TO DRY. I'VE BEEN standing next to him—brushing arms and laughing—at the sink for forty-five minutes now.

"The next time you cook for me, we will do it at my place —where I own a dishwasher."

"So, you're saying there will be a next time? That's encouraging."

His voice is flirty, way too flirty for a man who is supposed to be my head chef. And *only* my head chef.

"Well, I will have to try the menu when we change it, and I'd like to change it up at least twice per year, spring and summer, and then fall and winter." This is my feeble attempt *again* at boundaries.

"Oh, yeah...of course. Although I'm not opposed to cooking for you anytime—no need to wait for a menu change."

Once again, the flirtiness is in his voice, unmistakable.

"Thank you for your offer, and for tonight. I am glad I came, and you are an amazing chef," I say as I set down the towel I was using to dry the last pot. "But I don't ever want things to be awkward between us at the restaurant. I think we've been working well together, maybe because we do share a past connection, but I want to keep things professional between us. I hope you understand..."

I say the words, but do I mean them?

"Well, I'm happy to hear that you were able to pick up on

my attempt at flirting. I was afraid I'd lost that skill." He lets out a little laugh, which is endearing and vulnerable at the same time. "And yes, I do understand. *But*, sometimes, you get a second chance for a reason. You can't explain it. I didn't stop by the restaurant looking for you, but you were there. You were looking for a chef, but you weren't looking for me, yet there I was. Coincidences are one thing, kismet is another."

I say nothing and make my way to the living room to put on my winter coat. As I open the front door, I say in a tone barely above a whisper, "Thank you, Marcus. It was a lovely evening."

"I'm glad you came, Lynds...we *will* do it again."

Chapter Eight

I enter the restaurant kitchen, and I'm overwhelmed and overjoyed by a cacophony of "Yes, chef." There are six bodies behind the line, all receiving instruction from Marcus. His kitchen crew has been assembled for a few weeks now, but today is the first time they are all together, at their assigned stations. Marcus has brought them together to assess their strengths and weaknesses, see how they move together, make suggestions, and, most importantly, show them his ways and his vision for running 518 Farm-to-Table.

Marcus glances up, flashes a wide smile, and says, "Everyone, you remember Lyndsay Leach, the owner of this fine establishment."

Several laugh and all respond with a chorus of "Yes, chef," and "Of course." Most give me a polite nod or a small wave and continue with their work, while I say, "It's great to have you all here together. I'm so excited to have you on the team."

Most seem content with my welcome. With the exception of Blake.

He doesn't exactly scowl at me, but I can see his jaw set

and his lips tighten into a thin line. I'm sure he still holds some residual anger that I'm here and David is not, along with the fact that this kitchen now belongs to Marcus and not him. I hope this will not be a problem in the future. He can get over it or move on. This restaurant is now mine. David will never return here.

I stop to check in with Candace, who is working at the dessert station, to see if she needs anything, but she says all is well, although she would like me to sample a few new recipes she's considering bringing to Marcus later today. I gladly tell her to come find me, happy to taste any of her creations.

Heading into the dining room, I shrug out of my jacket and hang it over a chair. I open my computer and skim through my to-do list. It is still long, but we've slowly been knocking things off, and Marcus has assured me that every-thing will get done. I admire his confidence, even if it feels delusional currently.

I stroll back into the kitchen, where Marcus now stands at the stainless prep table near the pass, his sleeves rolled up, his tattoo visible to all. I take in his strong forearms as he clicks a pen and scans his clipboard, deep in thought. It's grounding to watch him work, even on something as mundane as paperwork.

"You're in early today," he says.

"Couldn't sleep," I reply. I stop at the counter, leaning over his shoulder, and ask, "How goes it with the kitchen crew?"

"They're doing fantastic. I promise, they'll be ready when we open."

I smile, feeling a warmth deep in my chest. I didn't antici-pate this. Marcus and I have quickly settled into a partnership without ever really having to name it. We move around the restaurant like a pair of ballroom dancers, never in each other's way, always there to help each other. Lifting one another up when the days are long.

Just as I'm about to ask him if the wine has been delivered, the back door opens, letting in a blast of cool air.

"Delivery!" a voice calls.

Marcus straightens. "That will be Tina."

Seconds later, she steps into the kitchen, a clipboard tucked under her left arm and a crate in her right hand, her long red hair pulled up into a ponytail. I'd guess she's in her mid- to late forties. She's dressed practically in jeans, leather boots, and a khaki barn jacket that's seen better days. But there's an ease about her that tells me she's been walking into kitchens like this for years.

"Morning, Bremerton," she says, a grin forming. "Tell me you're ready for me."

He laughs, heading her direction, embracing her, and says, "Always."

I tell myself it's nothing. Just a hug and a few words between friends, but is that all it is? And why do I care?

Tina sets down the crate and peers at her clipboard. "You're going to love what I brought you today. The chops are phenomenal. I made sure to bring you the best cuts."

She hands Marcus the invoice, their fingers brushing briefly as he takes it from her. The touch is casual, unremarkable, an interaction that happens a million times a day in a place like this. Between Marcus and his cooks. Between Marcus and me.

And still, I feel a twinge of something I shouldn't.

I watch Marcus as he scans the page, nodding, asking Tina a couple of questions. She answers him matter-of-factly. Like I'm sure she's done before, like I'm sure she does with all the chefs she sells to. Yet, I feel...

"Tell your dad that his butchering skills are on point." He

gestures to his kitchen crew and continues, "We're going to have some fun making these into culinary masterpieces."

"I know you will," she says.

Do I denote an undertone that shouldn't be there in those last words? Is she flirting with him?

I look down at Marcus's clipboard, scanning a list that does not require my input, trying to distract myself from how they are standing. I don't get to feel the way I'm feeling. Rationally, I know this. Marcus is my chef. He's allowed to have a life outside of work. He can laugh with vendors. He can have history. He can even have a history with Tina.

I'm his boss. Nothing else. Nothing that gives me permission to feel the faint ache that's forming in my stomach.

Tina looks my way, her smile growing bigger. "Oh, sorry. Hi. You must be Lyndsay."

I look up, startled. "I am. Hello."

"I'm Tina," she says, extending her hand. Her grip is confident, and I try to return her firm handshake, even though my confidence is buckling. "I handle most of the locally sourced pork around the area. Marcus speaks very highly of you."

I cough and spit out, "He does?"

Marcus gives me a confused look and says, "Of course I do."

The words are simple. Innocuous. Yet, they're what I needed to hear. And they make the ripplings of...jealousy—because that's what I'm feeling—fade ever so slightly.

Tina smiles at both of us. "This place is really impressive. You can feel it the moment you walk in. I know it's going to be a success."

"Thank you," I say, meaning it. Meaning it more than she probably realizes.

She finishes her notes and waves to the entire kitchen crew. "I'll see you next week," she says to Marcus. "Same time. Let me know if there's anything else you want to try as you nail down the menu."

Tina disappears out the back door, and the kitchen returns to its steady rhythm.

"You okay?" Marcus asks.

"Of course. Why wouldn't I be?" I say too quickly.

His eyes don't leave me, studying me for just a beat, then he nods. "I'm heading to the basement for a few things."

"Great," I say. "I'll...finish up here." Although what I'm finishing, I'm not quite sure.

He walks away, and his absence makes the kitchen feel empty. Emptier than it should. And I'm kicking myself for having these feelings. *Where the hell are all these boundaries, and why aren't they doing their job?*

I let out a deep sigh, pressing my palms against the cool stainless steel counter. This is stupid. There's no reason for me to feel jealous. No reason I should be replaying the interaction between the two of them. No reason I should be rehashing their words, searching for deeper meaning. I should've signed that damned imaginary contract!

My inner, more rational, voice whispers, *She's one of your vendors.*

I lift my head, acquiescing to what my inner voice has said, and walk back to the dining room to get busy with the things I need to accomplish. But my focus is gone. Instead, I fold napkins and polish silverware, the kind of tasks that don't actually need my attention, my thoughts still stuck on the morning delivery. I think about all the years I was married to David and never had these feelings. No jealousy. No wondering why he was spending so much time with his new pastry chef. No remarking on casual touches with waitstaff or hostesses. None of it. Not one red flag popping up when it should have. What does that say about me? And David? And Marcus?

Marcus emerges from the basement a few minutes later, arms laden with various spices and a few bottles of wine. He pauses when he sees me holding up water glasses to check for spots.

"You know those are fine," he says.

"I know."

He watches me for a second, head atilt, and I get the sense that he's about to say something else. Instead, one of the line cooks calls his name, asking about the beef delivery, and the moment slips away.

I tell myself I'm relieved, but I wonder what he wanted to say.

In the kitchen, I can hear the hubbub of his crew. Water is flowing from the faucet. Pans are being scrubbed. I crack open the swinging door to take it all in. There's a hum inside that reverberates in my chest like that of a bass drum.

Marcus moves through the kitchen with ease and authority. He checks stations, answers questions, makes small adjustments. I can't help but watch him. He's a natural, inhabiting the space like he's always worked here. This is his world. He fits in here effortlessly.

Will I ever feel that way? Will I ever truly belong here?

Tina's voice drifts back to me. *Tell me you're ready for me.*

I shake my head, annoyed at myself, once again. *What the hell, Lyndsay? Where is that "this restaurant is now mine" confidence you walked in here with this morning?*

I continue into the kitchen and head to Candace's station, hoping she's got some confectionery delight for me. She does. She hands me a blueberry tartlet with mascarpone cream and a pistachio shortbread crust, to die for. As I eat the last mouthful, Marcus steals behind me, close enough that I catch the familiar scent of citrus and smoke clinging to his chef's whites. He murmurs a quick, "Behind," his hand hovering at my back for a second longer than necessary.

The contact is brief. Innocent. A chef protecting a coworker from a hot pan. He would do this for anyone.

Still, my breath catches.

I'm furious with myself for feeling this way and step away before I can overthink it, retreating to the office under the pretense of paying invoices, even though I paid a large stack of them yesterday. The door clicks behind me, dulling the noise. I lean back against it, closing my eyes.

This is your own doing, Lyndsay. You should've sent him on his way, not invited him back into your life.

I HIDE OUT HERE MOST OF THE DAY, UNTIL I HEAR the din of dishes and knives begin to dissipate. Then I slink back out into the kitchen, acting like everything is normal. Because it is. At least I try to convince myself it is.

"What have you been up to today?" he asks.

"Oh, a little of this, a little of that."

He nods, accepting my answer, but I can see that he doesn't totally believe me. But he's not one to push. Never has been.

"Do you want to try the pork dish Blake put together using the chops Tina brought? I'd like to lock her in for the season. She's promised us a good price."

"Um, sure," I reply. I keep my voice even, my expression neutral. This is business. I can't let my earlier reaction become something it shouldn't be.

"She knows her stuff."

I nod as he hands me a plate with an oversized chop, the most gorgeous grill marks, and apple compote on top. "I believe you."

There's a pause. Not awkward, exactly, but lingering. He's studying me, and I wish he weren't.

"You sure you're okay? You've been kinda quiet today..."

"Fine, think it's just nerves with the opening coming up." The words sound plausible.

"We're in good shape," he says, throwing a reassuring smile my way. "Better than most restaurants are at this point."

"I know." He's right.

"What do you think?"

"About what?" I ask.

"The pork chop?" he says, confusion evident in his words.

"Oh, it's incredible." But the enthusiasm isn't there, even though it is amazing.

"I have an idea," he says.

I don't say a word, my mouth still full of this mouthwatering dish.

"I gave the staff the day off tomorrow. So, what do you think if we take a little road trip?"

"A road trip? Where to?"

"I want you to meet some friends of mine."

"Friends?" I repeat, curiosity and a smile building. He wants me to meet *friends*?

"Consider it a work field trip."

Friends *and* a work field trip?

"That sounds intriguing," I say. "I'm in."

Really? I'm in? Wasn't I just chastising myself about boundaries a few hours ago?

"Good. I think you'll like them."

"Where are we going?" I ask.

He shakes his head, "I'm not telling you. Just be ready at seven a.m. I'll pick you up."

"That's awfully early," I say playfully, feeling tension and doubt start to leave my body.

He shifts his weight, glancing around the now quiet kitchen. "It's a bit of a drive." I see a glint in his eyes, taking me right back to when we were young. When he would plan surprise dates for us, like the day we hiked Mt. Marcy, and he packed an incredible picnic lunch for us to eat when we reached the summit.

"I'll be ready."

We lock up and step outside, the air is cool, and I feel my mood shift from one of questioning to one of anticipation. And, for once, I let myself look forward to it without asking any more questions, of myself or Marcus.

Chapter Nine

The clock on my stove clicks over to 6:43 a.m., and he's already here.

Pausing mid-sip of my coffee, the mug warm in my palms, I stare out the front window. Headlights cut through the early morning haze. I slowly set my mug down and feel my bare feet on the hardwood as I move closer to the glass.

Of course he's early. And I appreciate it so much.

I glance back at the kitchen clock. He said seven. But he knows me, knows that I consider being on time late. I slide on fleece-lined boots and grab my coat off the hook by the door.

I consider inviting him in. Letting him step into my space again. But think better of it. The word *boundaries* screams at me not to do such a thing. Instead, I open the front door, frosted air filling my lungs, and make my way to his truck.

He reaches across the seat to open the door for me and hands me a paper cup.

"Traffic was light," he says.

"I'm sure it was. It's six forty-five in the morning," I reply, arching my brow and smirking.

"Didn't want to risk being late."

He says those words offhandedly, but they are not offhanded. Not one bit.

His truck is warm and smells faintly of coffee and something woodsy—his cologne, maybe, or just Marcus himself. I pull my seatbelt across my chest and focus on the click as it locks into place.

He pulls out of the driveway, like he's been here a hundred times before. Like early mornings and long drives and the silence that is settling in between us is normal. But it shouldn't be, should it? That ease only comes from being with someone for an extended period of time, whether it's a friend or a lover. Yet I feel it now, like there's no need to say anything. Is that weird?

I sip my coffee and stare out the window, watching my reflection flicker in the glass. The sky is purple and gray, the sun still deciding if she wants to show up today. The road is empty, making things feel strangely more intimate than it should.

"You good?" he says after a moment.

"With…?"

"A little adventure."

I huff out a faux breath of exasperation, wanting to keep things light. "I still don't know where we're going."

"Vermont," he says, "That's all I'm saying for now."

I turn to look at him. "That's not an answer."

"It is. Just not a detailed one." He chuckles under his breath, the corners of his mouth tipping up, and I find myself laughing as well.

We drive for a bit, and soon my curiosity can no longer be contained. I have to ask. "Who are we meeting?"

"Wouldn't you like to know?"

"Marcus, come on…just tell me."

He laughs softly. "I thought you liked surprises."

"I like control."

"That," he says, "has not changed."

But it has. Throughout my marriage, I didn't have control. David had it all. I had none. Loving him required me to abandon myself. And while I've been working to take control back, I'm not sure I've done that entirely. Hiring Marcus? I told myself I was in control of this relationship. Employer and employee. Yet, it's morphing into something more, without any effort. Is that because of me? Am I falling back into old habits? I swore I wouldn't let another man lead. But here it is happening again.

Am I making another huge mistake?

THE ROAD NARROWS AS WE HEAD DEEPER INTO Vermont, the landscape shifting from familiar to impressive. Hills roll out in front of us, fields that look like patchwork quilts ready for the spring planting, and maple trees standing tall, already having delivered their amber goodness. The scenery calms me. Enough that I don't ask more questions.

Marcus hums to the radio, Crowded House singing a song from our youth, and I marvel at how relaxed he is...with all of this, including me.

After a while, he signals and turns off the main road onto a gravel drive that stretches for what seems like miles. The tires crunch beneath us, disrupting the quiet that had settled in after Crowded House concluded.

"Okay," I say. "Now I'm officially intrigued."

"Good."

Soon, the drive opens up to reveal a farmhouse set back from the road, worn but solid, with a building nearby that I assume is The Evergreen Table, only because I can read the signboard standing by the front door. There is movement all around us. Delivery trucks, people carrying crates, someone crossing the yard with a clipboard in their hand. It may be early, but the place is fully alive.

Marcus parks near the edge of the lot and cuts the engine. For a moment, neither of us moves.

"Ready?" he asks.

I hesitate, just a beat. "For whatever this is? Sure."

He opens his door and steps out, scanning the property like he knows exactly where to go. I follow, hugging my jacket closer as the cool air hits.

The closer we get, the more I notice the details. There are herb beds lining the path, ready to be planted. There's a chalkboard hanging by the door listing the day's deliveries. Everyone seems to be moving with a purpose but not rushing. I like the way it feels.

A woman steps out of the building as we approach, wiping her hands on a towel slung over her shoulder. She has short, spiky dark hair, sleeves rolled up, and a commanding presence, even at a diminutive five feet five.

"Marcus," she says, a genuine smile coming to her face, "you're early."

He laughs. "Seems to be my m.o. today."

She turns to me, her gaze warm and assessing. "And you must be Lyndsay."

"I am."

"I'm Natalia," she says, extending her hand. "Welcome to The Evergreen Table."

The Evergreen Table? Yes, I had read the sign, but it now hits me like a lightning bolt. The Evergreen Table is the first restaurant in Vermont to receive a Michelin star. I remember reading the article in the *New York Tribune*. How it was such a feat, a restaurant not in a major city getting the coveted praise. I even asked David if he wanted me to book a table so we could taste her creations, but he declined, jealousy dripping from his emphatic "No."

As Natalia and I shake hands, a man comes up behind her. He's tall, with brown hair just below his shoulders, green eyes, and a relaxed manner.

"Thomas," he says, offering his hand next. "Front of house. Titan of tables. Keeper of customers."

"Debatable," Natalia replies dryly.

Their banter is seamless. Comfortable. I clock it instantly, the way you do when something works so well it's impossible not to notice.

Marcus makes introductions, though they don't need much filling in. Natalia and Marcus went to culinary school together, as did Thomas. But Thomas never completed school, deciding his skills were better served outside of the kitchen. They married a few years after Natalia got her degree, then opened up this place. Together.

"Come on," says Natalia. "We're just getting started. Kitchen's loud enough to wake anyone who's still asleep."

As we step inside, the warmth hits me first. Heat, sound, motion. It's busy without being frantic. Every person seemingly aware of their role. Natalia moves through it like a fish in the current, offering instructions, checking stations, answering questions, never breaking stride.

I find myself hypnotized by her. Not with envy, but with admiration. She's a strong and charismatic presence without being loud or overbearing or trying too hard. Much like Marcus. It's good to see that kitchens truly can be like this.

"This is incredible," I say quietly, mostly to myself.

Natalia hears me anyway. She smiles over her shoulder. "It wasn't always like this."

I look over at Marcus, only to see that he's locked on me, not the kitchen.

But why?

That's when I realize this isn't only a visit to catch up with friends.

This is a test.

Of what, I'm not sure yet. But I have my suspicions.

Natalia leads us past the line and into a quieter corner of the kitchen, the noise abating just enough that I can hear myself think again. The air smells like garlic and fresh bread and something sweet that I can't put my finger on. Comforting. Authentic.

"We try to keep the chaos contained to the mornings," she says. "This is the time for prep and problem-solving. Nights are for execution."

I nod because it makes so much sense. And I recognize that this is how Marcus runs our kitchen. "Marcus seems to subscribe to your philosophy."

She laughs. "It's a necessity."

Thomas appears beside us, holding two clipboards and a mug that says, *Feed Me and Tell Me I'm Pretty*. He hands one clipboard to Natalia without a word, their fingers brushing briefly in a way that's casual but intimate. It's a different touch than what I saw between Marcus and Tina. Confirming what I knew. I overreacted yesterday to something that wasn't there. And I'm mad at myself for the spiral I descended into for no good reason.

"We're on schedule," Thomas says. "Mostly."

"Mostly is a win," she replies.

They share a look. It's not long. Just a quick exchange of information and trust. Then they're moving again, each in a different direction, yet perfectly in sync.

I swallow, and Marcus steps closer, lowering his voice, he asks, "You good?"

"Yes," I reply quickly. "I just...this place has a vibe to it."

"That's them," he says. "They built it that way."

Natalia circles back, wiping her hands again. "So, we hear you run a restaurant, too."

"I do," I say. "In Lake George." But do I really? I *own* a restaurant. But do I really run it?

Her eyes light up. My response has not impressed her so much as intrigued her. "Seasonal stress. Tourists with lots of opinions."

This breaks the tension, tension I'm sure I was the only one feeling. And before I can stop myself, I laugh and say, "And expectations galore."

"That's the worst. That's one reason I'm glad we're off the beaten path. People have to seek us out. Of course, they still have lots of opinions."

"I'm sure they do. I can only imagine the scrutiny you face when you have a Michelin star."

"That certainly does add a new dimension to things," she says. "Follow me. I want to show you something."

She leads me through a side door and out into the back. Garden beds stretch out in front of me, frost still clinging to the wooden boxes. We enter a small greenhouse where someone is harvesting spinach and herbs. The smell reminds me of summer days, even on this brisk morning.

"We don't grow it all," Natalia says, "but enough to remind us where it comes from. The rest we try to source locally, support our community."

I lean over a bed of kale, my fingers brush the emerald-green leaves.

"I love this," I say.

"Marcus said you would."

I straighten and look at her. This is the second time in as many days that I learn he's been talking about me.

"Yes. He said you'd love it all. He talks about you the way people talk about things that matter," she says simply. "I know you two have a past. But when he speaks of you, it's not nostalgically. It's currently."

My chest flutters. Not because he's talked to her about me, but because of *how* he's talked to her about me. I look back toward the building, see him through the window, laughing at something Thomas has said. He looks content. This is his world. He knows where he fits. And suddenly, I wonder where I belong.

"Working with someone you love isn't easy, I should know. It hasn't always been easy between Thomas and me. We fight. A lot. But we always work through it." Natalia continues, her voice is gentle now. "I couldn't do this alone. And my guess is you don't want to do it alone either."

I don't reply. Because she's right. And because of that one little word she used. Love. I don't love him...do I?

When we head back inside, Marcus falls in step beside me. "You're quiet."

"Just taking it all in," I say.

He smiles, but his face indicates something else as well. Is it hope? I scold myself for reading into it. After yesterday, I know that I can overreact, overthink.

We rejoin Natalia and Thomas at a small table near the window, fresh mugs of coffee appearing like magic. The four of us sit, sunlight casting shadows across the scuffed wood.

"So," Thomas says, "Marcus tells us he works for you now."

I feel like the test has begun. I nod. "He does."

"And you're okay with that?" Natalia asks.

I'm not sure who she's posing the question to. I glance at Marcus. He takes a sip of his coffee, not answering. Waiting me out. Wanting me to answer honestly.

"I am," I say. "Because he shows up like this." I gesture toward the kitchen. "Present. Respectful." He finally looks at me, an expression crossing his face, something between appreciation and admiration.

Natalia smiles. "Then you're way ahead of where we started."

Sitting there, listening to Thomas talk about their early days and the fights he and Natalia had, listening to all of them reminisce about their days at the CIA, I realize what the purpose of this visit was. Marcus brought me here to show that love doesn't have to erase structure. And structure doesn't have to kill love. We have to trust one another. We have to choose the right framework. And believe that we can honor it.

AS WE WALK BACK TOWARD THE TRUCK, THE SOUNDS of the kitchen fade behind us. Marcus waits until we're both inside before starting the engine. He doesn't ask how I'm feeling. He knows my answer would be complicated, that I need time to digest what I've seen, experienced.

We pull back onto the road, once again engulfed in the kind of silence that's not awkward. I watch the restaurant disappear in the side mirror, soon taken over by rows of farmland and evergreen trees.

"That was...helpful," I say at long last.

He nods. "I hoped it would be."

I turn my head to look at him. "You didn't bring me there to impress me or even to meet your friends." It's part question, part statement.

"Well, I did want you to meet my friends," he says. "But no. I brought you there so you could see it."

"See what?"

"That it can be done," he says. "That you can care about someone and still know where the lines are."

I let that settle. "You're very clear about your place."

"I have to be. 518 is your restaurant, and I'm your chef. I don't want to make your life more difficult," he continues. "Or blur things in a way that puts you in a bad position. I know how easily that can happen. But I also wanted you to see the possibility of what might be."

I think about Natalia and Thomas. The ease. The respect. The way decisions are made without drama.

"I don't want this to be..."

And that's the problem. I just don't know what I want.

"Marcus, I can't pretend this is simple."

He smiles faintly. "Nothing worth doing ever is."

We drive for a few more miles before he speaks again. "For what it's worth, I'm not trying to change the structure we've created these past few weeks. If anything, I want to protect it."

"Why?" I ask.

"Because structure is the only reason this works."

I nod, knowing he's right. And that's what scares me.

Boundaries and structure are two different things. I put boundaries in place to keep him out. He wants structure in place to let me in.

As we cross back toward familiar roads, I realize something else, too. Marcus didn't bring me to Vermont to convince me we could be together. He brought me to show me that if we choose to be together, it won't be because we ignore the hard parts. It will be because we respect them.

And that makes the decision ahead of me feel heavier. And yet, strangely, more possible.

Chapter Ten

NEW RESTAURANT COMING TO BOLTON LANDING THIS SUMMER!

"Hey Marcus, did you see the article in *The Chronicle* about a new restaurant opening here?" I say as I push the door open between the kitchen and the dining room.

He's busy trimming steaks, but looks up and replies, "Yeah, I saw it. They didn't seem to have a lot of details. No mention of the chef or the concept—just that it was going into Maple & Ash. I asked around to see if any of my kitchen friends knew who had bought it, but they didn't have any scoop. It's too bad about Maple & Ash—their food was solid, but it just never took off."

Blake looks up from his station and gives me a strange look before quickly dropping his gaze back down and continuing with his prep work. Marcus says he's a very competent chef and that David trained him well. At least David was good for something. But that look was weird, and while I'd like to ask him what it was about, I don't have time. With seven days to go until we open, I really don't have time for anything— including who might be opening up a new place near us.

Things are way too harried for me to spend time trying to figure this mystery out.

I look down at my notebook with its ever-growing to-do list to see if there is anything I can check off. There's not. And my sparkly pen just seems to keep adding to the list instead of subtracting, and I find myself wondering how we are going to pull this off.

Well, I can check off #6 as Mom is here with a bunch of volunteers, and they're hanging artwork right now. She did a fabulous job—as I knew she would—and has chosen all land-scapes to be displayed throughout the summer. It's scenes from all over the Adirondacks, and each one of them captures something beautiful and unique to this area. The mountains, the meadows, the lakes, the wildlife. I'll be lucky if we have any artwork left by the time August rolls around. But Mom is prepared for that and has her artist friends ready to deliver more if needed.

Thanks, Mom!

"You're My Best Friend" starts playing, and I pick up to hear Chloe's voice.

"One week to go! Can you believe it? I'm so proud of you. You've made it all work. The restaurant, Marcus, everything!" Her excitement is palpable even through the phone, her voice bubbling over with enthusiasm.

"Thanks, Chloe. We couldn't have done it without you. You've been an enormous help."

Chloe has been interviewing all the front-of-house staff, and she has hired some fantastic people. She also took charge of collecting all their employment paperwork and getting them set up in our payroll system. There are not enough bottles of wine in the world to repay her for coming here to help us after she finishes her day job.

"I'll come up after work and double-check payroll forms

since your FOH staff starts training tomorrow. We want to make sure they all get paid on time."

Thank God. I can now cross #1 off my list.

"You are the best. I'll make sure Marcus has dinner ready for you!"

"Speaking of...how are things?"

"Things are fine, Chlo..." I say with a tone that indicates I know she wants to hear more about Marcus, but that I'm not going to tell her anything—not that there's anything to tell.

"Okay, just asking...as your bestie, I wanted to make sure I hadn't missed any new...developments."

"Nope, everything's status quo. Thanks for asking. Gotta run! See you tonight."

She's laughing as I hang up.

What I told her *is* the truth.

Since dinner at Marcus's place and our trip to Vermont, everything has been fine, better than fine. We've thrown ourselves into this restaurant for the last five weeks. Tweaking menus, scrubbing tabletops, discussing dessert plating. We've spent countless hours here together, sometimes until the wee hours of the morning, exhausted but wanting to make sure everything is perfect.

What can I say? We're like coffee and quiet mornings. We work well together.

Too well, maybe.

His flirting hasn't stopped. If anything, it's increased, but I'm not mad about it. A compliment here, an extended glance there. It's nice to have the attention of a man, especially one as handsome and talented as Marcus, and my elevated heart rate confirms this every time we're together. It's been good for my self-esteem and a nice distraction from a to-do list that seems endless.

But neither of us has crossed any boundaries—no matter how tempting it may be.

Still 100 percent in place.

Even if they're starting to feel more like suggestions.

I STAND ON THE RESTAURANT'S PORCH, STARING OUT over Lake George, the cobalt blue water still, no boats daring to create waves as it's still too cold to venture out. Ducks call in the distance, and the new spring leaves rustle on the trees. But mostly, it's quiet. Blissfully quiet. The kind of quiet that feels like holding your breath before something big.

With two days to go until our soft opening date of April first, tonight is big. It's friends and family night, and all I can think about is how I want this evening to go well. All the staff have invited the people they love the most to come and eat, while they wait on them and cook for them, and we figure out where the hiccups and glitches are. Better to figure those things out with people who love you than with guests who are paying for an unforgettable dining experience.

I don't need perfect tonight, but I need to know that we can do this.

That I can do this.

The pressure hums beneath my skin as I walk back to the kitchen. Marcus is behind the line, sleeves rolled up, towel over his shoulder, calm and poised. I give him a thumbs-up, and he answers with one of his own, plus an added wink. The wink moves the hum that was beneath my skin elsewhere. As I make my retreat, Candace shoots me a knowing look, all raised eyebrows and conspiratorial grin, as if she's in on our secret. Only there is no secret to tell. Not yet, anyway.

I draw in a breath and head to the dining room, where all the front-of-house staff have gathered, shiny and eager to get started. It's time to say a few words and open the doors.

Time to see if this dream can stand on its own two feet.

"You would think I would know exactly what to say on a night like this, but I am truly at a loss. These past six weeks have been a whirlwind, and without the help of each of you, we would not be here. You've come for training. You've helped unpack boxes. You've polished silverware. You've done everything I've asked and more—and I can't thank you enough. Tonight, as you wait on your family and friends, treat them just as you would our future guests. Make their experience unbelievable, and if problems arise, handle them with grace—and don't be afraid to ask for help. We're here to support one another. I know that each of you is going to be incredible. You were hired to work here because we know you have the attributes that we want 518 Farm-to-Table to be known for, so once again, all I can say is thank you. Now, let's do this!"

At that, everyone starts clapping and patting each other on the shoulder, ready to get this night underway. My hostesses head to the front door and let the crowd in.

It's happening!

We're serving actual guests!

"THAT WAS A *DISASTER!*" I PLOP INTO A DINING room chair, slide off my shoes, and let out a groan that echoes all the way back to the kitchen. My feet are throbbing, and my pride is somewhere under a pile of dirty dishes or drowning itself in a glass of Pinot Grigio.

Marcus looks...relaxed? "*That* was a friends and family night for a brand-new restaurant."

I shoot him a look. There's no panic on his face. No concern. All I see is amusement. In fact, I see that stupid little smirk of his starting to form as he takes a seat next to me.

"Lynds, what happened tonight is not uncommon," he says, as he drapes his arm over my shoulder in a reassuring way, the sleeves of his chef coat rolled up and his tattoo on full display. "And it's exactly why we do friends and family night—to see where the problems are."

I glance over at him, not ready to concur with his assessment of the evening. "You need to qualify that sentence to say a *plethora of problems.*"

This makes him crack up.

And soon, I'm laughing, too.

He gets up, taking his tattooed forearm with him, and I instantly miss that connection, his touch.

He grabs a bottle of wine from behind the bar and pours a glass for each of us. "Okay," he says, leaning back in his chair. "Let's talk about it. What has you most concerned?"

What *doesn't* have me concerned?

"We slammed the waitstaff and the kitchen when the hostesses seated parties too quickly. This, in turn, created major delays getting food out of the kitchen. The point-of-sale system is missing menu items, which means waitstaff had to go back to the kitchen to shout out orders like it was 1976. A couple of servers still can't remember what's gluten-free, and one of them told a guest we could make clam chowder without the clams."

Marcus chokes on his wine. "Please tell me you're kidding."

"I wish."

He grins, shaking his head. "Okay. Noted. Menu training, POS updates, pacing the tables. Anything else?"

"Music," I say. "Apparently, it's a rock concert in the main dining room and a funeral in the side rooms."

He laughs again, easy, unbothered, and says, "Really...I'm not upset by this. If we slow down the seating of parties, most of our big problems will solve themselves. You'll give relief to your waitstaff, and in turn, my kitchen staff will be able to handle whatever comes their way."

"You're not freaking out here? I'm freaking out."

"Nope. Did people have any good things to say tonight?"

"Yes, of course. They *loved* the food. Said everything was plated immaculately, and you received nothing less than five stars in terms of taste. They love our staff—which they would, after all, it was only friends and family. But our staff *is* good, they just need to settle in. They also said they love the decor with all the local art."

"See...all good things! We've got this, Lynds. Don't worry. Tomorrow, we'll do another run-through with the staff, and we'll get this right. Trust me. And don't forget, the soft opening on the first is only for about seventy-five local bigwigs, so not a full-on deluge of guests."

I lean back in my chair and drop my head down, letting out a huge sigh. "Bigwigs are the *worst*. Those are the people I want to impress the most. They're all locals with a lot of influence. And all fans of David. Of *David's*. They will go back and talk to all their friends about their experience here—and if it's a disaster, we're screwed."

He grabs both of my hands in his, trying to put me at ease, but all I can think about is how warm and strong they are. His thumbs brush over my knuckles, and for a second, the noise in my head quiets. "It *will not* be a disaster. Do you trust me?"

I look up into those azure eyes with the long dark lashes and say, "Yes, of course I do." But my voice sounds deflated and dejected.

Not letting go of my hand, he replies, "Good. I promise I won't let you down. I may have when we were eighteen..." His voice trails off for a beat, heavy with memory. "But I won't do it now."

I want to believe him.

No. I have to believe him.

∿

"I DON'T KNOW IF IT CAN EVER BE AS GOOD AS David's..."

"Her husband...amazing chef..."

"You mean soon-to-be ex-husband..."

"Marcus has REALLY big shoes to fill..."

"There's no way this can compete with David's..."

As I make my way through the dining room, I hear snippets of these conversations over and over again. Always trying to hush themselves as I approach, but they never shut it down soon enough.

This is what our local "bigwigs" think. The mayor, the editor of the local paper, members of the tourism board, numerous marketing agencies, several local hotel owners. They don't think that 518 Farm-to-Table can be as good as David's. And while I know they have all eaten Marcus's food before, and know of his immense talent, they still doubt. It's one thing to question my abilities to run a restaurant, but Marcus should not even be a part of the equation. He's more talented than David ever was.

I paste on a smile faker than the Prada bag the mayor's wife is carrying, and continue to stop by each and every table. I say hello, shake some hands, do dreaded double-cheek kisses, and then repeat it all over again. It's exhausting. Maybe it wouldn't be so exhausting if I thought any of these people were cheering me on, wanting me to succeed, but they seem to be here to revel in the possibility of my failure.

I head to the bar area to see if I can help. Servers are smiling and bringing out flights of local beers, glasses of wine, and I see many glasses of our spiked huckleberry lemonade heading to tables of six and eight. They may have loved David's, but they love free drinks more. My two bartenders assure me they have it under control and encourage me to mingle.

I make a few more rounds and can see that soup, salads,

and appetizers are on their way to tables. Based on what I see on the trays exiting the kitchen, the duck confit sliders, New England crab cakes, and Berkshire bacon and blueberry salad are extremely popular.

I wait a few moments and then decide it's time for me to once again eavesdrop.

"These sliders...I've never had anything so good..."

"I love the spices in the crab cakes."

"The staff is just delightful."

So far, so good.

Better than good.

Dare I say, they seem mildly impressed?

I head back to the kitchen to check on things. Marcus looks up from the order tickets and gives me a look that asks if everything is okay. I nod and smile, letting him know that all is well, not wanting him to worry about the butterflies that have invaded my core and are fluttering around more like bats heading out to feed for the night. As if he knows I need reassurance, he asks his kitchen staff, "Chefs...how's everyone doing?" In unison, they reply, "Good, Chef."

That's all I need to hear. While the bats are still flying, the kitchen is his domain, and if he tells me everything is fine, I know it is.

Back on the dining room floor, I see our local dignitaries biting into their entrées. There is almost a buzz in the room, making me wonder if there is a problem with the lighting. But it's not the lighting creating the hum, it's the people eating. It's a sea of "Mmmms" and "Aaaahhs" combined with contented sighs, slurps, and the smacking of lips.

Soon, staff are clearing plates, and coffee, tea, and desserts are being set down in front of people who look like they may pop like an overfilled balloon if they eat another bite—yet it doesn't stop them.

It's time for me to make one last pass through the dining

rooms and see what I can glean from the muted conversations that are happening.

"This place is amazing...

"I can't remember when I've had a better meal."

"...she pulled it off...better than David's..."

"I need to make a reservation for my anniversary."

"The pork tenderloin...incredible."

I don't need to hear any more. Our soft opening for the local muckety-mucks has left them better than speechless. It's left them ready to sing our praises and wanting more.

"I HATE TO SAY IT, BUT I TOLD YOU SO."

Marcus gloats as he cleans his knives. The rest of the staff have already left, and it's just him and me. All I can do is stick my tongue out at him like I'm five years old—which only proves his point more.

"Yes, you were right. I was wrong. Do you feel better?" It comes out in a faux-sulky tone, but the warmth behind it turns the words into something more playful than grudging, the grin tugging at my mouth giving me away.

"No, the question is, do *you* feel better? I had no doubts."

If you didn't know him, you would think his self-assuredness was cockiness, but Marcus is not cocky. Never has been. Even when teen boys used their bravado to get through the difficult years of awkwardness and uneasiness, Marcus never did. Maybe it's because he was never gangly and gawkish like so many of the other boys in our class, not that that really had anything to do with it. He just always knew who he wanted to be, something rare for teen boys. Never arrogant or abrasive. Always caring and confident.

"I do feel better," I admit. "The front-of-house did fabulous. They handled everything like seasoned professionals—

even when a few little glitches occurred. And your kitchen staff cranked out some dishes that made raving fans of our *distinguished* guests. Many made reservations before they walked out the front door. The mayor even asked if we would participate in the Lake George Wine & Dine Festival in June. What do you think?"

Eyes bright, he says, "I'm in! It will be great exposure for the restaurant."

"That's what I thought, too. I already committed us."

Marcus chuckles and finishes putting his knives in their carrying case, making his way to the back door, where I am waiting to lock up. Even though he has a key, we leave most nights together. It's practical. Habit. Nothing more.

He pauses, the scent of soap and smoke clinging to him, and he presses a quick kiss on my cheek and says, "Good night, Lynds." No waiting to see if I say anything. No pause to look at my reaction. Nothing. Just the sounds of his footsteps fading across the gravel driveway.

And all I can do is watch him walk away. Regretting that he had been in such a hurry. Thinking about his soft, warm lips pressed to my cheek. Wishing they had landed a few inches to the right.

Chapter Eleven

5 18 FARM-TO-TABLE A CULINARY DELIGHT LEACH'S NEW RESTAURANT A SMASH HIT

LEACH AND BREMERTON COMBINE FOR CULINARY CREATIONS NOT TO BE MISSED

These are just a few of the headlines from articles about 518 Farm-to-Table for the last six weeks. I pinch myself each time a staff member shares a new one with me. In my wildest dreams, I never believed we would hit it out of the park like this, but we have.

I glance at the list of this evening's reservations, once again, a full house. We've left a few tables available for small walk-in parties, but I note the 12-top coming in at six thirty, so that Maria, our head waitress, can take them, and the birthday celebration for a party of two at seven p.m. Need to make sure Candace sends out a complimentary dessert for the couple.

I walk into the kitchen, which is abuzz with activity. Looking down at his list, Marcus inquires about the status of various items for tonight's service.

"Have the strip steaks been trimmed?"

"Yes, Chef."

"Who made the apple bourbon compote? It's delicious."

"I did, Chef. Thank you, Chef."

"Are the brioche slider buns finished?

"Yes, Chef. Cooling right now, Chef."

I wait for a break and finally get my turn to say, "Can I have you for five minutes, Chef, so we can look at tonight's reservations?"

He looks up, not knowing I am here, smiles, and follows me to the dining room.

"You can interrupt me when you need something, Lynds. You don't have to stand there waiting for me to finish."

"It's okay, I don't mind. It's fun to watch you in your element. I like hearing 'Yes, Chef.'" There's a playful, bordering on seductive, tone in my voice. A tone that's been very prevalent for the last six weeks, ever since that kiss on the cheek.

That kiss on the cheek that's been repeated every night since.

It's become our ritual. Service ends. The clatter dies down. The lights shut off. I wait by the back door, even though he has a key. Pretend to check the lock. He presses his lips softly to my cheek before heading to his truck.

He never looks back, never says another word.

Every night, my face is flushed. Every night, I contemplate chasing him down in the parking lot to kiss him for real. A full-on kiss, so I can feel the heat of his mouth and taste the scotch that he sips as he cleans the kitchen in preparation for the next day.

But I don't do it.

Maybe it's because my divorce is not finalized. Maybe it's because I worry about what people will think. Maybe it's because I fear what mixing business and pleasure will mean for the restaurant. Whatever it is, it helps to keep the boundaries in place—no matter how much I want to cross them.

When I told Chloe about this nightly ritual, at first, she thought it was sweet—like something out of a slow-burn romance, all anticipation and restraint. But now, she just rolls her eyes. "You two are insane," she said. "I don't understand why two grown-ass adults aren't jumping each other's bones."

If only it were that simple.

Because no matter how long it's been, I still have a hard time thinking about sex with someone other than David.

And yet...

All I can think about is sex with Marcus.

When we were in high school, we were each other's first, and it was clumsy and awkward and sweet and romantic. With practice, it became intense and passionate and still sweet and romantic. What would it be like now?

"Lynds...earth to Lynds, what do we have for reservations tonight?"

Damn. Just how long have I been thinking about that kiss, which quickly drifted into thinking about sex with Marcus?

"We have practically a full house with a party of twelve at six thirty that has a tree nut allergy, and a party of two celebrating a birthday at seven p.m. Those are the only notes I have at the moment."

"Okay...no problem. If anything else pops up, just come let me know."

I watch him walk back into the kitchen, still reminiscing about our younger days and imagining him leaving a trail of kisses down my neck now.

My face betrays me, as do other parts of me, and I need a cold drink, which would serve me better if it were poured on me, instead of imbibed. But for now, a glass of ice water will have to suffice. I can take a cold shower when I get home.

IT'S SIX THIRTY P.M., AND ALL IS GOING WELL WHEN I sneak out to the porch to grab a breath of fresh air. It's still quite cool here in Lake George, and the porch is not open yet, so all the staff have been using it for breaks as needed. But it's ready to go. Everything is clean, the tables are set, and I expect by Memorial Day weekend, we'll be serving guests out here regularly. But for now, this is my escape when I have spent too much time "peopling" and my introverted self feels like she can't keep "it" turned on for much longer. Somehow, a few deep breaths, a moment spent staring at the calm, corn-flower-blue waters of the lake, and the sounds of the robins chirping are enough of a reprieve to send me back in with a smile to check on guests and ensure that all is running smoothly.

Just as I take my last peek at the lake, my phone begins to softly play "Tainted Love" by Soft Cell. This is Rebecca's ring-tone, which I assigned to her shortly after she gave me the keys to the restaurant. It was between "Eye of the Tiger"—which seemed too on the nose—and "Tainted Love." While both seemed like fitting choices for my divorce attorney, Soft Cell won in the end.

"Hi, Rebecca."

"Hi, Lynds. Got a minute? I assume you're at the restau-rant this evening. I've heard nothing but rave reviews. I want to get up there this summer."

"You have to come! Just let me know when!"

"I will, I promise."

She pauses, and I know the small talk is over. She has a reason for her call.

"I know it's been a few weeks since we've talked, but I haven't had much to report as I was waiting for the judge to put your divorce on his docket. He kept pushing it and pushing it, but today was the day. The court granted your divorce."

The words hit like a blow from a heavyweight fighter, leaving me bloodied and bruised. I try to speak, but my throat locks. I don't know what to say. Why am I reacting like this? I knew it was coming. I've been waiting for it. Wanting it, even —or at least telling myself I did.

At last, I manage to spit out, "Oh, wow. Thanks for letting me know, Rebecca. Is there anything else that needs to be done?"

"The 'Judgment of Divorce' will be mailed to me, and I need you to sign an 'Affidavit of Service,' and then you'll be all set. I can have the affidavit couriered up to you for signature— how's that sound?"

How does that sound? That sounds like the door closing on a relationship I thought I would be in forever. That sounds like the end of many dreams that David and I once had. That sounds like the official discontinuation of twenty years together. It sounds final.

"That sounds good," I say quietly. "Thank you for all your help, Rebecca."

"You're welcome, Lyndsay. I'll let you know when I'm in Lake George this summer."

We hang up.

I spend a few minutes collecting myself and my thoughts, still finding it astonishing that a marriage can end so quickly, like one of my books being closed before the final chapter is read, our marriage did not get the happily-ever-after.

I feel like an impostor. Years of writing about the happy ending, yet I can't make it a reality for myself. I thought I would handle the end so much better, but I'm bitter and angry, partly with David, but mostly with myself.

~

I WALK THE LAST PARTY OF FOUR TO THE DOOR, MY smile polished but fading, and thank them for coming. They gush about the meal and my staff, telling me they can't wait to come again.

I can't wait to lock the doors.

I need a glass of wine.

The restaurant is finally quiet—the hum of conversation replaced by the soft drone of the cooler behind the bar. I pour myself some Pinot Grigio and sit to look through tonight's receipts. The night went well, with the little exception of my divorce finalization.

Then I notice it—one check still open. A table of five ordered a ton of food and drinks. Why was their bill never closed out? Callie, who waited on this table, has already gone home for the evening. With a knot in my stomach, I head to the kitchen to ask Marcus if he knows the story.

"Marcus," I call, holding up the receipt. "Do you know why this check for \$672.19, a party of five that Callie waited on, is still open?"

"Yes, we had our first dine and dashers."

"What?" I say, anger evident.

"Dine and dashers, you know...a party that comes in and doesn't pay. Chew and screw. Whatever you want to call it, 518 had its first non-paying customers this evening." He says it with a smile on his face, almost amused by the happening, like we've joined an elite club or something.

I am not amused.

"Are you fucking kidding me? Dining and dashing? Here?! Why didn't Callie tell me? This isn't a fucking Denny's, for God's sake." My voice is strained, filled with more outrage and aggravation than this chew-and-screw situation deserves.

"We may not be a Denny's, but we were once a David's," Marcus quips, trying to diffuse the tension.

It doesn't work.

I snap. "Marcus, this isn't fucking funny, and I'm not in the mood for your stupid jokes."

He stops smiling.

"Lynds, calm down...it happens every once in a while. Fine dining restaurants are not immune to people coming in and wanting to pull a fast one."

Did he tell me to calm down? That's the kiss of death for most men, and tonight it might be for Marcus.

"Do *not* tell me to calm down in *my* restaurant. I'm the owner of this restaurant, and you will *not* tell me what to do." I know I'm overreacting to all of this, but I can't stop myself. I'm like a roller coaster off its tracks, unable to be stopped. "I expect to be told about things like this WHEN THEY HAPPEN, not hours after the fact."

Marcus doesn't engage with me, but glances at the kitchen staff and tells them they can head home for the evening, the remaining prep can be done tomorrow. Without a word, they pack up and scurry away like mice, not wanting to get caught in a trap.

I march out of the kitchen and back to the bar to pour myself another glass of wine.

I can hear the swinging door from the kitchen open, swishing back and forth between the carpeting in the dining room and the tile in the kitchen.

Then, I can feel Marcus right behind me.

"Want to tell me what the hell that was all about?" His tone is calm, but with an edge—an edge he doesn't use too often.

"Not particularly, no."

"Lynds, it's not like you to lose it, and you definitely lost it back there—so come on, spill."

"Did you not hear what I said? I don't feel like talking about it." I hate the inflection of my voice; he's not deserving of my wrath, but I can't stop myself.

Marcus knows better than to push and leaves me with my wine, heading back to the kitchen.

Even when we were young, and I had a massive blow-up with my parents or with Chloe, he would ask if I wanted to talk about it, to which I would always tell him no, and he would wait patiently for me to change my mind. I always did. And when I was ready, he would listen, eyes focused on me, leaning in like I was the only person in the world, never interrupting.

But I don't feel like talking tonight. The finalization of my divorce is a lot. I thought I had prepared myself for it mentally and emotionally, but it's obvious I haven't. My emotions are raging like one of those July thunderstorms that rolls in over the mountains and hits the lake with a vengeance, causing waves to swell and boats to bob up and down like little toy ducks in a bathtub.

I finish my wine, grab my purse and keys, and stand by the back door waiting to lock up.

Marcus grabs his jacket, kisses me on the cheek, skipping his regular goodnight, and heads towards his car.

I watch him walk away.

But then I'm overcome by the insatiable need to kiss him. It's something that cannot wait. The need is like that of air.

I run after him.

"Marcus, wait."

He turns around as he reaches his truck, and I pin him up against the door, my entire body pressed against his, kissing him like I'm eighteen again. He tastes like Macallan and memories, and possibly a mistake I don't care that I'm making.

And, while he's startled at first, he quickly responds, his hands finding their way into my hair, then gliding down my back, finally resting on my hips. His kisses deepen, and there's an urgency in the way we cling to one another, as if the years we've been apart have suddenly collapsed. My heart is racing, and all I can think about is the warmth of him, the taste of him. It's all so familiar, yet entirely new in its intensity.

He pauses long enough to ask, "Are you sure, Lynds?"

The air between us feels taut, pulsing, alive with possibility.

"Take me home, Chef."

Chapter Twelve

With a smile caught between smugness and sheepishness, Marcus asks, "Your place or mine?"

"Mine...it's closer."

When we arrive, my place is dark, except for the bed of stars overhead and the full moon shining like a beacon. Marcus circles to open my door, and I grab his hand—steady, warm, certain—and don't let go as I lead him inside.

We kick off our shoes, and the door closes with a soft thud. In the next breath, he presses me up against it, close enough that I can feel both of our heartbeats. His hands slide their way into my hair, kissing me like a man starved. For a moment, I'm self-conscious—the extra few pounds, the gray hair, things I didn't have back in high school. But his insistent lips move against mine with a relentlessness that leaves me breathless, and my insecurities fall away, and I find myself melting into the moment. Every touch sends shivers down my spine, igniting something within that I can't control. He presses closer, the heat radiating from him making me dizzy with desire.

I remove his chef's coat one button at a time, kissing his neck in between each unfastening. He lets out a moan that is low and raspy, like he is being freed from chains that have constricted him for way too long.

Then I slowly lift his gray, brushed cotton T-shirt over his head, running my hands over his chest and up to his shoulders, feeling the warmth of his skin under my fingertips. His muscles tense and relax to my touch, another soft groan escaping his lips. I take my time, memorizing every contour. Unlike our high school days, where we were constantly afraid of getting caught, there is no rush, and I can't help but notice how leaden the air in the room feels with anticipation.

Marcus forges a southern trail of kisses from my temple down my neck until he reaches my shoulder, and then he bends down to forge a northern trail, starting at my inner thigh. I'm so weak-kneed that I feel I may collapse, but his hands firmly grasp my hips, preventing that, as his lips move upwards towards my stomach.

When he reaches my abdomen, he grabs the belt of my red wrap dress and undoes it, leaving me exposed, letting it fall to the floor in a pool at my feet. My black Cosabella bikini and bralette are the only things keeping him from seeing all of me, any tentativeness long gone. I want him to see all of me. I slide the black lace bralette off my shoulders and lift it over my head, letting it join my dress. He drags his finger up my sternum as he begins to once again stand, and soon his lips are crashing into mine again, like waves in a storm, urgent and demanding, as his hands tease my nipples to attention.

It's now my turn to expose him, and I fall to my knees as I undo the top button of his jeans, grabbing the zipper pull and lowering it. I place my hands on his hips and peel back his faded Levi's, allowing them to drop to the ground. Using my fingers, I trace a path from his ankles to the back of his calves, to his inner thighs, until he can no longer take my teasing, and he grabs me, pulling me up from my knees, locking his eyes on mine.

Once again, he's kissing me like a scene from one of my books, both of us uttering guttural sounds that only make us want each other more. His kisses feel like electricity, charged, causing my entire body to feel ablaze like his knife tattoo. Our hands explore each other mercilessly as I lead him to my bed, always touching, never separating.

He sets me on the edge of the bed and lets his fingers run around the lace edge of my Cosabella's. I shudder with need, a need that can no longer wait. As I run my hands up his thighs and under his boxer briefs, I know that he can no longer wait as well.

I look at him and say, "No more waiting."

"I'm not...prepared for this, Lynds..."

I look at him knowingly. "I was tested after I found out about David's cheating. I'm good. And there's no chance of me becoming pregnant. That ship has sailed," I say.

He hesitates just a moment, then nods, "I am as well. I haven't been with anyone since my divorce."

This is the last moment of hesitation as it all falls away. Clothes, doubts, weeks of what-ifs.

He lays me down on the white chenille bedspread, murmuring, "You are a true wonder, Lyndsay Leach..." Then he inches his way inside me, gentle, shallow strokes making the anticipation of him fully inside me unbearable.

I grip his back like my life depends on it, as if letting go would make this dream end, and whisper in his ear, "Now... don't make me wait another minute longer."

And he doesn't. His lips on my breasts, his eyes watching me, he thrusts himself into me with a force akin to an earthquake, without the devastation, only pure elation. I reach for his chin and bring his lips to mine as we continue to come together, like two train tracks that once ran parallel, but now meet at a switch. It is only when we are both completely satiated that he stops, his body still wrapped up in me, caressing my face, once again calling me "A true wonder..."

We lay next to one another in a silence that is not awkward. In fact, I find it soothing, as must he, because he's soon asleep. I watch his chest rise and fall, curled up in his arms, feeling a sense of peace. His breathing is steady and calming, and I smile as I trace the outline of the chef's knife that adorns his body, finding the answer to my question.

He has no additional tattoos. This is the one and only, and with that, I soon fall asleep myself.

IN THE MORNING, I STRETCH AND REACH ACROSS THE bed to where I expect to find Marcus, but he's not there.

Where is he?

For a split second, I fear he has left without saying goodbye. But just as quickly, that thought disappears as the smells of fresh-brewed coffee and cinnamon waft their way to me, and I know he's in the kitchen.

I throw on a robe and go to join him.

"I have to say it's nice to walk into my kitchen and see a man without his shirt, making coffee and...is that French toast?"

He sets aside what he is doing and comes to kiss me on the cheek, yet this time the kiss is entirely different. Or is it? Maybe it was the same kiss these past weeks, but I was denying the intention behind it.

"Good morning, Lynds...and yes, it's French toast. I found that loaf of cinnamon swirl sourdough—which I'm assuming you made—and thought I would put it to good use. Coffee?"

"Do you even have to ask?" I head to the fridge to grab my

caramel creamer and pour it into the mug he hands me, making my coffee the color of a fawn in spring.

"You never weaned yourself off the creamer, huh?"

"Nope. I like my coffee the way I like my romance novels, light and sweet."

This makes him laugh, in turn making me laugh.

He soon places two plates of cinnamon sourdough French toast, scrambled eggs, and orange wedges on my kitchen table.

"This looks incredible...and you found all of the stuff to make this in my fridge?" I'm shocked that a breakfast this delicious could be concocted with the scarce provisions in my house. I've been eating most meals at the restaurant and have done very little shopping.

"I did. You have more in there than you think."

There's a slight pause, and then he speaks.

"So...can we talk about last night?"

"Which part?" I ask with a devilish grin.

"Well, I'd love to relive *that* part with you, but I was talking about at the restaurant..." His voice trails off.

I was afraid that was what he wanted to talk about.

My meltdown.

"Umm...yeah, sorry about that. I'm not quite sure why I lost it over that open check."

That's a lie. I know exactly why. And it wasn't because of a couple of stupid dine-and-dashers. It was because my marriage had officially come to an end. But I can't tell him that. He'll think I jumped into bed with him for that sole reason. And while it may have been the catalyst, seeing him naked in my bed has been something I've been thinking about for weeks. Maybe since he first walked into the restaurant, if I'm being entirely honest with myself.

"Lynds...it was more than that."

I don't want to tell him, yet the words come spilling out, just like when we were younger.

"So, yesterday, my lawyer called during dinner to tell me that the judge had granted my divorce. I'm officially divorced from David."

He doesn't say a word, waiting for me to continue.

I look down at my coffee, taking a big sip, needing to remove the tremble from the back of my throat.

"I really thought I had this all figured out. He's moved on, I've moved on. I've been throwing myself into 518, and everything has been fantastic. The restaurant is a success, and I'm happy to be out of the city and living up here full-time. But when Rebecca called...it felt like failure. Even though I don't want to be married to him any longer, it was a punch to the gut. It brought back all those feelings of inadequacy I felt when I found out about his affair."

He reaches across the table and puts his hand on top of mine, "I can understand that. When Val and I divorced, I felt the same way. It's why I left the area and started doing the pop-ups down South. I thought I could escape those regrets by throwing myself into something new, but really, they just followed me—and forced me to come back. I knew I couldn't get past them unless I dealt with them."

"Why *did* your marriage end?" This is a topic we have not covered, and I will take the door he has cracked open to learn more and take myself off the hot seat, even momentarily.

He winces at my question, and while I wonder if he will try to skirt the subject, he does not.

"It really was a case of two people growing apart. She had a big job doing big things with lots of travel, and I was throwing all my time and energy into The Sagamore. I felt like it was my one shot at doing something great as a chef, and my full attention was on making a name for myself. Eventually, we found that we loved our jobs more than we loved each other.

"But Lynds, you can't just ignore what you're feeling and

then blow up like a volcano. You have to let people in, me or Chloe, or someone—although I hope it will be me."

The tenderness in his voice is genuine, causing tears to well up in my eyes.

Once again, I look down at my cup of coffee, not wanting to make eye contact, and say, "I didn't want to tell you that my divorce was finalized, and have you think that was the only reason I kissed you last night...among other things."

He lifts my chin so that I can no longer avoid his gaze and continues, "To be honest, I knew something had triggered you. I was just hoping that you were overcome with desire after my nightly kisses on the cheek." He winks as he says it.

"They were rather enticing, I must admit. And there were several nights where I almost ran after you in the parking lot to give you a real kiss, but..."

He finishes my sentence. "You waited. You waited until you were officially done with David. I respect that."

"Yeah...it was stupid. I was worried about what people would think. I was worried about messing up things at the restaurant. I was worried about making a mistake."

"We are not a mistake."

He says this with such conviction that I want to believe him, but doubts about all of this are bouncing around my brain like a pinball.

"How do you know?"

"I just do. I knew it from the moment I walked into the restaurant in February. I told you, there is a difference between coincidence and kismet, and we are kismet."

I smile at him, and his use of the word "kismet" again. Is this really destiny? I don't know, but I can't stop myself from asking, "So...where do we go from here?"

"We take it day by day, Lynds, but I'm excited about the possibilities. You and I are good together."

He's right. We are good together. And if I can take the time to get over my fears, I think we can make a real go of this.

"MARCUS, HAVE YOU SEEN MY PHONE?"

He's just getting out of my shower, and I can't help but take a peek as he stands there in only a towel, drops of water running down his chest. I also notice the fingernail marks I left on his back. Good thing he wears a chef's coat at work... wouldn't want anyone to see those. Although he didn't complain when I was doing it.

I continue to look around but can't find it anywhere. I thought it was in the pocket of my wrap dress, but it doesn't seem to be amongst the heap of clothes we dropped by the door.

Marcus joins me in the living room, still clad in only a towel, and replies, "No. I didn't see it in the bedroom or bathroom. Want me to call it?"

"Yes, please."

He grabs his jeans from the floor and pulls his phone out of the back pocket and finds my number.

Immediately, I regret it as "I Hate Myself for Loving You" begins to faintly play from beneath the couch.

With a mischievous glance, he says, "Is that your ringtone?"

I reach under the couch, where it must've ended up after we undressed one another last night, and hit the decline button as fast as I can, my face red—and not from the minor exertion of stretching to grab my cell.

"No, that's *your* ringtone," I reply, which immediately sends him into hysterical laughter.

"Hmmm...interesting? Is it still true?"

"Ummm…" I'm not sure how to answer. I don't want to admit that I may still love him. That's too much, too soon.

Still laughing, he says, "Well, after last night, I think that needs to change," and he heads back to the bedroom to finish getting dressed for work.

Oh, man! He's right, that song no longer works. But what should his new one be?

"With or Without You" by U2. Maybe.

"Every Breath You Take" by The Police. Could work.

"Never Gonna Give You Up" by Rick Astley. A bit much.

"The Power of Love" by Huey Lewis and the News. Possibly.

But then it dawns on me.

"Time After Time" by Cyndi Lauper.

I delete Joan Jett, and Cyndi takes her place.

But Marcus doesn't need to know this, and I put my phone on mute.

Chapter Thirteen

ANOTHER NEW FARM-TO-TABLE RESTAURANT COMING TO THE AREA

"Lynds, your WTF lines are highly visible—what's up?"

"My WTF lines?"

I'm confused. What the hell are WTF lines?

"You know...those creases in your forehead that happen when you observe or read something that causes you to say WTF."

I laugh, but Marcus is right. They form a distinct V-shaped pattern directly above the bridge of my glasses whenever those moments occur, which is quite often, really. I don't have much patience, I'm not fond of stupidity, and I think common sense should be handed out by the bucketloads, and some people obviously missed it on the first round and need to go back for a second helping of it. You can imagine how many WTF moments I experience each day when I'm dealing with the public.

"Did you read the paper this morning?"

"No, I was busy helping you find your phone." He chuckles as he says this and squeezes my hand.

"Haha! Very funny, but seriously. A new farm-to-table restaurant is going into Maple & Ash."

"Really?"

"Yeah, there are no real details. The owners of Maple & Ash said they can't share much more until the sale is final, but that they're excited for 'the new owner to join the collection of fine restaurants in our region.'"

"That's cool. It's a nice space. I hope someone can make a go of it there."

He's so calm. Even magnanimous in wishing that someone could make the new restaurant a success.

I, on the other hand, am wary and more than a tad nervous. Another farm-to-table restaurant. We just opened, and I was hoping we'd have at least a year to solidify our concept, make raving fans of our guests. But someone coming in and competing with our same concept...just down the street. Ugh.

"It doesn't make you even the tiniest bit nervous that we'll lose some of our customers to this new place?"

"Lynds, restaurants come and go. Concepts come and go. What's important is the food on the plate and the staff that we put in front of our guests. I'm not nervous."

My WTF lines are still present.

"But...the same damn concept?" I feel like it's a personal attack on me. I don't know why. It's not like there aren't several Italian restaurants in the area, or several steakhouses, all very successful, all doing what they do in their own way.

I don't know.

"Lynds, don't worry about it. We're going to keep doing our thing, and whoever takes over Maple & Ash is going to do their thing."

He's right. I know he's right, but I can't stop thinking about it.

We pull into the parking lot of 518 Farm-to-Table, where my Jeep is still parked from last night—ah, nothing like a ride of shame. At least I have a new outfit on. Marcus cannot say the same.

Marcus reaches across the seat to kiss me and once again reassures me that there is nothing to worry about. "You all good? Relax those WTF lines, will ya? People are going to think that we're still fighting after last night's scene in the kitchen."

I exhale a nervous laugh. "Yeah...but Candace is already here, and I'm sure she's wondering where I am since my Jeep is here, but I'm not."

"So, what's the plan, boss? Do you want to come up with some sort of story, or are we walking in together and letting them talk?"

I hesitate, thinking that I would normally not want to be the subject of restaurant gossip. But I'm tired—tired of pretending, tired of managing optics, tired of worrying about what everyone thinks. At my age, you have fewer and fewer fucks to give. "We're walking in together and letting them talk."

The smile on his face says it all as he comes and opens my door, grabs my hand, and we walk into the restaurant... together.

SERVICE IS SMOOTH, AND I TELL MARCUS THAT I'M going to take off early to spend some time with Chloe, as I haven't seen her in almost two weeks. Marcus gives me a knowing smile and tells me to have fun. He knows that I can't keep our hooking up from Chloe for too long or she'll kill me.

Chloe has no sense of chill about these things, and these eighteen hours may already have put a crimp in our friendship. But I had Candace bake out a loaf of garlic parmesan sourdough for me—yes, my sourdough starter now has two homes—my lake house and the restaurant—and I'm bringing it as a preemptive peace offering.

As I'm walking out the back door, Marcus reminds me we need to finalize the menu for the Lake George Wine & Dine Festival this weekend. He yells to me to meet him at the farmers' market at seven thirty tomorrow so we can see what looks good. I wave and let him know I'll be there.

Now, I'm off to let Chloe know that boundaries have been crossed and that Marcus has a new ringtone.

CHLOE IS ALREADY AT MY HOUSE WHEN I ARRIVE, and I can see that she's let herself in.

I have a spare key hidden, not well, under a ceramic goose. The goose is an ode to our childhood when we were caught stealing an identical one from a neighbor's flower bed. Chloe gave me this one a few years back as a joke—which my mother did not find funny. I can still hear my mom as I opened the birthday gift and held it up to show everyone. "Do you two remember how mad Mrs. Lyons was and how I had to sweet-talk her to not call the police on you two? She thought you were a couple of hoodlums!" Chloe and I laughed until we cried.

But now I may need to rethink this whole key-hiding thing. If Marcus is going to be here more often...well, I don't want Chloe walking in on that. And most assuredly not my mother.

I can see Chloe's settled in on the porch, a bottle of Pinot Grigio and two glasses set up, enjoying the view of Lake

George. My home sits on the west side of the lake, so while we don't get to watch the stunning sunsets, I do love the sense of peace that evenings bring, with the water, and the mountains, and the sounds of the robins and the jays echoing across the bay. Now that Memorial Day has come and gone, the tourists are starting to flock to the region, but luckily, most of the boats are nestled in their slips for the evening, and the few that are still out drift lazily across the water, letting their occupants enjoy a sunset cocktail cruise.

"Hi Chlo...let me change, and I'll be right out."

I change into an oversized Lake George sweatshirt and Lululemon leggings and think about how I'm going to tell Chloe about Marcus.

So, my divorce is final, and I slept with Marcus last night.

I need to tell you that Marcus slept over last night—and it wasn't like one of OUR sleepovers.

Hey, Chloe...so, um...Marcus and I crossed ALL the boundaries last night.

I think I'll go with the third version. Like ripping off a Band-Aid. No hesitation. Just straight to business.

I snag a bag of chips off the counter and slide open the glass doors to be greeted by Chloe saying, "So, when were you going to tell me that you slept with Marcus?"

My WTF lines are back. While Candace saw us walk into the restaurant together this morning and gave us a knowing smile, she's not close friends with Chloe, and I do think Candace is a little more discreet than some others at the restaurant.

Hands on hips, I say, "How did you know that?"

"Are you admitting it's true?

I wear the mischievous grin of a cat with a feather still on its whiskers and flusteredly reply, "Yes."

"I knew it! I just knew it!"

"But *how* did you know it? Who told you?" We're both

laughing at this point, and it looks like my sourdough peace offering won't be needed.

"If I ever need a new career, I'm going to be a detective." She pauses dramatically, like she is about to reveal the murderer in a long-unsolved case. "When I came into your house, I went to the kitchen to grab a couple of wineglasses, but what did I see in the sink?"

Damn! I know exactly what she saw in the sink.

With the steadfastness of a prosecutor who knows he has the witness dead to rights, she lays out her evidence. "I saw two sets of dishes, both with remnants of maple syrup, plus a pan that had been used to scramble eggs. You, my dear friend, do not cook—and you *never* cook breakfast. This means someone cooked breakfast for you. Someone who knows their way around a kitchen. David was out, so I deduced it was Marcus. Case closed."

She looks so smug, but her detective skills are spot on. We were running late this morning, and I told Marcus to leave the dishes, I would put them in the dishwasher tonight.

"Yes, well, David is most definitely out of the picture. My divorce was granted yesterday." The sadness and anger I felt last night when my lawyer called have dissipated. I'm unsure if this is because of Marcus or because I've come to terms with the end of my marriage...officially.

"So, was Marcus an I'm-sad-and-need-comfort hookup or something more?"

Chloe always jumps straight to the heart of it. She's like an arrow seeking a target when it comes to finding out the emotional truth.

I curl my knees up to my chest, take a swig of my wine, and fill her in on my blowup in the kitchen. "When he left, I knew he was hurt, and it was like that saying about going to bed mad...I didn't want him to go home hurt or mad."

"No, instead you just wanted him to go to bed..."

I narrowly avoid spitting out my wine as I cackle at Chloe's assessment of the situation.

She's not wrong.

"Yeah, but I feel like it's been building for weeks, maybe since he first walked through the door of the restaurant."

"It has. You were just denying it. Insisting on these so-called *boundaries*..."

The way she says *boundaries* shows me just how much she did not believe what I've been saying for the last few months. "You don't have to say it like *that*...I was still a married woman."

"Lynds...Marcus is a good guy. I totally believe that. His actions at the restaurant, the way he's been all in, just prove it. I'm surprised it took this long. But enough about that, can we get to the good stuff now? How was it? Since my love life has been nonexistent for a period of time that may be longer than the Ice Age, I need ALL the details."

Chloe's not one to take to swiping right on Tinder, so she's not kidding with the Ice Age comment. I'm not sure she's been with anyone since her divorce. She jokes that five minutes with her vibrator is all she needs, but I really do want her to find someone. She deserves someone who will treat her well.

"I don't want to be someone to kiss and tell..."

"Like Marcus doesn't know that's exactly what you're doing right now!"

"But it was amazing," I say, letting out a sigh like a teenage girl who has just gone on her first date with her longtime crush.

"Yah? Do tell!"

In high school, Marcus was my first, and I was his, and there were plenty of awkward sexual...let's call them *discoveries*, as we figured things out, but eventually, we knew what to do to make each other happy. Last night was like that, but on steroids.

I must've been staring off into space thinking about last night, when Chloe interrupts the silence. "Okay, you don't have to give me all the details. I can see from that look on your face that Marcus knows how to please a woman, and while I'm a smidge jealous that you're getting some from that fine-looking man, I am also over-the-moon happy for you. After what David did, you need a little lovin' in your life."

"I do, don't I?" David's affair damaged my self-image to the point where I wondered if it could be repaired, but these last few months working side by side with Marcus started the recovery process. I no longer feel so fragile, so expendable. Yes, David is a total duplicitous dumbass, and I deserve a little joy in my life.

"So how did you leave things this morning?"

"Well, we said we would take it day by day and see where things went. But I really have a good feeling about this, Chlo..." And I do. Truly. But my mind drifts back to Vermont and Natalia and Thomas. Do we have enough structure to keep our relationship—both personally and professionally—in place like they do? I guess only time will tell.

"I'm glad to hear it. We have two final things to discuss. Does he have a brother, and what's his new ringtone going to be?"

CHLOE LEAVES A LITTLE AFTER TEN, AND IT'S BEEN another night that just reiterated how thankful I am for her. There is no competitiveness and no judgment. Just decades of history and the kind of friendship that can handle a few honest disagreements and still end in laughter. She's the sister I never had, the one who knows to pour the wine and when to tell me I'm being an idiot. Every woman deserves a Chloe in their life.

And she approved of my new choice of ringtone. "Time After Time" just seems to fit after all these years.

Before heading to bed, I make the mistake of checking my email. There's one from Susan: *The publisher wants to know the premise of your next book and when they can expect a first draft.* Reasonable questions, to which I have no answers. I've been playing around with a couple of ideas, but nothing has stuck. I get about 10,000 words in and then shelve it. It's not writer's block, it's a disconnect. I'm just not loving the ideas.

Maybe it was my marriage draining my creativity. Maybe it was subliminally rubbing off into my writing.

If it was my marriage, I can no longer use that as an excuse.

Perhaps this reconnection with Marcus will spark something in my writing. The spark, the sense of being seen again—it might be the very thing needed to wake something up inside me. Maybe in life, as in writing, you have to burn the first draft to find the real story underneath.

I'll reply to Susan tomorrow and hope that she can hold off my publisher for a hot second more. Tonight, I'm giving myself a pass.

As I climb into bed, all I can think about is last night. Even though he's not here, Marcus remains in my bed. I can smell his cologne mixed with bourbon and cinnamon, and the scent of char from the grill at the restaurant. It's distinctly him, and more than a little arousing.

But I told him I was hanging with Chloe tonight, and I will not give in to a booty call text—no matter how bad I want to.

As I try to banish all the sexy Marcus thoughts from my brain unsuccessfully, he texts me.

I hope you had a good night with Chloe. Was she surprised by this turn of events? Probably not, knowing Chloe. Anyway, I just wanted you to know that I missed closing with you tonight—amongst other things—and I'll see you in the morning.

I stare at the message, a smile tugging at the corners of my mouth. I send back a blushing emoji and a heart emoji and leave it at that.

It feels nice to be missed.

Chapter Fourteen

LYNDSAY LEACH AND DAVID MONTERO OFFICIALLY DIVORCED

CELEBRITY CHEF AND FORMER ROMANCE AUTHOR NO LONGER MARRIED

IS DAVID MONTERO'S NEW GIRLFRIEND WEARING AN ENGAGEMENT RING?

It's now internet official.

My publicist, Jill, sent me a text this morning, informing me that she had confirmed our divorce to several media outlets and that I should expect to see it in the news. What I was NOT expecting was the Mindi engagement ring announcement. I did go and read that article, and sure enough, the paps had snapped a photo of them in New York at some event, and there was a diamond on her left hand. It was of considerable size and shine. I chalked it up to David compensating for his small...well, let's not go there. I AM the bigger person.

Of course, David did a "No comment" for the article. I'm sure it's in hopes that the press will write another piece about him. He fucking loves being in the spotlight. He'll milk this as long as possible.

Hopefully, this will be the last of the articles where David and I are mentioned together.

I toss my phone on the bed. I need to stop scrolling and get dressed. I'm meeting Marcus in an hour at the farmers' market. And while the farmers' market isn't my usual type of shopping, I'm anxious to see my favorite chef do his thing.

STANDING AT THE SOUTH ENTRANCE TO THE farmers' market, waiting for Marcus, I look down at my watch. Not a newfangled Apple Watch, just an old-school one with hands and the date as writing requires me to limit my distractions. I'm ten minutes ahead of the chosen time to meet, to be expected. Punctuality has always been one of my less charming qualities. David said I had OCD about time, because he had no trouble strolling into an event late, making his grand entrance. I hated that about him. Especially when it was a gathering where he was not meant to be the shining star. Always stealing someone's thunder and thinking nothing of it. But he's not my concern any longer.

While I wait, I decide to fire off an email to Susan and ask if she can buy me a little more time with the publisher. A week, maybe two at the most. I know that time frame is probably not going to cut it, but I've never pushed off my publisher like this. I'm sure their patience is running thin with me. I don't want to risk breaching my contract, but I've got nothing.

I hit send, glance up, and there he is. Early by seven minutes. Marcus.

Faded Levi's. A pink V-neck T-shirt, showing off just a sneak peek of that delicious chest hair. A matching pink baseball hat of his favorite baseball team, the New York Yankees, sets off his blue eyes like a summer sky against cotton candy clouds. He smiles that easy smile, making my heart skip just a little more than it should.

"Hey," he says, handing me a caramel latte, "ready to go?"

If the way to a man's heart is through his stomach, then the way to a woman's heart must be coffee—or at least it is for this woman—and Marcus knows it.

"Yup, lead the way."

He grabs my hand, like it's the most natural thing in the world, his fingers intertwining with mine effortlessly. His long legs and eagerness to see what the market has to offer today have me about half a step behind him, grinning like I've just won the lottery.

Maybe I have—if there's a prize for gorgeous chefs.

"Sorry...am I walking too fast? Just tell me to slow down. I get a little excited about the farmers' market. So much good stuff."

As we make our way from stall to stall, Marcus spends time chatting with most, if not all, of the farmers and vendors. They all seem to know him and spend time sharing with him what's fresh and available today and what will be available later this week. We do a full loop without buying a thing—Marcus's version of reconnaissance—so he can make a plan.

"With the Wine & Dine Festival this weekend, I'd really like for us to keep it simple, but in line with the restaurant. We won't have a lot of space for equipment, and if it's like past years, the crowd will be huge."

"Agreed. So, what are you thinking?"

"Well, I'm thinking Berkshire pulled pork sliders. Candace could make the brioche slider buns. We could make a Texas-style barbecue sauce for that touch of the South and an apple and cabbage slaw with a slice of aged New York Cheddar. What do you think? Think we can pull that off? The good thing about doing pulled pork is that it can be smoked and pulled ahead of time and kept hot in warming trays."

"Wait! You're going to *make* barbecue sauce? Isn't that just something you pick up at the grocery store?"

His laughter tells me this is not the case.

"Yes, I'm going to make it. It will be a thousand times better than anything you've tasted from the grocery store."

"I believe you. Who's going to help you on Saturday?"

"You are." He says it as if the decision has already been made, even though I was never informed. "I already told Blake I'll be gone and that he'll be in charge of service that day, and Todd is more than ready to be second-in-command. Can you pull yourself away from the front of house? Can Maria handle it? It's supposed to be a gorgeous day, and it would be great PR if both of us were there. Plus, I think it would be fun."

"Oooohhh...I'm not sure that's your best move. I have limited cooking skills. Very limited."

"There are really no cooking skills needed. All the cooking will be done ahead of time. All you need to do is assemble. Come on! It'll be a good time."

"Okay, okay. I'll do it." It really doesn't take much convincing. The chance to spend the entire day with him sounds divine.

"Then it's time to shop. Tina said she has Berkshire pork butts available, but she'll have to deliver them to the restaurant tomorrow. Jay has some locally grown cabbage and apples that he's brought out of cold storage—so let's go back to his stand and clean him out. I believe he has enough if nobody beats us to it. I can call Meredith for some additional cheddar, and I should have everything I need for the barbecue sauce back at the restaurant. Oh! I'd better text Candace and give her a heads-up on slider buns. We're going to need about eight hundred."

"Did you say *eight hundred*? We're going to make sliders for *eight hundred* people on Saturday?"

"Yup...better wear your running shoes because it's going to be a fast and furious day."

"Are you sure you don't want to bring one of the other chefs?" Doubt is creeping in faster than the weeds in our restaurant herb garden.

"I'm sure. I want you."

My lips turn up into a slight grin at hearing the words "I want you," and Marcus says, "You know what I mean, Lynds..."

"I do, I do. But can't it be both?"

He likes my not-so-subtle flirting and says, "It most definitely can. Would you like me to show you how much I want you—maybe later today?"

The restaurant is closed this evening, and these are the words I was hoping to hear.

"I would—if you're free."

"I'm very free. What do you say to me fixing dinner at your place? Maybe we could take your pontoon out for a cruise this afternoon? Get a little vitamin D?"

This makes me blush, unsure if he's even aware of the double entendre from his vitamin D comment, but I roll with it—not giving him a hard time.

"Sounds like a plan. Can we get what we need for dinner here? You know what's in my fridge—not much."

"We can get it all here. Let's go shopping."

AFTER HITTING UP MARCUS'S FAVORITE VENDORS and grabbing everything we'll need for dinner tonight, we agree to meet at my place at two thirty to head out on the lake. The morning fog has cleared, giving way to full-on sunshine, and the kind of soft, golden warmth that makes you forget what day it is. Temperatures in the eighties, a light breeze coming from the south—an ideal June day off.

On the way back to my place, I pick up some ice for the cooler, a six-pack of beer, and some cheese and cold cuts for sandwiches. I'm not a cook, but I can stack turkey and Swiss between slices of sourdough like a pro. There's still a bag of chips in the pantry. I'm calling it good. Or at least good enough.

It's two p.m. by the time I finish packing the cooler, and I still need to change. I reach into my dresser for my swimsuit—torn between the black one-piece or the red bikini. I'm not usually self-conscious about my body—after all, every body is a bikini body—but is this red one a bit too much? I slap those doubts aside like an annoying mosquito and decide to go for it. Confidence is a choice, and today I'm choosing it. I find my black crocheted cover-up and sandals, and head to the linen closet to grab some towels for us both.

Soon, I hear Marcus's truck rumble into the driveway, and I head out to greet him, cooler and towels in hand.

"Hey there! Ready to head out on the lake?" I ask, taking in every ounce of him. Salmon-colored board shorts, not the extra-long ones, the ones that stop mid-thigh, allow me to once again gaze at his fit legs. He has on a T-shirt from one of the local breweries, a different ball cap from this morning—still showing his support for the Yankees—and aviators, which allow me to see my beaming smile, which I immediately try to dim, but can't.

"Ready!" he says, grabbing the cooler from my hand.

"Then follow me."

We make our way down the wooden steps to the oversized double-decker dock. The top level is where I spend lazy summer days reading, writing, and browning myself to a perfect shade of mocha. Below is a 2022 SunChaser 26' pontoon with all the bells and whistles.

"I know you told me you had a boat, but this is a BOAT," Marcus says, eyes wide.

"We used to have a speed boat, but then we got old," I say, laughing, "and a party barge just seemed like the right thing. No stepping down to get in. Super comfortable. Room for lots of friends."

He runs his hand along the rail. "You don't have to convince me. This thing is awesome!"

"I'm glad you think so! You can drive." I toss him the keys.

"Yes!" he replies with the enthusiasm of a teenager getting to drive solo for the first time.

I grab a seat at the bow while Marcus unties us, and then we're off. The lake opens up around us, deep blue and glimmering. It's Tuesday, so the water is calm, dotted only with a few kayaks and fishing boats, folks out soaking up all that the day has to offer.

"Which direction? To the village or up to The Narrows?" he calls.

"Captain's choice!" I holler back over the sound of the engine and the gentle breeze.

"The Narrows it is!" We head north on the lake.

It's my first time out on the boat this year, and I inhale the scent of the water and the wind and let the sunshine warm my face. The thirty-two miles this lake covers from Lake George Village to Ticonderoga are incredible, with everything from cozy family-owned cabins to hotels and motels to huge McMansions dotting its shoreline. The water is a brilliant shade of blue, somewhere between navy and cobalt, and so clear that you can see fish swimming beneath its surface. We glide along, the waves lapping against the boat creating a soothing rhythm, no music needed, and I feel a profound sense of peace.

We soon reach The Narrows and decide to drop anchor.

I reach into the cooler and grab us each a can of Common

Roots Lager, the perfect crisp and refreshing day-drinking beer. We cheers with a clink of aluminum, and the sound blends with the gentle caress of the waves and the distant call of a duck. I take a long sip, breathing in the summer bliss, wondering if there is a better way to spend a summer day.

There isn't.

Marcus sits on the bench seat, facing me, his feet at my feet, and there is a look upon his face that makes me curious.

"What are you thinking about over there?" I ask, tilting my head.

"You really want to know? I was thinking about all the parties we went to in high school. Out in the middle of the woods, handing someone a few dollars so we could get a red Solo cup and a few glasses of warm beer from a keg that would be kicked way too soon. And I was thinking how much better it is to be with you now—with cold beer on a warm summer's day on the lake."

Laughing at this memory, I say, "Yes, warm beer has definitely lost its appeal, that's for sure. But we had lots of fun at those parties."

"We did, for sure. But can you imagine parents today letting their kids go out to the middle of the woods to hang out and drink?"

Chuckling, I say, "Well, it's not like we exactly asked for permission. We were lucky it was before cell phones and the need to be in constant communication. We could get away with a lot more."

"So true. I think both of our moms would have killed us if they knew what we were up to."

Once again, that melancholy look comes across his face, the one I've seen before when he brings up his mom.

"You must miss your mom a lot," I say, knowing how lost I felt when my dad died, and I was forty-eight years old when it happened. To be only twenty years old...just way too young.

"I do." His gaze drifts toward the water. "It wasn't easy, but she taught me so much in the short time she was with me. She taught me about resilience and empathy and generosity. I live each day trying to make her proud."

My chest tightens, a mix of admiration and tenderness. "I'm sure she is."

He nods. "Well, since we're talking about all of the serious stuff," he says, "I saw that your divorce made the news."

"Ah, yes...nothing like a little unwanted press about the demise of your marriage."

Studying me, he says, "You can joke, but are you okay?"

I take a sip of my beer, buying a second before I answer. "Yes, I am. Really. I hate being in the news for this, for something I consider to be a failure, but I can't let it define me."

"Don't look at it like that. I'm sure not all your time together was bad. Sometimes you just need to focus on the positive things you received from your marriage, and what you can learn from the times that weren't so great."

"You are correct, oh wise one," I say, not wanting our conversations on death and divorce to set the tone for the afternoon and evening.

"Is that your way of telling me to change the subject?"

"It is."

"Okay. Consider the subject closed. Now, how about one of those sandwiches I spotted in the cooler?"

WE SPEND THE REMAINDER OF THE AFTERNOON IN A lazy rhythm, jumping into the lake hand in hand and then letting ourselves dry off next to one another in the toasty sunshine, only to do it again when our skin is sizzling and sweaty. There's no kissing, just subtle touches and hand-holding. It feels sweet and new and reminds me of when we first started dating.

We reminisce about high school days, and what college was like for me, and what the CIA was like for him. We touch on his time at The Sag, and, eventually, he asks why I gave up writing, since it was something I had dreamed about since I was seventeen years old.

I need to tell him.

"Well, that's the thing. I didn't exactly give it up." The look on his face is one of pure confusion, so I continue. "Can I trust you with something? You can never breathe a word of this. In fact, I'm probably going to have to tell Susan and my publisher, and there's most likely going to be an NDA involved. No probably—there *will* be an NDA involved."

He is bewildered but nods to let me know that I have his word.

"Early in our marriage, David asked me to give it up—so I could be his 'partner'—fully committed to the life we were building, which was really the life he was building. But writing is like breathing for me, and I couldn't give it up." I take a deep breath, remembering David's reaction when I confessed this secret when he filed for divorce, wondering if Marcus's response will be the same, but I go on. "I've been writing books under a pen name, Leona Lambert, for the last twenty years. You probably don't read these books. They're romance novels mixed with art heists taking place around the globe. They've been really popular, but no one knows that I'm the author of these books—and I want to keep it that way."

His eyes widen. "Wow!" He's quiet for a moment, letting it sink in. "First, I want to say that I'm glad you didn't give up your passion. Even when we were in high school, I knew you were destined to be a great writer—and you are. Second, what an asshole to want you to give it up. Third, your secret is safe with me." He says that last sentence while pretending to button up his lips, which makes me want to kiss them, but I resist, instead smiling at him, knowing this is the kind of support for my career that I've always desired.

But I don't want him to think that everything is all sunshine and roses with my writing career. He needs to know where things stand right now.

"Thank you, but currently, my writing is at a standstill. It used to be something I did without thinking. The stories and words were just...there. Waiting to be put on the page. But I'm struggling now. I have a contract and a book due, and I have no idea what I'm going to write about. In fact, I asked my agent to buy me some time—which I've never had to do. I really hate this feeling."

It's so easy to talk with Marcus about this, and I'm grateful for the fact that he doesn't interrupt me or offer advice, he just listens attentively.

"I read a book by Zibby Owens where her main character is a writer with no idea what she's going to write about, and she turns in a blank book to her publisher—and it's a hit. I'm almost to the point of trying to see if I can make this a reality. I really need to spend a few days where I put all my attention into my writing and not the restaurant or romance."

The minute those last few words pass my lips, I immediately regret them.

"I'm sorry if the restaurant and I have been pulling you away from your book." He's not hurt or upset. His words are genuine. "If you need to take some time off, just tell me. We've got good people at 518, they'll pick up the slack so you can work. And we can head back now if you want to get some writing time in this evening."

"Thank you. I appreciate all that you are offering, but I have no idea what my next book will be about—and staring at a blinking cursor doesn't help anyone. I'm just going to let things ride for now, until my muse returns."

At a level just above a whisper, Marcus says, "Maybe he already has."

WE GET BACK TO THE DOCK JUST BEFORE SEVEN P.M. and make our way slowly up the steps and to the house, Marcus holding my hand, our fingers loosely laced together, the touching subtle and comfortable. The evening light casts a purple hue over everything, tranquility setting in on the lake. If the day were to end right now, I would be content, but I'm thankful that he's not leaving.

"Ready for some dinner?" he asks. "I'm famished. Must be from all that sunshine and swimming."

I am hungry, too, but not for food. I want to taste his lips, which he denied me all day. I want to caress his back and run my hands up his thighs, hear him purr at my touch.

But I simply reply, "I could eat."

"Great. Why don't you go set the table on the porch, and I'll grill off the steaks and asparagus and a few slices of sourdough. Dinner will be ready soon."

Inside, he gets to work in the kitchen, while I remove two plates, silverware, napkins, and wineglasses from the cabinet next to where he is working. I grab a bottle of Pinot Noir from the wine rack and a corkscrew from the drawer and head outside.

I set the table on the porch and light several of the candles that are scattered around. Then I settle on one of the daybed swings, a light blanket in my lap, the sound of the lake and the fading light washing upon me, and reflect upon the day.

I can't believe how utterly perfect it was. The morning at the farmers' market, watching him talk with people who are so obviously important to him, and not just because of the food they provide him, but because of the relationships he's established with them. The knowledge he has of their families, their kids, their lives. The afternoon on the lake, reveling in the sunshine, talking about everything under the sun, literally and figuratively. Remembering the constant small brushes against one another makes my lips draw up in a smile. I've smiled continuously today, so much so that my cheeks hurt.

I want more days like this.

I want all my days to be like this.

The sun has now set, and dusk is turning to dark, making me wrap the throw around my shoulders as the temperature drops. I listen to the sounds of the waves swashing against the shoreline and a woodpecker searching the trees for its own dinner. This is why I love it here. Nights just like this.

Marcus steps through the sliding glass door carrying a platter filled with rare rib eyes, grilled asparagus with sea salt and fresh ground black pepper, and toasted sourdough with garlic butter. It smells heavenly, but I no longer want dinner. I only want him.

"Can you put that down for a moment and come sit with me?" I ask.

He looks confused but doesn't deny my request.

He scoots next to me on the daybed, and it gently rocks.

"Not hungry?" he asks.

Without saying a word, I move from next to him to on top of him, my legs straddling his waist. I place my hands on his cheeks and kiss him with a need that startles me. He responds in kind, meeting my urgency, maybe even surpassing it.

When we finally pull apart, we are both breathless, and I lift his T-shirt up over his head, placing it gently beside us, then trace a line from the nape of his neck to his hip. He mimics me, removing my cover-up and bikini top, drawing the exact same line down to my left hip.

"The only thing I want at this very moment is to feel you

inside me with the breeze brushing our skin and candlelight flickering around us. Does that work for you, Chef?"

"Completely."

∼

AFTER SPENDING HOURS WRAPPED UP IN ONE another under a couple of lightweight blankets, staring at the reflection of the sky full of stars on the lake, the goosebumps from the night air are more than I can take, despite the heat that radiates from him. We move inside to enjoy our dinner. Cold steak and garlic bread fill my empty stomach, just as making love to him filled my soul.

With a fork in hand and a mouth full of food, because now I am overcome with true hunger, I say, "Do you know how badly I wanted to kiss you all day?"

Leaning into me, he replies, "Not as badly as I wanted to kiss you. But I promised myself this morning that I would let you set the pace. I didn't want you to feel pressured after the other night."

"I appreciate that," I say, smiling. "But I never would've invited you back to the 'scene of the crime,' so to speak, if my intention wasn't to have a repeat performance."

"Lyndsay Leach...you are a wonder." He looks at me with eyes that are both vulnerable and filled with admiration. It's as if he sees every part of me and cherishes it all, even the parts I try to hide.

"Why do you say that?" I ask, not understanding the mix of awe and sincerity in his voice.

He tucks a lock of my hair behind my ear, his smile soft. "Lyndsay, you are kind and strong. You love with your whole heart, and even after I broke it, you found a way to forgive. You're a wonder to me—quiet, steady, and real—and I'm grateful I get to see that again."

Chapter Fifteen

"Lynds, can you grab that tray of brioche buns? I think that's the last of it for the Wine & Dine Festival today. And, by the way, I signed the NDA you had your publisher send over. That thing is pretty ironclad."

He's right about that. If it's like the one Chloe and my mom—and David—had to sign, it says that the publishing house will not only sue the person who breaks the NDA for some ungodly amount of money, but that they will claw back every cent I've earned. Financial annihilation, essentially.

But there's no reason to worry about this. I know my people. They won't share my secret. And David? He's too fucking greedy to risk losing a payday—so he'll keep his damn mouth shut.

Candace hands me the final tray of glossy slider buns, winks at me, and tells me to have fun, but not too much fun. I give her a knowing smile and a quick wink back.

No promises.

I hand the tray off to Marcus and make my way to the passenger side of his truck. It's eight thirty a.m., and we have a few hours to set up everything before they start letting people through the gates. My stomach does a slow somersault. I feel nervous, like the first day of school nervous, and I don't know why. It's ridiculous. Marcus and the kitchen staff have done all the heavy lifting over the last few days, and Marcus has assured me that it's just a lot of assembly and then putting on my best politician's face and kissing a few babies and shaking some hands with the public. As Marcus put it, "Pretend you're at a book signing, not a restaurant event." I can do that.

When we arrive at the site, it is a flurry—no, a snowstorm—of activity. There are over forty restaurants and wineries participating, and everyone is hustling to get set up and make things perfect. The air crackles with energy. Chefs are slicing and dicing. Vintners are uncorking bottles. The aroma of seared meat, citrus, and herbs mingles with the sweetness of fresh flowers and the crisp notes of various wines. Intoxicating!

One of the festival leads, iPad in hand, waves us to our spot, and we begin unloading. Marcus and I manage to muscle the mobile hot box food warmer out of his truck and slide our pans of Berkshire shredded pork inside, along with a backup tray of barbecue sauce. I'm still amazed that he MADE barbecue sauce. Barbecue was something David never really enjoyed, so Sweet Baby Ray's was always our friend when I requested ribs or barbecue chicken in the summer. But I'll never go back to store-bought after tasting this smoky, tangy perfection that Marcus has concocted.

Our setup looks sharp. I had the printer make a large sign that reads, *Berkshire Pulled Pork Sliders with a Cabbage Apple Slaw and New York Extra Sharp Cheddar*. Additionally, there's a QR code that will take anyone who scans it to our website, where they can check out our full menu or make a reservation. I'm hopeful this festival will bring us even more customers.

And with about fifteen minutes to spare, I'm happy to see that we're ready.

Standing in front of our booth, I grab my phone to take a picture. "Say cheese, Marcus!"

He turns to the camera and flashes his biggest and brightest smile. Click! I quickly check the photo and it's fantastic. No filter needed. So stunning in his chef's whites, slightly bronzed from our day on the lake, his eyes shimmering in the sunshine. He's magnetic, and his charisma practically pops through my screen. The kind of man who makes everyone else fade into the background.

Soon enough, ticket holders begin to enter, and the race is on. From us, it's a lot of:

We hope you love it!

Yes, that's homemade barbecue sauce!

Oh, the cheddar is from Meredith at Lower Adirondack Milk & More.

You must come to the restaurant.

Just scan the QR code to make a reservation.

For sure! Apples and cabbage are a great pairing.

And then, from the crowd, it's:

Are you Lyndsay Leach? Why did you stop writing? (I didn't, but I can't tell you this.)

You are so handsome. Here's my number. (This happens several times to Marcus.)

Are you ever going to write more books? (Maybe.)

Do you cater private events? (This was strangely only asked of Marcus and by some very attractive women.)

You two look good together. Are you dating? (We just smile and don't reply as we quickly hand the next person in line their slider.)

The day is a total blur of making the sliders, handing out the sliders, answering questions about the sliders, and trying to keep the sliders away from a raving fan with long golden hair, who answers to Linus. His owner is very apologetic when he comes to claim this lovely retriever, who is waiting like a good boy in hopes that we will pay the cheese tax just one more time.

By the time five o'clock rolls around, there are only a few sliders remaining, and I'm exhausted.

"You ready to pack up, Lyndsay?"

How does he still look energized, and I look like I'm ready to take a nap as long as Rip Van Winkle's?

"Yup! It was a good day, wasn't it?" Chaotic? Yes. But satisfying as well.

"It was! Amazing! I love events like this, a chance to get out of the kitchen and talk to people..."

It's obvious that this day has given him a dopamine hit like no drug could. I, on the other hand, feel drained, having expended all of my energy for the day on smiles and small talk. I've always struggled to put myself out there, my introverted self being much more comfortable behind a keyboard, which is why writing under a pen name worked so well for me. No book tours. No interviews. Just bless and release.

But him...he loves this stuff.

Not wanting to share how tired I am, I perk up and say, "And get a few phone numbers from some beautiful women?" My tone is pure jest, but it only takes Marcus a second to come up beside me and lay a big kiss on me, which is followed by *click-whirr, click-whirr.*

The sound of a camera taking our photo—mid-kiss.

"I didn't know you two were an item?" the reporter says, glancing down at his camera to make sure he's got the shot.

Neither Marcus nor I respond. I think we're too stunned that we've been caught kissing in public.

The photographer continues, "Would you like to comment for the piece that's going in the paper tomorrow about the event?"

Marcus chimes in, knowing that I'm tired and my fuse is short, saving me from saying something I might regret. "It was a fantastic day with so many great restaurants and wineries participating. The crowd was awesome, and we can't wait to come back next year."

So diplomatic.

I want to rip the camera out of his hand and delete the pics, but that's not going to happen.

"Any comment on the kiss?"

"Nope, thanks for asking." His reply is brusque and punctuated by Marcus turning his back to continue packing our stuff into the truck.

Once again, more diplomatic than I would be. How about: *It's none of your fucking business, jerk!*

I climb into the passenger seat and let out a frustrated sigh.

Marcus glances over. "Was that directed at me?"

"No, of course not." I rub my temples, looking out the windshield. "I was just hoping to keep this—us—whatever *this* is—under wraps a little longer."

"Can I just say that we're officially an *us*. And you're an adult who is officially divorced. You did nothing wrong." With that, he shifts into drive.

He's right. I know he's right, but things seemed...*safer*...is that the word I want, when it was just him and I—and Chloe and Candace—who knew. I can guarantee by tomorrow it will be on *The Pulse* that I'm dating some mystery man, unless the reporter provides him with Marcus's name.

"It's just...we're so *new*." My voice is timid.

"But are we? I don't feel like it's new. I feel like it's right, and I don't care who knows we're together."

Once again, he's correct. It's starting to become a pattern. One I can't even be mad at. And I love that he doesn't care who knows. It's proof that he's all in.

"Okay...I'm adopting your attitude! We are dating." It

sounds so strange to say at my age, "And whoever knows, knows."

He reaches over, squeezes my hand, gives me a peck on the cheek, and we head back to 518-Farm-to-Table.

~

BY THE TIME WE CRAWL OUR WAY FROM LAKE George Village to Bolton Landing, it's almost six thirty p.m. The single lane road and summer tourists make it a slog, but Marcus's '80s playlist has us lip syncing to Def Leppard, KISS, and Motley Crüe like we're back in high school. (Yes, I *loved* me some metal. My high school look was teased hair, plenty of Aqua Net, ripped jeans with a bandana tied around the thigh, and an overabundance of eyeshadow. It was a look.)

We pull into the back lot, laughing, still mid-chorus of "Pour Some Sugar on Me," when the kitchen door bursts open.

Candace yells, "Marcus! Marcus! We need you NOW! We're deep in the weeds!"

In an instant, the music cuts off, and Marcus runs to the kitchen to find total havoc. Tickets are lined up for miles. Waitstaff are yelling for the dishes that they need. None of the kitchen crew is at their regular stations. And Blake, who was supposed to be in charge, is nowhere to be seen.

"Where's Blake?" I ask Candace, scanning the kitchen. "He was supposed to be in charge this evening."

Candace is running the fry station and shrugs. "He never showed up. So, we all just kind of jumped in, but it's a mess, and we're way behind on orders and...I'm sorry. We should've called you, but we thought we could handle it."

Marcus doesn't waste a moment. "Deep breath, everyone. We can do this."

He has everyone slide back into their normal positions,

with him taking on his head chef role and Blake's sous chef role, and he begins to get a handle on the array of tickets in front of him.

"Lynds, can you go out to the dining room and give each guest a free drink on the house? Tell them that we had a little problem in the kitchen, but that we expect to be back on track momentarily."

He's so confident and assured that the only thing I can say is "On it!"

I track down each member of the waitstaff and tell them to offer all of their tables a complimentary drink. They breathe a sigh of relief, knowing that a free cocktail will calm the angry upheaval coming from the dining room. Soon, the clamor has quieted, and there are only the normal murmurs coming from the tables.

Just as I'm about to head back into the kitchen, Maria, my head waitress, intercepts me. She's perturbed, which is so out of character, and I detect some agitation in her voice. "Can you stop by table 12? The guest has requested to speak with you. He's sent his steak back twice already."

FUCK! She needn't say more. I have a sneaky suspicion I know who it is. Tonight? Of all nights?

Making my way through the main dining room to one of the smaller alcoves where Maria is working, I see the back of a very familiar head seated at table 12. Auburn hair peppered with gray, just long enough to show you the relaxed waves he takes such pride in, just short enough to let his bronzed skin peek out above the collar of his pale blue Lacoste golf shirt.

David.

The minute Maria said he sent his steak back *twice*, I knew it was him. Knew it deep in my David-hating soul. He believes that every decent restaurant should know how to cook a steak to the diner's desired doneness, and there should never be a need to send it back. Anything less than perfection made the restaurant a complete and utter failure in his book. This has been his litmus test for as long as I've known him.

Before I have a chance to turn back and come up with a game plan for dealing with him, he turns around and flashes a smug smile my way, his brown eyes dancing with glee at the events of the evening.

"Lynds...I was wondering when you were going to show up."

Of course he was. I nod at him, unable to produce a snappy comeback without sounding like a total bitch, and he continues.

"So, *this* is what you've done with David's?" he asks, his voice slick with condescension. "You've taken my restaurant and created a space of complete and utter chaos. It's a three-ring circus in here. I've sent my steak back twice already. Your kitchen is a complete disaster—despite the early buzz I've heard to the contrary."

Fuck him.

My pulse spikes, but I keep my face neutral. I own 518 Farm-to-Table now, it's no longer *his* restaurant, and I can refuse service to anyone I so desire, and my desire is to show David to the door.

I inhale and steel myself for what I'm about to say. "I'm sorry your steak wasn't cooked to your liking. That being said, I wouldn't want you to eat anywhere that doesn't meet your standards, so please let me show you to the door."

The smugness leaves his face and is replaced by astonishment, but rather than making a scene, David replies, "No need. I know exactly where the door is, Lynds. You don't need to show me the way around my *own* restaurant."

"Don't you mean *former* restaurant?" I reply.

His jaw twitches. "You bet I do. I wouldn't want my name associated with this disaster," he says as he pushes in his chair. "And really, I'm surprised that you do."

I don't respond, just stare at him with a look that tells him not to say another word.

But he does not heed the warning.

With a snicker, he says, "If your cooks need a lesson on how to prepare a steak properly, just let me know. I'll give you a discount on my consulting fee."

"That won't be necessary," I reply, keeping my tone civil in front of the other two tables seated in this room, who I know are hanging on every word. Lucky guests. Dinner and a show this evening.

Before I can stop myself, I take a step closer to him and whisper in his ear, "Don't ever come back here again, David. This restaurant is no longer yours, and you are no longer welcome." Stepping away, I flash a smile that would win me an Academy Award and tell him, "Have a great evening."

He flashes me that *Crown of the Kitchen* fake and forced grin that endeared him to so many and heads to the front door.

I signal to Maria. "Bring me his check and reset the table," I say, which she does without question.

At the bar, I pour myself a generous glass of wine and take a long, steadying sip. My heart's still racing, but it feels...good. Strong. Triumphant. Like I've reclaimed a piece of myself.

By the time I head back to the kitchen, I find that calm is slowly being restored. It's not exactly a spa back there, but it's also not the raging five-year-old's birthday party we walked into. Marcus's tone is even-keeled, no yelling, just his commanding voice providing clear instructions to his staff. The captain righting his ship.

I walk back out, knowing he has it under control, and make my way to each table, apologizing for the backup, slipping back into my role of smiling restaurant ambassador. Thankfully, most of our guests are very gracious and understanding, just a few Persnickety Pams, who seem much happier when I volunteer to comp their checks. This night is going to cost me a pretty penny, but it will be worth it to save ourselves from some negative reviews.

Once law and order are reclaimed, I return to the kitchen, again, wanting to see how the back of the house is doing after an anarchistic hour. Marcus is commending his crew for rising to the challenge, telling them that things like this happen and that, as a team, they will work to do some more cross-training this week.

He takes full responsibility for what happened—which he doesn't need to do.

This is ALL on Blake.

Where the hell is he? Why didn't he show up?

BY THE TIME THE LAST GUEST LEAVES, WE'RE ALL running on fumes. Front of house, back of house, everyone. Equal parts wired and wiped out. We gather in the dining room for an end-of-shift drink and some food—because they didn't get a family meal since Blake never made it—and we talk through all that happened. The exhaustion settles around us like steam on concrete after a storm, but there's laughter as well—the kind that comes when you've survived something together.

I look around the room, and I'm more than thankful for this crew. Every single person offers ideas of what could've been done to make a bad situation better and how we can put some stopgaps in place that will prevent it from happening again. They're problem-solvers, not complainers. Rock stars, all of them. And, they've all agreed to come in on their day off so we can make service better than ever. I'll be dropping a little bonus into everyone's check this week to say thank you.

We say goodnight to Candace, who is the last of the staff

to leave, and Marcus pours us each two fingers of scotch. I still haven't told him about David's unexpected visit, and I don't think I will, at least not tonight.

I tell myself it's because the problem is over. I handled it. David came, he stirred the pot, and, instead of me hitting him over the head with said pot, which I wanted to do, I showed him the door. There's nothing to be gained by rehashing it. But the truth is less tidy. I'm not telling Marcus because I don't want to hand David any more space in my head—or in our evening. The last thing I want is for Marcus to see that smug smile in his imagination and feel anger on my behalf. I'm done giving David power. Tonight belongs to us and this little team that pulled off the impossible.

"Did you try to call Blake?" I ask, still wondering why he never showed up.

"I did, straight to voicemail. I also texted him a couple of times—no reply." He frowns. "I'm a little worried. He assured me yesterday that he would be here and could handle it. Do you think something happened to him?"

Leave it to Marcus to be worried while I'm sitting here ready to burn Blake's chef's coat and direct him to the unemployment line.

"I'm sure he's fine, but a heads-up would've been nice. I could've sent you back to the restaurant this afternoon when things slowed at the festival. We wouldn't have been in such a jam."

"Agreed." He takes a sip of his drink. "How were the guests by the end of the night?

"98 percent of them were happy—free booze will do that. And the 2 percent who weren't satisfied with a free cocktail were very happy when I comped their checks. I think we'll be fine and suffer minimal Yelp and Google Reviews damage."

"That's all we can hope for. You ready to go home?"

When he says this, I smile. I know he means my house, but I love how he calls it *home*.

"I sure am. Let's go. I'll drive. You look like you've been rode hard and put up wet."

"I look like *what*?"

"What? You never heard that phrase when you were down South?"

"Can't say that I have, but I'm going to assume it means I look worn out, which I am. Of course," he says, leaning in, eyes sparkling, "If you'd like to be rode hard and put up wet, I can probably rise to the challenge."

Laughing out loud, I wink at him, swat him on the ass, and say, "Let's go home, Chef."

Chapter Sixteen

DAVID MONTERO'S EX CAUGHT KISSING HER HEAD CHEF
NEW LOVE FOR LYNDSAY LEACH?
LOVE AGAIN IN THE KITCHEN FOR LYNDSAY LEACH?
FORMER AUTHOR LYNDSAY LEACH DATING LOCAL CHEF MARCUS BREMERTON

That is the first round of headlines I wake up to this morning, all accompanied by the same photo of Marcus and me locked in a very public kiss at the Wine & Dine Festival.

But these aren't the worst. Not by a long shot.

There's a whole other set of headlines that grabs my attention, hitting me like a gut punch.

DAVID MONTERO OPENING NEW RESTAURANT IN LAKE GEORGE
CELEBRITY CHEF DAVID MONTERO HAS BOUGHT MAPLE & ASH
CELEBRITY CHEF OPENING MONTERO'S MEADOW IN FORMER MAPLE & ASH
ANOTHER FARM-TO-TABLE RESTAURANT

COMING TO LAKE GEORGE WITH MONTERO'S MEADOW

My jaw clenches, and I can feel the heat rising off my skin.

That son of a bitch!

He's the new owner of Maple & Ash.

He's opening a new farm-to-table restaurant.

So close to mine.

Un-freaking-believable.

Marcus is still sleeping, but he must be able to feel the tension radiating from my side of the bed. He rolls toward me, gravelly voice still full of sleep, and asks, "What's up, Lynds?"

He looks so delectable. No shirt, mussed up hair, a couple of days' worth of growth shadowing his jawline, the perfect mix of black and gray.

Focus, Lyndsay.

"Well, where to start? Our kissing photo has made *The Pulse* and several other sites. I hope that photographer made some good money from that pic. I will say, we do look good—so I'll give him that."

Lead with the positive, right?

Marcus lets out a sleepy laugh, rubbing his eyes. "That so?"

"But that's not all the media is reporting this morning," I continue, the change in my tone as noticeable as a drop in air pressure when a storm is coming. "They have announced the new owner of Maple & Ash. Do you want to know who it is?"

"From the look on your face and your tone of voice, I have a sinking suspicion I already know."

"It's David," I say, each word clipped. "That asshole is opening a new farm-to-table restaurant at Maple & Ash that he is calling Montero's Meadow. Are you fucking kidding me? Same concept, just a few doors down from 518. And what kind of name is Montero's Meadow? Is he serving grass and wildflowers? That pretentious idiot just wanted to get his name out there again."

My anger is boiling over like an unwatched pot of water. This is his way of getting back at me for taking David's. This isn't business. It's personal. He's lain in wait like a lion stalking its prey, and just when I thought everything was going so well, he attacks.

I took his baby, and now he wants to show me who's boss.

I get out of bed and start pacing. Muttering, more for my benefit than Marcus's, I say, "He's got some balls. But he's not going to win. We've established 518 as a fantastic restaurant in the last couple of months. He may have his celebrity name to cash in on, but we've already created fans."

Marcus reaches for my hand, his thumb tracing steady circles against my skin. "You are 100 percent right, Lynds. We've got this. But this is probably why Blake no-showed last night. I'm sure David has wooed him back to working for him."

"Damn it! You're probably right." The puzzle pieces are all clicking into place. "I'm sure the release of this information was all perfectly timed, and Blake just took the opportunity to throw a wrench in last night's service, knowing you weren't going to be there. Which is why David showed up last night to watch the carnage. Blake and David, Lake George's own Beavis and Butthead."

Snickering at my *Beavis and Butthead* reference, which is spot on, Marcus says, "Why didn't you tell me David was at the restaurant last night?"

Whoops. I forgot that I didn't tell him.

"I meant to," I say, wincing. "Then things ran long, we were dead tired, and honestly…I didn't want to give him more oxygen. I handled it. I showed him to the door and told him to never come back."

His expression is unreadable, and I wait for him to say something, only to hear, "Okay then."

That's it. No lecture, no judgment. Just trust. I think he's impressed that I handled David without the need for backup from my boyfriend—as am I.

I didn't need rescuing.

I didn't need to defer or defuse.

I faced David head-on—and won.

"Since you seem to be ready to do battle, there are some things we need to talk about," Marcus says, sitting up and running his hand through his hair. "Mainly our vendor relationships. I don't think any of them would sell to David based on past experience, but I want to reach out to them this morning. I don't think we can push any of them to sign exclusive contracts with us, but maybe they can reassure us that they won't sell to David." Sliding out of bed, he continues. "I'll hop in the shower, and then we can get a plan together."

"Oh, I hadn't even thought about that. Yeah...you go jump in the shower, and I'll go start some coffee."

I'm still enraged, but it's starting to ebb thanks to Marcus's calm demeanor. I don't know how he can do it. No matter what comes his way, he's as steady as a rock. His calm is a balm to my seething.

Take a breath, Lyndsay.

I need some coffee.

As I reach for the coffee and my French press, I get a text from my publicist. For over twenty years, Jill's had it pretty easy. Just making sure the captions that accompanied photos of David and me were correct. But she has earned every damn cent these last several months. She wants to know if I want to respond to any of the David news, advising me that it would be best if I just wish him good luck on his new venture. I text back that as long as that is secret code for "Eat shit and die,"

I'm good with it. The three bubbling dots are quickly replaced by the laughing-crying emoji and that she'll get something out within the hour to the media. She also sends me back a happy face, kissing emoji, and eggplant emoji with *Need more details on that new chef of yours.*

I send back the shushing face emoji and set my phone down, needing an immediate infusion of caffeine.

When the coffee is ready, I pour myself an oversized cup. After the addition of caramel creamer, it looks like Caribbean sand, and the first sip begins to restore my peace like a trip to the beach. I exhale and sit down, only to be interrupted by the sound of a key in the lock of my front door, and the sound of "Darling, are you home? Did you see the news?"

My mother.

Of course, I'm home. It's seven a.m. on a Sunday.

And I am no longer leaving that key stashed under the goose.

"In the kitchen, Mom."

I pour her a cup of coffee without even being asked, adding a splash of creamer. She likes her coffee to be more of a deep brown, the color of mahogany.

She bustles into the kitchen like a child looking to tattle-tale on a sibling. "I'm sure you saw the articles about David? Did you know this? Did you know he bought Maple & Ash? And what is going on with you and Marcus? I saw the picture of you two kissing at the Wine & Dine Festival."

Marcus. Shit. She doesn't know he's here because we drove my Jeep home and left his truck at the restaurant. Maybe I can get her out the door before he's out of the shower.

Yeah, that's not going to happen, who am I kidding?

"Good morning, Mom. Thanks for letting yourself in without knocking."

"Lyndsay, this is practically an emergency," she says, placing her hand on her chest dramatically, her voice already pitched in an urgent, overly concerned way. "I *had* to let myself in."

Her definition of an emergency and mine are vastly different, and this difference just solidifies the fact that the spare key needs a new hiding place.

"It's not an emergency, Mom. No one is dying. No one is sick. David has bought Maple & Ash. I will deal with it." Wow! I sound so calm. So different from twenty minutes ago. Marcus must be rubbing off on me.

"Fine, fine. You'll deal with David. But what is this whole kissing photo of you and Marcus? Are you two dating?"

As she says the words, Marcus walks out of the bedroom wrapped in only a towel and says, "Lynds, Meredith just called. She says David..."

He stops mid-sentence when he sees my mom.

"Oh, hello, Mrs. Leach. I didn't know you were here. I'll be back in a minute," he says, hightailing it back to the bedroom to get dressed.

My mom turns to me, eyebrow raised, a look of disapproval on her face.

"So, he's sleeping over, is he?"

Her mother-judgy tone can probably be heard across the lake. "Yes, Mom. We're adults. He's sleeping over, as you put it."

"Since when has he been sleeping over?"

"Since my divorce was finalized."

Shit! I forgot to tell her about that, too! But I'm sure she saw it in the news.

"Yes, I did *read* about that in *The Pulse*." Once again, her voice says it all, confirming I'm at the top of the least-favorite child list. Thank God I'm an only child, so I can be on that list and the favorite-child list at the same time. "A phone call from you to tell me would've been nice."

In the nick of time, Marcus enters the kitchen, in his standard attire—faded jeans and a brushed cotton T-shirt. This tee is ice blue and does wonders for his eyes.

"Can I make you ladies some breakfast?" he says, winking at me as if he knows he's saving me from saying something I shouldn't say to my mother.

"That would be great. Mom, would you like to stay for breakfast?"

"No, no. I can't stay. I'm meeting Leanne for coffee at Spot. I've got to run. You two enjoy." And just like that, she's gone, leaving behind only the spare key and a bit of motherly reproach.

"Sorry to walk out with just a towel, I didn't know your mom was coming by this morning."

I roll my eyes like I'm sixteen. "That makes two of us."

I pick up the spare key she used to let herself in and drop it into the junk drawer. No more spare key outside.

"Breakfast?"

"Yes, please."

Marcus begins making bacon and cheese omelets with the groceries I had delivered, and I drop some sourdough in the toaster.

"So, as I was saying before I walked out half naked in front of your mom, I spoke to Meredith. She said that David reached out to her yesterday about supplying all the cheese for his restaurant. Meredith declined."

Thank God for small favors.

Marcus continues, "He even tried to say he would tell other restaurants how she 'does business,' and Meredith told him to take a flying leap. While she said she couldn't go exclusive with us, she will *never* sell to him. She also said she has a new goat cheese that she would like to offer us exclusively... which is really cool. God, I love working with her. She's salt of the earth for sure. And Tina will never sell to him. He turned her down multiple times in the past."

"That's fantastic. If we could at least get all our vendors not to work with David, that would help."

"I don't think we have to worry. I'll reach out to everyone this morning and see if they've been contacted. But due to his past actions, I don't think anyone we work with will do business with him."

That's so satisfying to hear. I thought all the spitefulness had left me when I took David's from him, but it's come back—roaring like the engine of a Ford Mustang GT—now that he is opening up a restaurant with the same concept.

We sit down to enjoy the meal Marcus has fixed, and I continue, "Okay, so what else do you think we need to do to protect the restaurant?"

"Well, I think we need to create a few more specials—just to add a little oomph to what we're already offering. And I need to go make sure Blake is the only hit we've taken in the kitchen."

That last sentence comes out with more worry than I was hoping to hear.

"Everybody else was there last night? You don't think he's poached other members of the kitchen crew, do you?"

"It wouldn't surprise me. I'm sure he's looking to take a cheap shot at you, and in Lake George, stealing staff is the ideal way to do it. If he leaves us shorthanded, that is just about the biggest loss we could suffer. Trying to hire going into peak season is tough."

I dread having to hire more staff and hope that Blake is the only one who's left for Montero's Meadow. I now say Montero's Meadow with the same tone I say *Mindi*. The bitterness is profuse and pervasive, but I won't let it ruin my breakfast.

While I wish I could crawl into a cave and stay there, I need to know if the restaurant has taken any more hits. "Let's finish up here and head to the restaurant and see what the damage is. Hopefully, it's minimal and only Blake."

WHEN WE ARRIVE AT THE RESTAURANT, EVERYONE— well, *almost* everyone—is in the kitchen, prepping for tonight's service. The clang of pans, the whoosh of the vent hood, the controlled cadence of knives—it's business as usual, except for two empty stations that stand out like missing teeth.

Blake and Anthony.

Anthony's apron is neatly folded on his workstation. Marcus doesn't say a word, but I can feel his disappointment.

Candace is elbow-deep in biscuit dough for the blueberry shortcake, but stops kneading long enough to say, "He came by early this morning. Said he really couldn't pass it up. David offered him double what he's making here. For someone with his background, that kind of money talks. It will help his family out a lot."

I nod, throat tight. I get it, but I wish he had given us a chance to counter David's offer, or just to have a conversation.

Marcus lets out an audible exhale. "Did David try to woo all of you away?" I can hear the dejection in his voice that Anthony has left. Marcus treated him like a son, teaching him as much as possible in the last few months, and Anthony showed a real aptitude for the kitchen without any formal culinary experience, besides what he brought from his stint in prison.

All of them nod.

Candace steps forward, wiping her hands on her apron, speaking for the group. "A text message went out in the group chat to meet at The Barrel. Most of us were too tired to go after the disastrous dinner service last night, but Anthony went. Blake was there, too. He told Anthony about a 'new opportunity' and threw out an hourly rate that was too good to turn down. Sounds like anyone who showed up at The Barrel received similar offers."

Marcus's lips press into a hard line. "Well," he says, finally, "Now we know what the new business opportunity was. And I can't thank you all enough for not jumping ship. Lyndsay and I talked about the possibility that David would try to poach you guys, and as a thank-you for not going, there will be a bonus in your check this week." Something we talked about on the way in this morning. "And a considerable bonus mid-September, once we get through the summer rush."

Candace, once again acting as the leader for the kitchen staff, says, "Thank you. Really. We appreciate it, and we want you to know we're in it for the long haul. We believe in you, Marcus, and you, Lyndsay, and we love 518. We're not going anywhere."

I let out a huge sigh, feeling an immediate relief, gratitude welling in my chest, that we have kept the majority of our kitchen staff. They could have fled to the land of celebrity chefdom, but they didn't. They *chose* to stay here. Obviously, we need to replace Blake and Anthony, but everyone in the kitchen has agreed to reach out to their contacts and see who might be looking for a job.

Candace turns back to her station, then pauses. "Lyndsay, you should know that it looks like he took a couple of the waitstaff, too. Mandy and Justin dropped off their aprons this morning; they're in the dining room. I tried to talk to them, but they were acting kind of cagey. I'm pretty sure they're going to work for David, too."

Damn. But I guess it could be worse.

With a forced smile, I say, "Thanks for the heads up, Candace—and for trying to talk to them."

"No problem." She nods and goes back to work on her biscuits.

The kitchen smells like butter and betrayal. But not because of these folks. They're sticking around, and I'm grateful.

Marcus and I make our way to the dining room, the quiet a stark contrast to the noise of the line, to discuss what we have learned.

"So...it was a coordinated attack," I say, pacing. "With David using Blake as his henchman. They both knew exactly what they were doing. Blake learned everything he could about this restaurant while he was here—our menu, our operations, our customers—and then took it all back to David. I feel like an idiot. I should've just thrown his application away when it came in back in February. I never should have trusted him." Was this David's plan the entire time? Has Blake been working as a double agent since the get-go? Once again, how could I have been so stupid?

"Lynds, you can't live your life not trusting everyone you meet." His tone is firm, but gentle. "I was the one who hired him. We took a gamble, and we lost. We need to move on. I'm going to do some massive cross-training of the kitchen crew this week and get a couple more people hired. It's going to be okay. We are going to pick ourselves up and do what needs to be done. Go place some ads for kitchen help and servers. Take a look at the waitstaff schedule and adjust as needed. Make sure we've got enough people scheduled to cover reservations, and if we have to, we can close to walk-in guests. Also, see if anyone is willing to pick up extra shifts. I'm going to reach out to our vendors and make sure we're all good there. You okay, Lynds?"

I nod. I want to believe him, but I feel defeated. It's like finding out David cheated on me all over again, but this time with the staff I had entrusted the restaurant to. We ate dinner together almost every day. I knew about their kids, broken dishwashers, and vacations to Orlando. They weren't just employees. They were family.

And losing family never gets easier.

But as Marcus's warm and calloused hand finds mine again, I remind myself—neither does rebuilding.

And that's exactly what we're going to do.

Chapter Seventeen

After yesterday, I need a break. Time away from the restaurant. Time to question my life choices—like why the hell did I ever think running a restaurant was a good idea? I'm a writer, and right now I'm not even that.

Which is another reason I'm taking a day off from 518. I need to figure out what this next book is about before my publisher loses complete faith in me. In the past, my books have all centered on my protagonist, Fiona, a thirtysomething art expert who helps museums recover missing or stolen artworks. Each book takes place in a different, well-known locale and has her working to find a well-known painting or sculpture or piece of jewelry. Of course, Fiona always has a romantic dalliance—sometimes with the bad-boy thief, sometimes with the oh-so-handsome police detective, sometimes with the studious but sexy museum curator. Yes, it's very much like *The Thomas Crown Affair*, but with a lot more spice and smartassery and a happily-for-now ending.

But I'm bored with it.

While my readers still devour it, it's so formulaic. Pick a

famous city, pick a famous piece of art, decide who Fiona hasn't slept with in a while, rinse and repeat. I'm tired of it.

I pour myself a cup of coffee and head out onto the porch, inhaling the bittersweet aroma. The lake is still this morning, the kind of still that makes you think it's holding its breath. I sit down, hoping the morning air and quiet will spark something. It hasn't these last few months. But maybe today will be different.

As I sit in my Adirondack chair and listen to the robins chattering, I contemplate just sticking to what I know. Fiona can go to Budapest (she hasn't been there yet), the thief can steal "The Esterházy Madonna" by Raphael, and it's time for her to sleep with the detective. Maybe I could spice it up, and she could sleep with the detective AND the thief.

This is the best you've got, Lyndsay? She sleeps with two men?

Ah, desperation is setting in.

I take a sip of my coffee and try not to think about how stale my ideas have become. That's when my phone rings.

The lyrics to "Take On Me" break the silence. Susan is calling. Your agent calling can be either good or bad, and this early in the morning I'm thinking it's the latter.

"Hi, Susan! What's up?" I say, trying to sound like I'm busy writing. Can that actually be conveyed in the tone of someone's voice? Yeah, it can't. And definitely not convincingly.

"Hi Lynds..." Her voice is low and serious, not her normal gung-ho and gangbusters timbre. "I spoke with the publisher, and, well, they're going to need something from you and soon."

"Okay...define something and how soon?" I ask, not really wanting the answer, hoping that Susan will somehow get cut off and we'll get disconnected.

"They want to know where Fiona is off to, what art is

stolen, and who she's sleeping with—and they want that by the end of the week. They want first chapters in three weeks."

Of course they do. Same old Fiona. Same old formula. Same old me.

"Umm...yeah, I can do that." But my voice lacks enthusiasm, and Susan doesn't miss a beat.

"You don't sound so sure," Susan says.

I have my opening, and I need to take it.

"Susan," I say, my voice quieter now, "I'm not sure. I don't know if I want to write about Fiona and her escapades anymore."

I have just dropped a huge bomb on my agent, and rather than there being an explosion, I'm met with silence on the other end of the line.

Her quiet is unbearable, so I fill it. "It's just...the last few months have changed me, and I don't want to write the same old stuff. It's...I don't know. So unoriginal. I mean, come on, even my publisher only asked for three pieces of information."

Finally, Susan exhales. "Lynds, if you don't want to write about Fiona, that's fine. She's had a good run. But I need something. They are expecting a book, and I'm not dumb. I know you haven't written anything in months. And contracts and deadlines are real things, and while I don't think they'd claw back any advances, and I know they want to keep you as one of their writers after all the money you've made them, you need to decide what you're doing. It's time to put on your big-girl panties and get back to work."

And she's back...with the tough love I've come to expect.

"Yup, I hear you," I say, forcing some steadiness into my voice. "I'll have something by the end of the week. I promise."

But when the call ends, the silence returns. Thicker this time. I stare out over the lake and wonder if this is a promise I can keep.

I sure hope so.

~

I SPEND THE DAY PING-PONGING FROM THE Adirondack chair to the outdoor dining table, with my laptop in hand, but no words on the page. I even tried the daybed for a while, where I became lost in thoughts involving Marcus and very few clothes. That was my cue to relocate. There's no time for steamy sentiments. He's working, and I need to do the same.

By six p.m., I'm no closer to having a book idea than I was in the morning, and I'm grateful Chloe is coming over for gourmet grilled cheese and wine. Yes, I did manage to bake some bread today. It was a needed distraction.

Maybe I could write a book where Fiona gives up her adventurous life to open a bakery?

Who the hell would read that?

Chloe arrives just after six. I've already poured us two glasses of wine, and we head out to the porch, the evening air soft and golden around us.

"So," she says, tucking her legs beneath her, "I see that Dipshit is opening a new restaurant just like yours. Is he so out of fresh ideas that he has to copy you? For fuck's sake, he's an asshole."

"That he is. And he had Blake recruit some of the staff." I take a long sip of wine. "I know I shouldn't be surprised. I know I should've expected something like this when I took his pride and joy away from him, but I was hoping he was soooo happy with *Mindi* that he would just slink away and leave me alone." I slide down in my chair, letting my feelings of defeat come to the surface.

Chloe rolls her eyes. "This does not take away from your

success. If David is living by the mantra that imitation is the sincerest form of flattery, then congratulations. You've just become his idol."

"Yeah, which is crazy because I'm not a chef. I'm not a restaurateur, in fact, most days, I'm not even sure what I'm doing." No truer words have I ever said. *What the hell am I doing?*

"But you're making it work—and work well. Don't doubt yourself, Lynds."

I smile faintly. "Now you sound like Marcus."

There's a twinkle back in Chloe's eye as she asks, "And how is that fine-looking chef of yours? I feel like you've got your own *Bear*."

I can't help but giggle as I've thought this very thing myself. Who hasn't binge-watched *The Bear* and wanted their own handsome chef?

"He's wonderful...so calm and grounded. A true master in the kitchen."

"And in the bedroom?" Chloe asks, giving me a look that demands an answer.

"I have no complaints."

"I'm happy for you, my friend. You deserve nothing but good things."

"Could you tell my publisher that?" I laugh, but it comes out more weary than cheery. I feel like I've been nothing but a Debbie Downer this evening, but if you can't talk with your bestie about things, who can you?

"Why? What's up there?"

I lay it all out for Chloe. The lack of writing, the lack of ideas, and how I don't think I want to write about Fiona any longer.

"Then I think it's time to say goodbye to Fiona and write something new," says Chloe, like the supportive friend I've come to rely on.

"I agree, but I have no idea what." There is frustration in my voice, even though I don't want it to be there. I love writing, I do. But currently, I don't like it.

"Okay...hear me out on this," Chloe replies, a glint in her eye. "But I think you should do a memoir."

I must have a puzzled look on my face because she continues, "You've been through a lot in the last six months, and I think your readers would love to learn more about you, what you've been going through, how you handled it, how you've built something new. And yes, you can be a little spiteful and mean about David at the same time."

This time I do let out a genuine laugh. "So, a *revenge* memoir?"

"A *healing* memoir." Chloe grins. "With a satisfying side of revenge."

I swirl the remaining few sips of my wine, thinking it over. I have to admit that the idea is intriguing. I love reading memoirs, but writing one of my own?

"Seriously? You think people would read it?" There's more than a sprinkle of doubt in my voice.

"YES! Your *original* readers love and miss you, and you've been in the news because of the breakup of your marriage, your new restaurant, your new love...you have a lot to share. Readers are going to find you so relatable."

"I don't know," I say, even as the wheels in my brain are starting to turn. "Writing about myself isn't in my comfort zone. I write fiction, where I can hide behind my characters, and this seems a bit...scary." And while I say those words, I also think about how delicious it would be to give David a taste of his own medicine, talk about taking his favorite restaurant, my new love, how well I'm doing post-divorce.

"It is scary, and it should be. But you are in a season of change, and why not change up what you write—at least for the moment."

I take in a deep breath and contemplate the idea for a split second longer before I hold up my glass in a mock toast and say, "You're right. I'm calling Susan and telling her that I want to write a memoir. What's the worst that can happen?"

A memoir.

I'm going to write a memoir.

Chapter Eighteen

CELEBRITY CHEF DAVID MONTERO'S NEW RESTAURANT OPENING THIS WEEKEND

After almost a month of speculation as to who the new owner of Maple & Ash would be, this Friday night marks the return of celebrity chef David Montero to the Lake George region. Montero bought Maple & Ash and is opening Montero's Meadow, a new farm-to-table dining experience, in Bolton Landing.

We had the pleasure of sitting down with Chef Montero at his new restaurant to ask him a few questions before the grand opening.

Reporter: What made you want to return to the Lake George region?

Chef Montero: I love this area of New York—it's such a special place. I've missed having a culinary connection to the community and couldn't imagine not being here this summer.

Reporter: Will this be a re-creation of David's? Everyone loved David's and the food.

Chef Montero: Oh, no. Definitely not a re-creation of David's. David's was unique and special, but sometimes, you need to evolve. Montero's Meadow is focused on farm-to-table and showcasing local products.

Reporter: You must be aware that your former wife has taken David's and renamed it 518 Farm-to-Table. Is your new restaurant a way of competing with her?

Chef Montero: Definitely not. I don't see that restaurant as competition. Lyndsay is a smart woman, but she is a writer—not a chef or restaurateur. I think our guests will notice a *distinct* difference in the menu, in the quality of food, in the presentation. Montero's Meadow will be the crème de la crème in farm-to-table dining.

Reporter: That's very exciting. Would you care to give us a sneak peek at your menu?

Chef Montero: While I'd love to, it is a surprise. Guests will have to come dine with us and see what's in store.

Reporter: Thank you for your time, Chef Montero. I'm sure our readers will be clamoring for reservations.

Montero's Meadow opens this Friday, and reservations can be made by going to their website or using OpenTable.

I roll over and slam my phone on the nightstand so hard that my hand cream, which had been resting there on the corner, falls to the floor.

Doesn't see me as competition? What a sanctimonious asshole! I am most definitely his fucking competition!

Leave it to the local reporter to fawn all over him. And that photo of him! Smiling like he just conquered the world, in his chef's whites, his smug grin, so confident. It's infuriating. Why doesn't anyone see through his facade?

I stare up at the ceiling, still enraged. 518 Farm-to-Table is good, better than good. It's fabulous.

And David is not going to win.

I swing my legs and plant my feet firmly on the ground. Determination pulses through me. It's time to head to MY restaurant and make sure everything is in order.

But first coffee and a call to Susan.

I need to pitch this memoir.

Then the Restaurant Wars can begin.

"YOU'RE GOING TO WRITE A MEMOIR?" SUSAN'S TONE is neutral, and, unlike most of our interactions, where she can be easily read, her voice today gives nothing away.

"Yes," I say emphatically, hoping to remove any niggling doubts that may have been present in my initial statement of this new development. "Really, it's going to be a snippet into my life—the last six months of my life, to be exact—starting with finding out David was cheating."

I'm starting to feel excited about this project. I think it's got great potential. I think women in their forties, fifties, and sixties who undergo a life-changing event are often underestimated. But these women are resilient, inventive, thriving, and nobody should minimize or undervalue them.

What I really mean is that I don't want anyone to misjudge or misperceive me.

Susan's silence is killing me. I can't take it any longer, and ask, "So...what do you think? Do you think they'll go for it?"

Once again, there's a pause, and the line is quiet before Susan says, "YES! I love this, and I think they will totally go for it. This is soooo good. Lyndsay Leach writes a memoir."

Phew! Thank God. This was the reaction I was hoping for, and I'm glad that Susan is fully on board because she's now got to get my publisher on board.

Susan continues, "Lyndsay, I can tell you the first question that the publisher is going to have, and that's 'How soon until it's done?'"

She's right. Nobody wants to read a memoir about the breakup of my marriage ten years from now, not even three years from now. They will want to read it as soon as possible.

"If they're willing to buy into this memoir, I can have some preliminary chapters to them in a few weeks. I really think if I buckle down, I can have a first draft in eight to twelve weeks."

I know that will be a push, but I've done some Fiona first drafts in shorter timeframes than that.

"Okay...that will make them *very* happy. I think they would be willing to crash this book to get it in the hands of readers. Let me call some folks and see what they think, but if I were you, I'd start writing."

I MARCH INTO 518-FARM-TO-TABLE WITH MY HEAD held high, shoulders back, as if I own the place—which I freaking do! The kitchen hums with motion and noise. Cooks moving from station to station, offering words of encouragement to one another. The team is in the middle of cross-training, and I make a point to greet each one of them as I pass. "Looking great, everyone. Appreciate all of your hard work," I say, flashing the kind of smile that's equal parts support and pride, the kind that comes from knowing where we started and where we are now.

Then I grab Marcus by the elbow. "Dining room. Now."

He leaves a few parting instructions to the crew, wipes his hands on his apron, and follows me out.

"What's up, Lynds?" he asks, although I know full well he read the article about David this morning.

"Oh, you know," my tone a little sharper than intended.

"Just your average morning—coffee, emails, and finding out your ex-husband is opening his new restaurant this week." I'm back to fuming, even though I thought I had calmed down on the drive over here. "Apparently, he doesn't seem to think we're any sort of competition for his new endeavor."

Marcus has a look on his face that's a cross between a grimace and a smirk, but he knows from my tone where I'm going with this.

"I don't want him to think we're not his competition. In fact, I want him to think of us as his number one rival, a rival that is going to kick his ass," I continue.

That earns me a full-on grin.

"That's what I wanted to hear, Lynds," Marcus says, nodding. "I wanted to know that you were fully in on trouncing him and his new restaurant—because we can do it. I know we can. We have a great menu, great staff, and to be honest, I think he's rushing this whole thing. It's pure ego. And that will backfire on him."

Yes, I agree that David seems to be rushing things. This is not his normal modus operandi, to rush an opening. He's methodical. Calculated, usually to the point of obsession. But he must be pretty pissed at the success we're having. I'm not unhappy that I got to him. I'm rather enjoying it.

"Okay, I'm glad to hear we're on the same page," I say, feeling that competitive spark ignite inside me. "That being said, I don't want us resting on our laurels. I thought we would have some more time, but we need to implement some of those things we talked about, maybe have some nights where we offer a four-course prix fixe meal with wine or beer pairings, and whatever other ideas you may have that will push us to the top of the farm-to-table scene."

Marcus's smile widens. "Like it, like it. We can do that. And with the summer season upon us, tourists and locals alike will love this. I think we focus on doing a prix fixe menu on

Monday nights in June and July—since that's usually the slower night around the area, and I'll talk with the kitchen crew to come up with some specials for the rest of the week. What do you think?"

"I think," I say, letting out a deep breath, "that we're going to make David regret underestimating us."

Marcus turns to head back to the kitchen, but I grab him by the elbow, knowing I'm not done. "Now, I do have some other news to share with you, and I need to ask for some help, which I'm not good at—as we both know—but I need to get back to writing. This morning, I called Susan and pitched a brand-new book to her, which is a *huge* departure from all the books I've done previously, but I know I can do it."

"Lynds, you can do whatever you put your mind to," Marcus says, boosting my confidence with his words and his endearing smile.

"Thank you," I say, returning his smile, "but I want you to know that I'm writing a memoir, essentially about the last six months of my life, which means it's going to talk about David, his cheating, the restaurant, and...you."

I watch as the smile fades from his face, but is soon replaced with a thoughtful look as he says, "That sounds like a book I'll want to read."

"You don't have any concerns? Questions? I promise, what I say about you will be all positive—from the restaurant to our relationship. Nothing but good things." And I mean those words. Marcus has been a true North Star these last few months. I can't imagine where I, or this restaurant, would be without him.

"I trust you to tell the story honestly," he says gently.

"I promise I will. But this also means I need to dedicate some time each day to writing. I'm a morning person and do my best writing then, so I plan to work from home until about two thirty each day, and then I'll come here."

He nods, practical as always. "You do what you need to do. Writing is your passion, always has been, and I don't want me or the restaurant to be a distraction from that passion. We can handle things here. We just need to let the team know that you won't be around as much."

"Okay," I say, feeling my shoulders relax for the first time today. "Tonight, at family meal, I will share what we've discussed with everyone."

Marcus squeezes my shoulder, gives me a kiss, and heads back into the kitchen.

I feel relieved, beyond relieved, that he took all of this so well. Now I just need to make sure the team is on board.

CANDACE PREPARED FAMILY MEAL TONIGHT— chicken alfredo with broccoli, a fresh salad, sourdough bread, and raspberry brownies for dessert, and the entire 518 crew is loving it. Plates are filled with heaping portions, and forks are eagerly digging in. But the part that makes me so happy as I look at them all is the conversations that are occurring. Kitchen crew, bussers, waitstaff, dishwashers, hostesses, and bartenders are all talking with one another, engaged in lively chats about their families, college courses they'll be taking in the fall, and upcoming birthday plans. In the few short months, they truly have become a family.

They've become *my* family.

I clang my water glass with a knife, like I'm about to make a toast, and chitchat falls away to a curious hush.

"Sorry to interrupt all of the good conversations you were having, but I wanted to say a few words before we start service this evening."

All eyes swing to me, and I can see that some of them appear to be a bit nervous, no doubt rattled from the news of

David's new restaurant and the handful of staff he poached. I hope what I share will settle any unrest they may feel.

"I want to start by saying that all of you are valued and important to me and this restaurant. Without each and every one of you, 518 Farm-to-Table would not be the success that it is." A few smiles start to appear. I press on. "Now, I'm sure you've seen that we've got a little competition coming our way." There are a few groans and grumbles coming from around the table at the mention of this. "But I just want to say one thing...We are going to kick this new restaurant's ass."

At this, the entire room erupts, hooting and hollering in complete agreement. I hear a few "Oh, yes, we are!" and "No doubt!" coming from my staff—and one "Fuck yeah!" coming from Todd. I am filled with a fierce and grateful love for these people.

"Marcus and I spoke today, and we're going to make some additions to the menu for July and August with a special four-course prix fixe menu on Monday evenings, which will include a special wine or beer pairing. Additionally, we are going to add some seasonal specials to our menu that will rotate weekly, depending on what's available. All I ask is that you keep doing what you're doing—providing the best possible experience to our guests. We need to be killing every aspect of service. From the moment our guests walk through the door until they leave, we need to be acting as if we are a three-star Michelin restaurant."

Heads nod, and Marcus chimes in with "We've got this, Lyndsay," to which everyone replies, "Yes, we do!"

Because they're more than staff, they're family, I continue, my voice softening. "I also want to let you know that I am going back to writing. I have a new book that I'm working on, so I will not be coming to the restaurant until midafternoon. This means I need to shift a few responsibilities, and I will reach out to a few of you for help if you're up for it." I make eye contact with a few of my most trusted staff members, so they know I am speaking to them. There are a few subtle nods, and I know they will gladly take on some additional duties to help me.

"Finally, I want to say that once we get through August and the tourist season dies down, and this momentum holds, each of you will be receiving a bonus. That means we keep our guests happy and the online reviews at five stars—can we do it?" I say as I place my hand into the middle of the table, hoping they will all join in stacking hands—and they do.

Restaurant Wars have begun.

And my crew is going to kick David's ass.

Chapter Nineteen

The lake is calm this morning, so calm that you wouldn't know what an incredible tantrum Mother Nature threw the last two days with her lightning and thunder and rain and wind. She was so riled up that whitecaps graced the shoreline. Now the only residual evidence is the heavy air, still humid and thick, as if it could rain again at any moment. But the sun is peeking through the clouds with her golden streaks, and I can tell it's going to be a summer day that will soon have the tourists flocking onto the lake. I need to soak up the quiet while I can.

I have my coffee and my laptop, and I'm determined to start this memoir. Hopefully, Susan will call and tell me that she got the go-ahead. Even if she doesn't get it, I think I'm going to write it. I need to do it for me. For every woman who's ever been blindsided by the unraveling of her own life.

The words flow easily this morning, and before I know it, I have several chapters completed. They are not perfect chapters, but they are written from my heart, from deep within, and they are an honest reflection of the demise of my marriage. Unguarded. Raw. I will never look back on what David did and give him a pass, never. But I can see how I helped close the door that let someone else in.

I stretch, head back into the kitchen for another cup of coffee and a slice of sourdough with peanut butter, when my phone buzzes. It's Susan.

Got a few minutes to talk?

My stomach drops. Damn. Are they not going to go for it?

I call her. "Hey, Susan, what's up? What did they say?" I can hear the anxious edge in my voice, and I'm sure she can, too. I need them to okay this book. I can't write another Fiona story. I just can't.

"Well," she says, dragging it out longer than necessary, "I will tell you they were...caught off guard by the idea. Sam especially. He totally wants another Fiona book—for obvious reasons."

Of course, he does. Fiona brings in the cash. It's a business. I get it.

Susan continues, "But...he came around. You can write your memoir, and, as I suspected, they're going to crash this book to get it in the hands of readers as soon as possible. You better be typing like your life depends on it—because your literary life kind of does."

Relief and adrenaline fill my body. "I won't let you—or them—down. I actually started this morning. The words are coming. I hesitate to say it, but it feels easy. Maybe because it's my life, but for whatever reason, I feel inspired again."

"I'm happy to hear it. I'll touch base at the end of the week and see how things are going. Just know that you need to get this right. I went out on a limb for you today when I told them you didn't want to write about Fiona. They're expecting big things."

Before I can respond, Susan hangs up.

Nothing like a little added pressure, as if writing didn't have enough of it as is.

~

PULLING INTO THE PARKING LOT AT 518, I'M SMILING. It was a good day creatively, and I feel a high from writing that I haven't felt in...I don't know when. And now I get to see Marcus. Even though the restaurant was closed yesterday, our last full day off before we kick it into high gear for the summer, he didn't spend last night with me, insisting that I wake up and have all the uninterrupted time I needed to focus on my writing. While I appreciated it, the empty bed felt foreign. I missed the weight of his arm around my waist, the cadence of his breathing, which has become my needed white noise. Missed drifting off to sleep to some old '80s movie that lets us reminisce about our teen years. And God, I missed my morning wake-up kiss that makes me almost forget about coffee. Almost.

I climb out of the Jeep, still smiling, but the second I round the corner toward the back door, it hits me. A smell so foul it stops me in my tracks. It smells like rotting onions mixed with rancid tuna fish, all topped with curdled milk. It's horrible, and I find myself gagging as I dash past the dumpster and head for the inside of the restaurant.

The kitchen is not much better. Fans roar in every corner, attempting to push sour air out. Something's wrong.

Marcus is on the phone, pacing, his frustration evident by the cadence of his words.

"When can you get here?" he says, voice gruff. "We need this fixed as soon as possible. We're essentially shut down until it can be repaired."

My pulse spikes. What is he talking about? What needs repaired? Why are we shut down?

He hangs up, exhales, and meets my eyes. His look tells me it's bad.

"So," he says, running his hand over the stubble on his

chin, "The storms fried the compressor to the walk-in cooler. And because we were closed yesterday, we didn't know. We lost everything."

My eyes widen. The smell, the fans, the tension. It all clicks. The storms. The spoiled food. The oppressive heat.

"Oh, no," I breathe. "All of it?"

"All of it," he confirms. "The temps were too high to save anything. Between the lightning strike and the power surge, it's a total loss."

I sink against the counter, the weight of what he's telling me settling in.

"Are you sure it was the storm?" I ask. I don't want to say it aloud, but the thought is there. David. I didn't think he'd stoop so low as to open a competing restaurant down the road with the same damn concept, but he did. Would he enter the depths of hell and resort to sabotage?

Marcus shakes his head. "It was the storm—hit by lightning. We're lucky that it didn't start a fire, Lynds. You could've lost the restaurant."

The good news, it wasn't sabotage. The bad news, Mother Nature had to show off her power on my cooler.

"You're right. I'm glad there wasn't a fire. When can someone get here to fix it?" I ask.

"Tomorrow," Marcus replies. "That's the earliest I could find anyone."

Damn it! This is not how I pictured kicking off Restaurant Wars.

"Okay...and then we need to replace all of the food and stuff?" He knows I'm looking for some sort of time frame as to when we can reopen. I'm looking for him to calm my anxiousness.

"Yes, if it's fixed tomorrow. We can let it get back to temperature and restock it the next day. We could probably open that night, but I'd rather wait until the day after—that way, we can be sure we're all set."

Three days. We're going to be shut down for three days. At the height of the season. And with a list of reservations as long as my arm.

Resigned, I let out a sound, halfway between a sigh and a growl. "Alright, then, I guess I need to look at the reservations and see who I can rebook for later this week."

I head through the dining room and print out a list of the reservations for the next few nights. One by one, I begin making calls. Most of the people I speak with are lovely, understanding, and happily allow me to rebook them with the promise of a complimentary dessert. A few are cantankerous, letting me know of their displeasure in no uncertain terms, and while I'm irritated by their irritation, I also can't help but feel pride in the fact that they want to dine here so badly.

As I get to the last few reservations on the list, I gasp at one particular name.

Huck Monahan.

My breath catches. Could it be? It has to be. I don't know of any other Huck Monahan.

Just THE Huck Monahan of *The New York Tribune.*

Huck Monahan, the food critic.

He made a reservation for 518 Farm-to-Table.

And I'm about to cancel it.

This can't be happening.

I storm back into the kitchen, where the crew is disinfecting stainless steel, and the stench of decay is dissipating, finally. "Did you know that Huck Monahan has made a reservation?" I ask, trying to sound casual, and failing miserably.

Marcus's head snaps up.

"No, but let me guess...it's for one of the nights we're going to be shut down?"

"Yes."

He winces but recovers quickly. "Okay...don't worry. I cooked for him a few years back when I took over at The Sag. He's a tough critic, but he'll understand."

My eyes narrow. "You've cooked for him before? When were you going to tell me?" I ask.

He rubs the back of his neck, sheepish. "I didn't tell you because it wasn't my finest hour. We received two and a half stars. I was overly cocky, and the pressure of cooking for him definitely got to me. I served him overcooked shrimp and a steak that wasn't properly trimmed." I'm surprised to hear Marcus say he was cocky because it's not like him, but love that he just owns it.

He continues, "Plus, his waiter that night was so nervous that he brought him a Pinot Grigio when he ordered a Pinot Noir, then forgot to bring him a steak knife, and last, but not least, spilled a glass of cold water on his dining companion. Overall, a disaster."

Great, just great. Not the reassurance I was hoping for. Why couldn't he tell me that he and Huck were old friends? That they send each other holiday cards and share recipes via text?

"But why is he coming up here? Why is he not down in the Hamptons or in the City?" I'm pacing now. A Huck Monahan review could make a restaurant. Or it could break it.

"Every few years, he comes up to the area to review some of the newer dining hot spots. Lake George attracts a lot of tourists from the City. It makes sense that he'd include us. I'm sure that's why he's coming. And probably Montero's Meadow, too."

At the mention of David's restaurant, my stomach twists more than it did when passing the dumpster. Huck has reviewed all of David's restaurants in the past, giving him four-star reviews—which is pure gold from Huck—and one five-star review—which made that restaurant a pilgrimage for foodies and David its god.

If we don't get this right, Restaurant Wars could be over before we've even had a chance to battle. I need Huck Monahan's dining experience here to be stellar.

"Lynds, what are you thinking?" asks Marcus, studying me.

I meet his gaze, steady now. "I'm thinking that I need to call Huck Monahan and reschedule his reservation."

Because when Huck Monahan dines at 518 Farm-to-Table, he's going to have the best damn meal of his life with the best damn service to match.

And when his review hits *The New York Tribune*, David Montero won't know what hit him.

Chapter Twenty

Today's the day, or should I say, tonight's the night. Huck Monahan will be dining at 518 Farm-to-Table this evening. When I called him and explained that we would need to change his reservation due to the failure of our cooler, he was a complete and total gentleman. Told me it was no problem; he would swap nights with another restaurant where he would be dining. We concluded the conversation by confirming a reservation for two people, Saturday night, at seven p.m., at the table of my choice.

And as soon as I hung up with him, I let nerves and worry overtake me. To say I've been obsessing about Huck Monahan for the last few days would be the understatement of all understatements. Is the weather going to be nice enough that he and his dinner companion can be seated on the porch? He loves a good Pinot Noir—do I have several acceptable bottles he can choose from? (I do...I have more than enough wonderful bottles.) I've nagged Marcus about the fish that will be on the menu and making sure it will be fresh that morning. I've bugged Candace to make sure she has an entire selection of fresh desserts and that she is not to serve anything she made yesterday. The bartenders have made sure that all our local beer selections are available. I even created a special playlist for Saturday night with no Taylor Swift tunes because I read on a Reddit thread for restaurant owners that he doesn't like Taylor Swift. (This alone should make me question Huck's taste. Who doesn't like Taylor Swift? But I'm going to give him a pass on that one—for now.)

Of course, with all this obsessing, it's been hard to focus on my writing, yet I forced myself to buckle down each morning and push aside the thought of Huck Monahan.

But as soon as my writing is complete each day, I go back to doing my deep dive into Mr. Monahan and his reviews. Let me just say, if he doesn't like your food or the service or the ambiance, you are going to know about it in no uncertain terms. Some people have accused him of being cruel in his reviews. Perhaps. But the restaurant business is no place for the weak or the meek, and if you're at the level where Huck Monahan wants to dine at your establishment, then buckle up. In one review I read, he said the chef had the "palate of a baby swine and that the food he served was no better than leftovers scavenged from a dumpster behind a greasy spoon." His words are sharp and unforgiving, but I can't help but love the weight his expertise carries. For a restaurant, a positive review from him is the pinnacle of praise. Much like a glowing book review from the *New York Times* for an author. Badges of honor.

And we are going to get that badge, and I am going to wear it like a beauty pageant contestant wears her winning crown. Huck Monahan is going to LOVE us. Failure is not an option. If we fail, we lose to David, and I am not going to lose.

∾

I WALK INTO THE KITCHEN, AND IT'S BUSTLING WITH activity. Everyone is deep in prep work...except Marcus. He's nowhere to be found.

"Hey, Candace, is Marcus in the dining room?" I ask.

Busy putting a sprinkle of extra fine sugar on her biscuits before popping them into the oven, Candace replies, "No. He left about an hour ago. Said he'd be back soon."

He left? On the biggest day ever at 518 Farm-to-Table? On the day we're expecting Huck Monahan to walk through our doors. What is going on? Where the hell did he go?

Not wanting Candace to know that I'm out of the loop, slightly concerned, and more than curious, I say, "Okay... thanks. Do you guys need anything?"

"We're good, Lyndsay. Marcus gave us our assignments before he left. We've got it under control. We're ready for Mr. Monahan," she says, giving me a quick wink to let me know that I shouldn't worry.

If only her wink was all I needed to make the jitters go away.

I make my way to the bar, where my head bartender has come in early to make sure everything is stocked and set. I can see that he has the bar polished to a high-gloss shine and is checking wine glasses for water spots. These small details matter. Huck Monahan eviscerated a restaurant that served him wine in a glass with one minute water spot (yes, he took a picture—he takes LOTS of pictures). There will be no water spots this evening.

In the dining room, two of the waitstaff have come in and are checking each and every place setting—shining silverware, refolding napkins, making sure the water glasses are also free from spots. Seems that everyone got the memo.

Maria, my head waitress, asks, "Lyndsay, where are you thinking of seating Mr. Monahan tonight?"

I've thought long and hard about this. Do I seat him

inside where he can see our staff hard at work, along with some other diners, or do I seat him on the porch, overlooking the lake, with a smaller group of guests?

It's a perfect seventy-five degrees today, and the sun is out. There's a slight breeze, which will keep the bugs at bay, and the temperatures are not supposed to drop much this evening. It really makes my decision easy. Huck Monahan shall be seated on the porch.

"We're going with the porch tonight, Maria, and you will be waiting on Mr. Monahan and his companion." I can see excitement, tinged with fear, in her eyes, but she shouldn't worry. She's excellent at her job. She knows our menu inside and out. And she's going to crush service. Wanting her to know that I have complete faith in her, I squeeze her arm and add, "You've got this, Maria. Why don't we go take a look at what table we should give him?"

We head out onto the porch, and I can't help but pause to take in the view. Looking at the blue waters with the sun reflecting off them like a million shimmering diamonds, I am reminded why Lake George is called "The Queen of American Lakes." She is stunning. This view will certainly not hurt Mr. Monahan's dining experience.

Maria stands by a table for four located in the center of the porch, but away from where waitstaff enter and exit, and says, "Lyndsay, I think this is the spot. He'll still be around other guests this evening, but away from the commotion of the door, and the view is spectacular. Plus, a four-top will give him plenty of room for all the dishes he tries."

This is why she's waiting on Huck Monahan this evening. She thinks like I do. She's also the perfect combination of attentive, but not fawning, professional, yet warm. She knows how to anticipate a guest's needs without hovering, and she always remains calm, even when those around her are not. She's exactly the kind of server who can handle the pressure of catering to the discerning and often unforgiving palate of someone like Huck Monahan.

"Yes, you are 100 percent right. That's the perfect table. Please grab a reserved table tent and place it there. I will let the hostesses know that this is where he will be seated." Not that they will be bringing him to his table. I will be doing that personally.

Maria walks away to grab the tent and continue preparation for tonight's service, while I head back into the kitchen to see if Marcus has returned.

He has.

"Hey! Welcome back," I say, the emphasis I put on *back* indicates that I am wondering where he was on such an important day.

He looks up and gives me a nod, and continues checking the prep that each of his kitchen staff has completed in his absence. If I didn't know better, I would say he is mad at me, but I'm not the one who took off during prep when Huck Monahan is dining with us this evening.

I walk over to him and ask, "Is everything okay?" I'm trying to figure out if something has happened, and that's why he was gone, or if he's miffed at me for some unknown reason.

"Everything's fine, Lyndsay."

His voice is curt, and I know everything is not fine. But I don't have time to deal with this at the current moment, nor do I want to look like one of those needy and controlling women, constantly having to know every move of her partner.

Service starts in sixty minutes, and Huck Monahan will be here in three hours. Whatever is bugging Marcus will have to wait.

At six forty-five, I walk through the dining rooms, greeting our guests and checking in on all our staff. Everything is going well. Meals are coming out of the kitchen looking like they belong on the cover of *Bon Appétit,* and guests are laughing, and staff are smiling.

The kitchen is running like clockwork as well. The atmosphere is light, Marcus is joking with his crew, but when I walk in, his demeanor changes.

"Do you need something, Lynds?" he asks.

I suddenly feel very unwelcome in the kitchen of *my* restaurant.

"No, just wanted to make sure everyone was set here. Huck Monahan is due within the next fifteen minutes."

"Huck Monahan will receive the same excellent service that every other guest has received this evening," Marcus replies. Once again, his tone is brusque, just shy of being rude.

"I have no doubt," I reply, trying to put on a cheery front, even though I want to ask him what the hell his problem is this evening. But I don't. Instead, I make my way to the hostess area to wait for Huck Monahan.

At seven p.m., on the dot, in walks Huck Monahan. I recognize him from the Instagram stalking I've done in recent days. He's in his late thirties, about six three, and very thin, thinner than any man who is a professional food critic should be. He wears his blond hair in a man bun, and he's dressed in a crisp white button-down shirt with dark blue jeans, a Louis Vuitton belt, and brown Cole Haan loafers. It says professional, but also well-dressed summer tourist.

With him is another man, also in his late thirties, but with dark hair and a more relaxed vibe about him. He's in an aqua Ralph Lauren golf shirt, jeans that are much more faded than

Huck's, and boat shoes. They're both laughing and seem relaxed as they enter 518.

Brooke is currently at the hostess station and has picked up from my nervous energy that this is Huck Monahan and greets him in a warm manner, asking if he has a reservation, like she would any guest.

"Yes, I have a reservation for seven p.m., Huck Monahan."

"Of course," Brooke replies, "We have you sitting on the porch this evening, unless you'd like something inside?"

Huck looks at her and politely smiles. "No, the porch will be fine."

I can't tell from his response if it's truly fine or not. His demeanor gives away absolutely nothing.

"Fantastic! Lyndsay will show you the way. We hope you enjoy your dinner," says Brooke as she hands me menus so that I can take Huck Monahan to his table.

Huck makes eye contact with me. I'm pretty sure he knows who I am. To break the ice, I say, "Follow me, gentlemen. It's a gorgeous night to dine outside."

In a deep baritone voice, Huck asks, "Are you Lyndsay Leach?" as we make our way to the porch.

"Yes, I am. I'm the owner of 518 Farm-to-Table, and we're very happy you're dining with us this evening."

He smiles, another polite smile, and says nothing else. Once again, no indication of whether he's happy to be here or not. I wish I could read this man. But I guess when you have a job as one of the most influential restaurant reviewers on the East Coast, you try not to give anything away.

They both take a seat, and I hand them their menus. While placing the wine menu on the table, I can't help but notice that he does take in the incredible view. Mother Nature is putting on a stunning show tonight, unveiling her calmer demeanor after the storms earlier this week. I also sneak a peek, hoping the calm blue water will assuage the jitters that overcame me when Huck walked through the door. There's perspiration running down my back solely from nerves.

I let them know that Maria will be their server this evening and that she will share this evening's specials. Huck gives me a short nod, and I know that I have been dismissed.

I've done all I can do. It now rests on the shoulders of my staff.

Please, God, let this go well. Please.

AFTER WHAT SEEMS LIKE AN ETERNITY, BUT REALLY isn't, Maria walks back into the kitchen and says, "VIP. Table P7," as Marcus rips the ticket off the order printer. I wait to hear what's been ordered.

"Fire three apps. Duck sliders, scallops, and the app special —Southern clams casino." This is followed by a chorus of, "Yes, Chef."

I see Todd look up from his station at the mention of the clams casino—his signature dish—and smile. He looks thrilled that Huck Monahan is going to try his food. To give it a Southern flair, he's using crumbled jalapeño cornbread instead of breadcrumbs and Tabasco for some additional kick. I tried it before we opened tonight and loved the change-up from what many would consider to be a passé dish.

I grab Maria and ask how it's going. She nods and says fine. Any nerves she may have had earlier in the day are gone, they're just another table to her. A table she will treat to a wonderful dinner.

I can't help but ask, "What else did they order?"

Maria explains that they ordered a bottle of Domaine de Montille Bourgogne Pinot Noir and that Jack, my head bartender, who is also a sommelier, was delivering it as we speak. Jack knows his stuff, and I'm sure he's relishing the chance to serve Huck. Maria says that his dining companion ordered a flight of local craft beers and that after the appetizers, they would be having the New England lobster salad and the Berkshire bacon and blueberry salad, two of our menu staples. For their main courses, they've ordered pan-seared trout, the strip steak medium rare, and the chicken and waffles —trying a variety of things to make sure all of our kitchen staff is up to snuff. But I have confidence in my crew and know that Marcus will double-check everything before Maria takes it to table P7.

Finally, Marcus looks up from his station and gives me a reassuring smile. Whatever bug crawled up his ass earlier seems to have found its way back out. I still wonder where he was this afternoon and what happened to put him in such an uncharacteristic bad mood, but I can't get caught up in it now.

I step back out onto the dining room floor and decide to leave the kitchen crew alone. I need to busy myself while this goes down.

~

I watch as the appetizers head out to the porch, and they look amazing. Plated perfection.

After a little over twenty minutes, Maria passes me on her way back to the kitchen, carrying the three appetizer plates from Huck's table. They have tasted everything—several times —but there is plenty left on the plates. Why is there so much left on the plate? Did they not like it? No, I tell myself, don't panic. They can't eat everything, especially with all they ordered. Surely this must be how food critics operate and how Huck stays so thin.

Maria has been fantastic—attentive but not overbearing— and shares with me that Huck and his companion snapped lots of pictures of each dish with their phones. I know from my research that Huck writes an article for the *New York Tribune* with his review, but that he also shares his dining experience on his Instagram page. If he likes you—and by you, I mean the restaurant's food and service—you can expect that there will be several posts and a reel, and many photos shared to his stories. If he doesn't like you, there will be nothing but his review ripping you to shreds like a feral cat with a well-worn blanket and the pictures to prove it.

Several moments later, Maria breezes by with the salads for our VIPs. Once again, they look fabulous. The cold lobster meat is white with a hint of coral, not translucent, firm, yet not overcooked. It has been draped over a bed of crisp mixed greens, and I note that Huck or his tablemate has ordered the lemon herb dressing on the side. I'm sure it's a test to make sure Maria and the kitchen are paying attention. The blueberries on the other salad are plump, and I can see the lardons of Berkshire bacon and blue cheese crumbles. My mouth is watering, even though I'm too nervous to eat.

As the door to the kitchen breezes open and closed with other staff bringing food to our guests, I can hear Marcus sharing that they are in the homestretch with the VIP table, complimenting them on a job well done, and saying how the pressure will soon be off and onto Candace. Candace laughs and assures Marcus that they will love whatever desserts they order. He tells her he has no doubt.

Whatever Huck writes about us, he can't take away the love and respect I have for my team. They have risen to every challenge, from staff leaving to new menu items to a VIP guest who could make or break us.

Soon, Maria is back with salad plates. These are a touch emptier than the appetizer plates, which I interpret as a good sign, but maybe this is all food critic mind games.

Maria looks at me and gives me a quick wink and says, "As

I was bringing the main courses to table 6 on the porch, I heard Huck's companion say how much he loved the clams casino. They were whispering, but Huck also commented on how the lobster was extremely well cooked. Everything is going great, Lyndsay."

I let out a sigh of relief. I'm so glad Maria put her owl-like hearing skills to work to gather these two little tidbits of information. I feel the bubbles in my stomach start to dissipate. Not enough to eat anything yet, but they are certainly calming down, giving me peace of mind.

Maria heads to the bar to get them some sparkling water and allow them a few minutes to let their food settle, while I go and make a quick pass through the dining room to check on the rest of our guests.

ALL IS WELL, AND BY THE TIME I POKE MY HEAD INTO the kitchen again, I see Marcus is double-checking the three main courses that will be heading to table P7. He adds the garnishes, wipes the plates down, and says to Maria, "They're ready!"

She loads them on her tray, making sure to grab the extra Vermont maple syrup that was requested, and as she turns around to head out to the porch, she bumps into Hannah, another server coming to pick up, and the three plates go crashing to the ground.

To me, it appears to happen in slow motion. The steak, the trout, and the chicken and waffles slowly tumbling, unable to be recovered. Then the sound of ceramic plates breaking.

Hannah's hand immediately goes to her mouth, and she says, "Please tell me that's not for the VIP table?"

Maria nods that it is.

Before another word can be spoken, I yell, "Fire those three VIP meals on the fly!"

A chorus of "Heard" rings through the kitchen.

Marcus looks stunned by my commanding tone in what is most definitely his domain, but he and his staff immediately get to work.

The timing won't be ideal, and I'm sure Huck will notice the delay in receiving his dinners, but what can we do?

Soon enough, Marcus and his team are high-fiving each other as the new plates head out the door. But as quickly as the high fives are completed, they go straight back to work. Just because the entrées are on their way out to our VIPs doesn't mean service is over. There are still tickets coming in and many meals that need to be prepared.

I catch Marcus's eye and mouth the words, "Thank you." He smiles, a big smile this time, winks, and mouths back, "You're welcome."

All seems right again.

I make a loop around the dining rooms again and greet our new guests, asking people how they are doing, if they're enjoying their meals, what plans they have for tomorrow—the standard surface-level table talk I make with all our guests.

After about thirty minutes in the dining room, I beeline for the porch, being sure to start at Table P1, so I can casually make my way down to P7 and see what's happening there. The guests on the porch have no idea who Huck Monahan is, and while this is something I always do—checking in with the guests—I want to make sure it looks like nothing extra special is being done to gain favor with the illustrious food critic.

A lovely elderly couple is seated at P5, and they stop me for a good fifteen minutes, talking about how long they have been coming to Lake George, all the fine restaurants they have dined at, and how this is the very best meal they've ever had. If I had paid them for these kind words, I could not have planned it better. Plus, since they are both hard of hearing, I'm sure Huck overheard them. Heck, I think people in the dining room heard them.

I finally make it to Huck's table, where Maria is just topping off their decaf coffee, and they are enjoying a slice of blueberry shortcake, some apple bread pudding, and the goat cheese and strawberry cheesecake that Candace created special for this evening. I did not try the cheesecake, but from the number of bites that are missing from it, I would say it was a home run. As Maria steps away, I say, "I hope you are both enjoying your evening at 518 Farm-to-Table, and I trust that Maria has taken good care of you. If there's anything that we can do to improve your experience in the future, please just let me know."

Huck's dining companion smiles and says that everything was "lovely." I see Huck bristle, giving him a bit of side eye, as if to say, "You're not supposed to let her know we enjoyed our meal," which makes my heart happy. I'm fine with that "lovely"—it's all I need for now. As for Huck, he just nods and gives me a terse smile. Once again, I've been dismissed.

HUCK AND FRIEND LEAVE AROUND NINE P.M., JUST AS I'm walking the elderly couple from the porch to their car. This little old couple makes me think about how I hope Marcus and I will grow old together, finishing each other's sentences like these two. I smile thinking about Marcus and me dining out together in our eighties and talking to all the staff at our favorite restaurants. This sweet couple asked to make another reservation for early next week, telling me they were bringing their daughter and her husband because "everyone should come here. It's so delicious!" If I had a twenty in my pocket, I would've slipped it in her purse because her raves cannot help but be heard by the departing food critic. Next week, when they return, I will send some prosecco their way.

Huck's car is parked near the elderly couple, and as I hurriedly walk back toward the restaurant—so I can get Maria to spill the tea—I say a quick goodnight to both Huck and his friend. They both say goodnight, then jump into Huck's white Tesla and take off.

ONCE ALL THE GUESTS HAVE LEFT, THE KITCHEN crew, Maria, and I sit down for a bit of scotch and a debrief. The tension that was present earlier, especially coming from me, has melted away. Maria, who tells a great story, walks us through Huck Monahan's meal, detailing the entire evening with a play-by-play that would make the most veteran sports announcer jealous, and Marcus's crew jumps in with color commentary to recount exactly how each dish was prepared and what role they played. Marcus gives each of his crew a heartfelt thank-you and lets Maria know she did an incredible job in what could've been a very stressful situation. Everyone is pleased—more than pleased—about the way service went. With the exception of the delayed delivery of the main courses, there were no missteps that anyone could see, and we dissected every minute of their time here.

We toast to our success, knowing we did fantastic. The execution wasn't flawless, but it was close.

And while our part is over, the anticipation for the review may just about kill me. Recognition from Huck Monahan could catapult 518 into the spotlight. A scathing review could have us closed by Labor Day.

Silently, I say a little prayer that Huck Monahan finds us worthy of a positive review and a feature on his Instagram.

MARCUS CAME HOME WITH ME LAST NIGHT, BOTH OF us too tired for anything more than the comfort of *Sixteen Candles* on the television as we fell asleep. In high school, I always thought of him as my Jake, so handsome and popular. It was comforting to watch it again with him, as we had so many nights when we were dating during our teen years.

This morning, as I roll over and touch the left side of the bed, heat is radiating from him, and he is snoring, which he only does when he's exhausted. I quietly slip out from under the blanket, slide into my robe, and head to the kitchen to make coffee for us.

I still want to ask him where he was yesterday afternoon. When he came back, he wasn't himself. He appeared rattled, which is so unlike him. When he said, "Everything's fine, Lyndsay," I knew that it wasn't. His tone immediately took me back to June of our senior year, when he was hiding his mom's cancer diagnosis and his lack of future plans. I didn't pick up on it then, but every time someone would ask him how things were going or what his plans were, he was brusque and evasive. At the time, I chalked it up to the stress of the end-of-the-year and final exams. It wasn't. It was something much bigger that he just didn't feel comfortable sharing with me at the time. Is the same thing happening now? Is he keeping some sort of secret?

I pour myself a cup of coffee and throw some sourdough in the toaster, grabbing the peanut butter and jelly. When I turn around, Marcus is standing behind me in only a pair of gray sweatpants, his hair disheveled, and the perfect amount of stubble on his cheeks. I kiss him quickly and pour him a cup of coffee as well.

"Good morning, sleepyhead. You must've been exhausted," I say. "You were snoring this morning."

"Sorry about that. I was tired last night, more tired than I thought. I guess the stress of Huck Monahan dining with us got to me more than I let on."

I turn to hand him his coffee, and while he's said the right thing to account for his exhaustion, I feel there's something more.

"So, where were you yesterday afternoon during prep? I arrived, and your crew was hard at work, but they said you had stepped out." I sound like my mom when she used to try to catch me in a lie in high school. To make matters worse, he looks down, avoiding eye contact. This makes my stomach churn. Marcus has eyes that seem to peer through you, and he's always been big on eye contact during conversation. He says a person's eyes tell you all you need to know.

"Oh, it was nothing. I just had to go run a quick errand. I know it wasn't great timing, but everyone knew what they needed to do."

His eyes tell me he's lying, hiding something.

Do I push and try to get the truth from him, or let it go?

Once again, I ask, "Everything's okay?"

"Yup. Can you pass the jelly?

I guess we're changing the subject. It's obvious he doesn't want to talk about whatever happened yesterday. This is how he avoided talking about important things our senior year.

And it was the end of us. Are we heading down this road again?

No, no. I'm reading too much into this. He's allowed to go run an errand. He doesn't have to account for every minute of his day with me.

I pass him the raspberry jam and ask, "What are your plans today?"

"I'm heading to the farmers' market to see what looks good. I've also got a meeting with a couple of vendors. How about you?"

"Writing, writing, writing. I need to get at it soon. Susan has put me on some very tight deadlines to make my publisher happy."

"Well, I'll grab a quick shower and get out of your hair," he says as he pops his last bite of toast in his mouth and heads to the bedroom.

I know he said everything is fine, but it's not, and I need to figure out what's up.

Chapter Twenty-One

I wake up and immediately reach for my phone. Today is the day. Today is the day that the *New York Tribune* publishes its "Upstate Summer Dining Guide." Someone from the *Tribune* emailed me yesterday saying it was coming out.

After ten long days of distracting myself, I will finally hear what Huck Monahan thinks about 518 Farm-to-Table.

I look over at Marcus, who is sleeping soundly, and decide not to wake him, though I can't imagine how he can sleep knowing the review is coming out today. It's been the only thing on my mind since the email yesterday telling me when I could expect Huck's review to go live. I barely slept last night.

I type "New York Tribune" into Google and click to go to their website. The link to the dining guide is on the front page, and even though I'm not a religious person, I make the sign of the cross before going to the special section.

There we are. On the very front page.

RESTAURANT REVIEW: 518 FARM-TO-TABLE

This is how Huck Monahan titles each of his reviews. There is no indication of whether he liked it or not based on the title. You have to read it—for better or for worse. I pull up the duvet so only my eyes are showing, as if I need to hide from Huck's words, and begin reading.

Each summer, new restaurants come and go from the Lake George region. The restaurant business is hard, the guests are even harder to impress, and creating a sustainable restaurant in a tourist area may be the hardest feat of all.

So, when my editor said that I would be, once again, heading Upstate after a several-year break, I had to do some research as to what restaurants had come and what restaurants had gone.

Of course, one of my favorites from previous visits, David's, is one of the restaurants that has left. Due to a very public affair and divorce, chef-owner, David Montero, lost David's to his former wife, Lyndsay Leach. In February of this year, she took ownership and renamed it 518 Farm-to-Table.

Did he have to mention David and David's in my review? Of course, he did. It was one of his favorites. Huck loved David's. But what did this mean for me and 518? I continue reading.

While I was nervous walking into 518 Farm-to-Table, as I am when I walk into any restaurant that is not owned by an experienced chef or restaurant group, I was immediately struck by the sense of professionalism and warmth. We were greeted by a young hostess and then personally escorted to our table on the porch by the owner, Lyndsay Leach.

The porch setting is perfect for those who love to dine al fresco. The waters of Lake George were calm that evening, and there was a slight breeze, which kept the mosquitoes away and allowed my dining companion and me to watch several sailboats enjoying their time on the lake.

Okay. So far, so good.

Nowadays, I find the concept of farm-to-table dining, while trendy, to be often overdone and underwhelming. Ingredients are often not locally sourced, and there can be a distinct lack of uniqueness. That is not the case here. 518 Farm-to-Table has found a refreshing and authentic way to showcase an abundance of local farmers and vendors that are prevalent in the region's agricultural heritage. The menu at 518 sets itself apart with the unmistakable Southern flair infused by head chef Marcus Bremerton, giving it an extraordinary twist to an otherwise overly familiar concept.

YES! YES! YES!

The appetizers set a high bar for the rest of the meal. We started with duck sliders, scallops, and Southern clams casino. The dishes were meticulously prepared and beautifully presented. The Southern clams casino, in particular, stood out with its innovative use of jalapeño cornbread and a hint of Tabasco. What could have been your typical outdated 1970s dish was flavorful and made for a great update. It was a delightful start that showcased the kitchen's ability to blend traditional and contemporary flavors seamlessly.

I may have laughed to myself about Todd's signature dish being clams casino when he initially interviewed, but he just impressed the ever-so-hard-to-impress Huck Monahan with it!

Service throughout the evening was of the caliber I would expect. Maria, our server, was attentive, not intrusive, managing every detail like a seasoned professional. The bartender/sommelier (I didn't ask for his qualifications) was knowledgeable (though slightly too chatty for my taste) about the bottle of Domaine de Montille Bourgogne Pinot Noir and presented it well, while also explaining the curated flight of local craft beers my dining partner ordered.

Our salads, which followed, the New England Lobster and the Berkshire Bacon and Blueberry, were fresh and contained an array of local produce. No iceberg lettuce to be seen. The lobster was perfectly cooked, with a firm but tender texture, and the bacon in the second salad added the necessary crunch, crispy without being overdone. These dishes appeared to hold up to the restaurant's pledge to use fresh, locally sourced ingredients.

Woohoo! Maria had heard him correctly with her secret eavesdropping! The lobster was perfect.

However, the main courses were slow to arrive. An unfortunate kitchen accident delayed the arrival of our pan-seared trout, strip steak, and chicken and waffles. Despite the hiccup, when the dishes finally did make their way to our table, they were beautifully presented and worth the wait. The pan-seared trout was cooked well, the strip steak was the proper temperature and very flavorful, and the chicken and waffles, served with Vermont maple syrup, which I usually view as a brunch dish, struck the proper balance between savory and sweet. The southern influence was evident, but not overpowering, adding a delightful twist to each dish.

I'm not mad about this. Sure, would I have liked the meals to go out on time? Yes. But he said they were "worth the wait."

That's high praise from Huck Monahan when he could have just gone on and on about the delay.

Dessert was the final payoff of an outstanding meal. We tried the blueberry shortcake, apple bread pudding, and a goat cheese and strawberry cheesecake. The blueberry shortcake was light and airy, the apple bread pudding was rich and comforting, and the cheesecake was a nice blend of savory and sweet. No complaints with any of these three thoughtful desserts.

Candace is going to lose her mind when she reads this!

Throughout the evening, the staff's passion was evident. Despite the delay with the main courses, the overall experience at 518 Farm-to-Table was impressive, especially for a newcomer to the industry. The farm-to-table concept felt authentic here, a rare feat in a world where everyone thinks it's their ticket to success. Chef Marcus Bremerton's Southern twist added a unique flair, elevating the dining experience.

While the main course delay was a minor setback, the quality and creativity of the dishes more than made up for it. The fresh, locally sourced ingredients, with a hint of Southern home cooking, show that 518 Farm-to-Table is in it for the long haul. If you want a taste of farm-to-table dining with a distinct Southern flair in a stunning Upstate New York setting, 518 Farm-to-Table is a destination worth visiting. The combination of exceptional food, attentive service, and a beautiful setting makes it a standout in the crowded farm-to-table landscape.

Rating:

I drop the duvet that was covering my face and begin kicking my feet like a child who just found out she is going to Disney World. Holy shit! We did it! Four stars from Huck Monahan! Four fucking stars! Five would've been incredible, and practically unheard of for a new restaurant, so I will take my four stars and be EXTREMELY happy! Over-the-moon happy. Kid on Christmas happy.

All my happy kicking wakes up Marcus.

I shove my phone in his face and say, "Read it! Just read it!"

By the look on my face and my kicking feet that woke him from his peaceful slumber, he knows the review is good, but I want him to read Huck's words, not hear them from me. After all, we've been a team in this since the beginning. This would not have happened without him and the incredible job he's done leveling up the kitchen staff from what some would consider to be a band of misfits to a team of culinary wizards.

I watch his face. He's pleased. I do see him frown slightly at the delay of the main courses, but he's soon over it and beaming with pride.

"Lynds...this is the best review *ever*! This exceeds any expectations I had for the night, especially after the main course debacle. But Huck didn't ding us too badly for that... and he said, 'worth the wait.' Damn right it was worth the wait!"

I laugh. "I know. I can't believe it. He loved us!" I say as I reach over to give him a hug and well-deserved kiss.

He kisses me back with a passion that I thought was missing these last few days, but I'm glad for its return. While he's been with me and at the restaurant physically these past ten days, his mind has seemed elsewhere, his kisses mere pecks. And while I've tried to figure out what's going on, he hasn't opened up, sealed up tight as one of those fresh clams we receive in our daily deliveries. Always saying he was tired from the summer grind and that it was nothing.

I know that's not the case, but I can't force him to open up.

"Have you read any of the other reviews?" he asks.

"No, just ours. I didn't even check to see what other restaurants Huck visited while here."

Yes, now that we've received a fabulous review, I'm going to refer to him as Huck, not Huck Monahan or Mr. Monahan. After all, we're friends now, aren't we? Four stars surely make us buddies. I continue, "I'm sure he stopped in at Montero's Meadow, and I'm sure they received a rave review, but as long as they don't get more than four stars, I'm all good."

I truly mean it. If David doesn't receive a score higher than 518, I will be extremely pleased. It will show that I can play his game, compete in his world.

"Hmmm...let me see," says Marcus as he begins scrolling again. "He hit that new German place. Of course, The Sagamore and that little Mexican cantina with the amazing margaritas and birria tacos." He pauses and smiles because that little cantina is owned by one of his former sous chefs from The Sagamore, and it's a true joint. Nothing fancy. But Marcus looks like a proud father as he skims their brief review. Then he continues. "He visited Acqua Calma. Yikes! Looks like they did not have a good night. The brew pub got great reviews on their beer, not so much on their food. Oh, here it is. Are you ready?" Marcus pauses and then asks, "Do you want me to read what Huck had to say about Montero's Meadow?"

I brace myself for the inevitable incredible review. "Can you just give me the highlights? I don't think I can handle Huck gushing over David."

Marcus clears his throat, as if he's about to announce the

entrance of the President at a black-tie event, a smile forming on his lips, and begins to read.

My recent visit to Montero's Meadow, Chef David Montero's newest endeavor, had me salivating all day in anticipation. After all, my past meals have been nothing short of wonderful. Yet, my meal at this new "farm-to-table" restaurant in Bolton Landing was...nothing but a disappointment. As a critic with a deep appreciation for locally sourced dining, I had high expectations, especially given the owner's reputation. Unfortunately, the evening was a glaring testament to the fall from grace of a once-great chef.

I'm not ashamed that a smile as wide as the Grand Canyon has spread across my face. Marcus shares that he's skipping over what Huck said about the hostess and waiter, which was less than complimentary, and moves straight to the food.

We began with three of the recommended appetizers: Hudson Valley duck pâté, the Adirondack mushroom tart, and a "seasonal" garden salad. The pâté was something I would not serve my cat (not that I have one). Dry, crumbly, and lacking salt, the toast points were the only saving grace. But toast points? Should I have to mention toast points? I guess if I need to find something positive to share, then I must. The mushroom tart description said that it contained locally foraged mushrooms, yet had the unmistakable taste of tin. (Not to mention, an overwhelming amount of button mushrooms.) And, while I would not normally order a simple garden salad, the menu promised a "celebration" of local produce, something I very much needed after a week of eating at some of Lake George's most touted restaurants. Unfortunately, it was a mix of limp lettuce and flavorless cherry tomatoes. Nothing more depressing than a restaurant that can't produce a decent salad.

I'm listening to the words Marcus is saying, but I can't believe them. Huck found Montero's Meadow to be subpar. Below subpar. Montero's Meadow was a failure. I'm ecstatic. And the best part? We're not even to the main course. I mean, maybe he recovers, but it doesn't sound like that's going to happen.

> Our entrées did not improve things. I ordered the pan-seared trout, which arrived at the table looking like it had died a slow, painful death. It was a sad, lifeless piece of fish, void of any freshness. The vegetables were a soggy, bland mess of zucchini and carrots. So bad that I don't want to waste more space here on them. My dining companion's Catskill Mountain lamb chops were simply overdone. Not a hint of pink to be seen. Someone in the kitchen covered them in a generic rosemary sauce, probably hoping to disguise their mistake, but it did nothing to mask the meat's poor quality. I felt sorry for the poor lamb that was sacrificed for this meal. He (or she) deserved better.
>
> Hoping for some glimmer, we turned to dessert. But we were met with only further disappointment. The maple apple pie, while having excellent flavor, had a crust so soggy it might have been used as a sponge. The blueberry cobbler was no better, with a doughy undercooked topping and blueberries that tasted as if they had been picked out of season.

Whoa! Huck Monahan is holding nothing back. This is the critic that chefs fear.

This review is incredibly...awesome if you're me, and humiliating if you're David. I encourage Marcus to jump to the end. I need to know how many stars Montero's Meadow received. It's killing me not knowing.

> My visit to Montero's Meadow was beyond disappointing—it was a culinary catastrophe. The combination of atrocious service, subpar dishes, and the blatant failure to uphold the principles of farm-to-table dining left a sour taste in my mouth. It is a stark reminder that reputation alone cannot sustain a restaurant; authenticity and genuine effort are crucial. I suggest that diners save their time and their money for an establishment that truly values its customers and its cuisine.
>
> Rating:

Marcus looks over at me and says, "Wow! That's worse than his review of Acqua Calma, and he said that their fettuccine 'left a greasy film on the palate and an overwhelming sense of regret.'"

By this time, I am maniacally laughing, laughing so uncontrollably that people would think I need to be committed if I were in public, but I'm not. I'm home, and I'm savoring every bit of David's evisceration by my ol' pal, Huck. So good! So good that I may have to send Huck a bottle of Dom, maybe two, one for each review.

Marcus glances over at me and can't help but laugh himself. He's not one to usually take pleasure in someone else's misery, but even he can't resist.

"This is fantastic. This review makes me even happier than our own," I say. "I don't know how he'll recover from this. Of course, nobody should ever count David out. Somehow, he always finds a way to smell like roses. But for now, he's deep in the shit, and I love it."

I look over at Marcus, and his smile has disappeared, and

he looks quite serious, as if the weight of the world is suddenly back on his shoulders.

"What's wrong?" I ask.

"Nothing. Nothing at all," he says, pasting on a smile that in no way looks genuine. "I guess I'd better get up and get moving. My guess is things are going to be busy at the restaurant today. Plus, you need to do some writing."

He heads for the shower, and while I know I need to figure out what's up with him, I just need to take a few more minutes to revel in our excellent review and David's horrible one. This day makes up for all the crappy days of the last six months.

I have bested David—and it feels fucking amazing.

Chapter Twenty-Two

"Oh my God! Is the phone ever going to stop ringing?" my sweet hostess says with a tiny grimace on her face and a touch of exasperation. But she's got this, and the moment she reaches for the phone, her entire face is a smile, and any trace of tetchiness is gone as she says, "Hello, 518 Farm-to-Table, how can I help you?"

Of course, she knows what they want. A reservation. Which is nearly impossible at the moment. If I'm not mistaken, she's booking into September. I stopped looking two days after the review came out because the pace at which reservations were gobbled up was unfathomable, like Cookie Monster with chocolate chip cookies. There are none to be had in July and August. We were busy before Huck Monahan, but we have reached a whole new level of demand. I know it wasn't a Michelin review, but it feels like it. 518 Farm-to-Table is a bona fide success thanks to all our hard work and some kind words from Huck Monahan.

Huck's accolades ten days ago also meant that we had to hire. I've hired three more hostesses, additional waitstaff, more dishwashers, and two experienced bartenders, and Marcus has added to his kitchen staff, too. Luckily, it's not like when I was trying to hire in February. We are receiving stellar applications. People *want* to work here. People know this place is something special.

And while it's exciting, like hitting the bestseller list exciting, it's also exhausting.

I've been kissing Marcus goodbye every morning as he heads off to the restaurant or the farmers' market or to meet with vendors. I then sit down to write until two thirty p.m., at which time I send my pages immediately off to Susan because they are being edited on the daily. I thought my publisher was insane for wanting to do it this way, but when your publisher takes a chance on you and gives the green light to crash your memoir—you get on board.

After that, I grab a quick shower and I'm here by two thirty, giving me time to check the reservations, sit down for family meal, and catch up with everyone, before the madness of the evening service begins.

And it is madness. We now open at four p.m., trying to squeeze a few more guests in each night, and people are waiting to get in at three forty-five. We always have a few without reservations who give our hostesses the saddest puppy-dog eyes (and usually a fifty- or hundred-dollar bill) in hopes of gaining favor. Luckily, we keep a few tables open, and they can usually slide in a couple celebrating an anniversary or a party of four who want to have a birthday meal together.

But I don't know how much longer I can keep up this pace. Yesterday, while I was Zooming with Susan, she must've seen my weariness because she asked, "Lynds, do you want to be a writer or a restaurateur?"

I didn't know how to answer her.

For as long as I can remember, I've wanted to be a writer. I went to college for writing, and when I graduated, I made it happen. With hard work and perseverance, and more than a little luck, because nobody becomes a bestselling author without a little luck—no matter what they say in interviews—I achieved my dream.

But it's a dream I haven't been able to share with anyone for the last seventeen years. Nobody knows that I'm Leona Lambert, the writer behind all the Fiona novels.

Is it time for something new? A new dream?

Susan didn't make me give her an answer, but her question has been weighing on me like the stack of books on my TBR pile.

I leave the hostess desk and walk back into the kitchen to grab Marcus.

"Hey, got a minute?" I say, smiling at how handsome he looks in his white chef's coat that brings out the silver in his hair.

"Always for you," he says, giving the kitchen staff a few final instructions and telling them to start plating family dinner.

He gives me a quick peck on the cheek and says, "What's up?"

I'd like to ask him the same thing, but it's not going to get me anywhere. Something is still up, but he insists he's fine.

I know it's not the case.

While I may have been naive in high school and missed all his deflecting and secretiveness—mainly because I was so absorbed in my own little world—I can see it now. After the review came out, I saw him take a couple of phone calls in private, purposely moving out of earshot, and he once again disappeared last Thursday afternoon without letting anyone know where he was going. It's so unlike him. He barely heads to the walk-in cooler without letting his staff know where he is.

"Nothing, no VIPs this evening, and only one anniversary celebration. They'll be seated in Michael's section, and he knows to comp them a dessert. Anything I need to know?"

He pauses for just a millisecond, and I get my hopes up that he's going to spill whatever he's been hiding from me, but he doesn't. "Nope, all our deliveries came in today, so we don't have to 86 anything. We should be good."

"Okay, sounds like we're all set then." My voice trails off, wanting him to jump in and tell me that we're not all set, that something is going on, but he doesn't.

Like trying to be both a writer and a restaurateur, I'm not sure how much longer I can go on like this. I keep waiting for him to break up with me like he did all those years ago. I may have missed the signs then, but I'm not missing them now.

It's ten thirty p.m., and the last of the front-of-the-house staff has just left. They once again killed dinner service this evening and have the dining rooms and porch set for tomorrow.

I head back to the kitchen to see where they are with cleanup. Everyone is busy wiping down their stations or wrapping sauces in plastic wrap. I can hear voices in the walk-in cooler and peer in to see Todd showing the new guys where everything should be placed. He gives me a nod, and they get back to it. I look around once more and see that Marcus is nowhere to be found.

"Candace, is Marcus still here?"

She's wrapping up the few slices that are left of her Nutella and strawberry cheesecake, which this evening's diners loved, and says, "Yeah...I think he's out back, probably just grabbing some air."

It is full-on summer here in Upstate New York, which means summer temperatures. And while the kitchen has air-conditioning, it never seems to be enough when you are cranking out hundreds of meals each night. I'm sure he stepped out to suck in a few lungsful of the cool evening air.

I proceed to the back door and slowly pull it open, where I expect to find Marcus on the back step with a glass of scotch in hand. "Hey, Mar...," My voice dies away as I look to see Marcus deep in conversation.

With David. *What the hell? Why is David here?*

David is smiling, a smile that tells me he's up to something. It's mischievous, almost wicked. Marcus looks like he's been caught sleeping with my best friend—which might actually be better than this unholy alliance—and his eyes drop to the pavement to avoid my glare.

But my intrusion doesn't stop David from speaking. In fact, he's like a bottle of Coke that's been shaken and needs to be released. "It's good to see you, Lynds," he says.

And while I wonder why he's here, it doesn't take him long to speak again, going straight for the jugular, "I just stopped by to talk to the new head chef of Montero's Meadow."

A rush of blood and anger and a good dose of hurt makes its way to my head...and my heart. I hear nothing else. Not a single word. Not from David or from Marcus. All I can hear is "new chef of Montero's Meadow." It echoes in my brain like the sound of a lone loon on the lake at night.

This is why Marcus has been so secretive, so distant, so deceitful.

He's going to be David's new head chef.

This is one and the same as breaking up with me. But how can this be? We're a team. Or I believed we were? So much for this partnership. So much for this *structure* that was supposed to protect us.

Get it together, Lyndsay. Don't give either of them the satisfaction.

I don't know how I do it, but I finally bring myself back to the moment and see that Marcus has his hand up to stop David from talking, but David is babbling on about something, which I can't hear over the anger rattling inside my brain. And, more importantly, Marcus is not denying what David has said. I raise my hands and look directly at Marcus and say, between gritted teeth, in a tone that indicates my rage, but not my hurt, "Get your knives and any other personal items you have inside *MY* restaurant and get the fuck out. Leave your keys with Candace. Your services are no longer needed."

We're over—both personally and professionally. I've been stabbed in the back by one of those razor-sharp knives he carries in his knife roll. But I won't give him the satisfaction of seeing me bleed in this parking lot.

I walk to my vehicle, not looking back. Once again, David has fucked me over—and the betrayal hurts more than learning he cheated on me because it involves the man I love. The man I thought I had a future with.

I throw my Jeep into reverse, leaving both men in kicked-up gravel and myself in tears.

Chapter Twenty-Three

O nce I get home, I sit in my Jeep, the tears still falling silently. I quickly text Candace and tell her to expect Marcus to give her his keys and that she should not leave the restaurant this evening without them. I ask her to be at 518 at nine thirty a.m. tomorrow and to tell Todd the same. I can see the three little dots blinking, telling me she's typing a response, but I swipe delete. I can't deal with questions this evening. I just need her to get the keys.

Then I immediately call Chloe.

It's late, but she picks up right away. "What's wrong? Is everything okay?" she says, her voice lowered, her pace slowed, knowing that I would only call this late if something dire had occurred.

I squeak out, "Can you come over now?" in between sobs, my crying no longer silent.

Over the sound of my own blubbering, I hear her say, "Be there in fifteen minutes."

When she arrives, I'm still sitting in my Jeep, head on the steering wheel, mascara running down my face, like the tire tracks I left in the restaurant parking lot. Without a word,

Chloe unhooks my seatbelt, grabs my purse, and helps me into the house.

She sets me on the couch and grabs two glasses from my kitchen and the bottle of scotch from the bar cart, pouring us both more than two fingers.

"Is your mom okay?" she asks. Completely natural to think something has happened to my mom, as we are of that age.

I shake my head and say, "She's fine."

She looks relieved, momentarily, and then says, "Is it Marcus?"

I drain the scotch, determined to get these waterworks under control, and nod.

"Okay...I'll pour you some more. You go wash your face, and then tell me what happened."

I follow her advice, which is the same advice she gave me when she found me crying after Marcus broke up with me in high school—minus the scotch—and return to my spot on the couch after wiping away the so-called waterproof mascara.

She offers me the glass, which I decline, and then asks, "What's going on?"

"Marcus is going to work for David."

I say the words but can hardly believe them, and I can see by the bewildered look on Choe's face that she can't believe it either. She's struggling to understand what I've come to terms with. History doesn't guarantee loyalty. Not with David. Not with Marcus.

"What the actual fuck? He's going to work for David? Is this some cosmic joke?"

I wish I could tell her it was, but I heard the words straight from David's mouth. Marcus is going to be the head chef at Montero's Meadow. "It's not a joke," I say, grabbing a pillow and squishing it into my face, as if that will make this all go away.

I relay everything that has been happening with Marcus over the last few weeks. The disappearances from the restaurant without explanation, the phone calls he always took away from prying eyes and ears, the passionate kisses that had turned to measly pecks.

"I thought he was breaking up with me, to be honest, that's why I thought he was so distant. I figured he was just sticking it out until the end of the busy season. But going to work at Montero's Meadow is the ultimate betrayal because now he's working for my cheating ex, and it's the end of us, or what I thought was us." This betrayal by Marcus feels identical to that of David. No, he wasn't cheating on me per se, but it is an infidelity. In terms of intimacy, loyalty, and choosing someone else over me…it's the same.

Chloe is quiet, letting me sit in my misery before she speaks. "It doesn't make sense, Lynds. Marcus is crazy about you. I can see it in his eyes."

I thought I had seen that in his eyes as well, but how wrong I was.

WHEN I WAKE IN THE MORNING, I AM STILL ON THE couch, covered in a fuzzy, blue throw blanket, and there's a note from Chloe on the coffee table that reads: *I didn't have the heart to move you. Call me later. I'm here for you. Love, - C*

She is always here for me. These last six months, she's been my biggest supporter, helping me pick up the pieces of my tattered and messy life.

But I need to pick myself up. I need to come up with a plan for the restaurant. I need to continue writing this book. (Man, this newest development is going to make for one helluva chapter.) And I need to swear off men for a while. (No matter how good they look in a chef's coat. In fact, no more chefs. Ever.)

Once I'm showered and dressed, I roll out in the Jeep with Phil Collins' "Against All Odds" coming from the speakers. My brain flashes back to the last time Marcus hurt me like this. I listened to this song on repeat on my Sony Discman. I only stopped listening to it when Chloe broke the CD in half and said, "That's enough Phil Collins."

Now, the lyrics hit me like a punch to the gut, each word resurrecting emotions from thirty-five years ago...and from last night. Heartbreak. Anger. Bewilderment. It feels all too familiar. I'm once again reliving the past. It's a cruel loop that I can't seem to get myself out of.

As the chorus swells, I can almost hear Chloe's voice, her version of tough love telling me to snap out of it. But I can't. The tears well up, but I do my best to blink them away, refusing to let them fall.

I'm stronger than I was back then, or at least that's what I whisper to myself.

It's only seven forty-five when I get to the restaurant, and the place is quiet. I haven't been here at this time of the day in a few weeks, since I went back to writing, but I do love it like this. Without all the commotion. No tickets printing. No knives chopping.

I grab the sourdough starter from Candace's prep area. It's in an enormous container now as Candace uses it to make much of the bread we serve our guests. Today I need to immerse myself in the process. Starter, flour, salt, and water. Four simple ingredients that make something so extraordinary.

By the time my dough is mixed and resting, Candace has arrived. She's early. As I knew she would be.

"Good morning," I say, my voice soft. She's looking at me, questions dancing around in her eyes, but she does not ask, only matches my greeting, as she places Marcus's keys in front of me without saying a thing about them.

She grabs her apron and asks, "Thanks for starting the dough. What type of bread are we making today?"

"I was thinking sun-dried tomatoes and mozzarella, and cinnamon raisin," I reply.

"Sounds like a plan. I need to make some biscuits for today and a batch of pies, but I can keep an eye on the dough if you have other stuff to do."

"I'll be here all day, so between the two of us..." My voice fades away as Todd walks through the back door.

"Morning, Lyndsay. What's up? Do we have an early morning kitchen meeting?" he asks. He must've been gone before Candace collected Marcus's keys. He has no idea that the man he looks up to, who has taught him so much, is no longer working here.

"Something like that," I reply. "I need to talk to you and Candace."

Candace puts down the all-purpose flour she was scooping into the industrial mixer and stands next to Todd. I can see the look of fear in Todd's eyes, most likely, he's afraid that he's being fired for some unknown reason. Little does he know he's getting a promotion—even if he's not quite ready for it.

I pull in a breath, letting it sit in my chest long enough so I can compose myself, and then say, "Marcus will no longer be working at 518." I'm unable to prevent the quiver in my voice or a tear from sliding down my cheek.

Nervousness manifests in Todd's eyes at the realization that his mentor—and friend—will no longer be in this kitchen. Candace's eyes reflect confirmation of what she thought was happening last night. They are both silent, waiting for me to say more.

"This is not what I had planned, but this is the situation we are in, and I'm going to be relying on the two of you to help fill the gap here in the kitchen." Gap might be the understatement of all understatements. This is a chasm of epic proportions.

They both nod, neither wanting to ask why, yet still desperately wanting answers I'm not ready to give them. All I can do is offer my leadership as the owner of this restaurant, so that's what I do.

"Todd, you will be moving to Marcus's station starting today. That means you will run this kitchen and the team. If you need additional hands until you can get your feet under you, then call in who you need. Candace, you will work with Todd to take on all ordering for the restaurant. There's a book in the office with all our regular vendors, and you can also hit up the farmers' market as needed. I believe you've been with Marcus in the past?" My voice is cool and even, despite saying his name, despite the chaos swirling in my chest.

Todd has a blank, lagging expression, still trying to comprehend the fact that he will be running the kitchen this evening, and I'm afraid I may have dropped him in the deep end before he's ready. But he does know how to swim. Marcus has shared with me how talented he is, so now he gets to show me. Candace grabs the notebook she keeps in the pocket of her apron and replies with a quick "Yes. No problem, Lyndsay." She's all business and knows this is her opportunity to showcase the skills she has that don't involve her baking a soul-crushingly delicious tart.

By the time Candace walks away to check the walk-in cooler for ingredients, Todd has come to the surface of the water I just dropped him in and says, "I won't let you down, Lyndsay."

I hope he's right. I'm not sure how many more letdowns I can take.

DINNER SERVICE IS...A BIT ROCKY, BUT NOT THE complete disaster I had feared it might be. Some delays getting meals out to guests, one steak that was sent back, and a couple of incorrect side dish substitutions, but nothing that I couldn't smooth over.

What is difficult about the night is seeing how much the staff misses Marcus. How much I miss Marcus. No pats on the back from him at family dinner. No laughter tonight as staff members move from the dining room to the kitchen and back. No winks when I steal a salad from the cooler. It feels like we are all grieving in a way. I guess we are. A member of our restaurant family is no longer with us.

As the crew wraps up, I am sure to thank them all for a job well done, which I can see they appreciate, even if they aren't sure as to why things are like they are. By tomorrow, I am positive they will know exactly what is going on. It doesn't take long for the local restaurant rumor mill to pass along the latest scuttlebutt—and Marcus going to work for David will be the talk of the town.

But I need to stay above the fray. I need to keep my restaurant at the Huck Monahan rating it has earned...without Marcus Bremerton at the helm. And I am determined to do just that.

Chapter Twenty-Four

When I get home, I fall straight into bed, emotionally wrung out, physically spent, bone-deep tired in a way that convinces me I'll be asleep in a matter of minutes.

Since Marcus's departure, it's been months of living a life lit from both ends of the candle. Writing in the predawn hours, then to 518 by midmorning to help Candace and Todd. A few more stolen moments throughout the day, where I manage to jot down a few words between paying bills and processing payroll. Then it's family dinner, dinner service, cleanup, and time to do it all again.

The early weeks were brutal. Marcus was a significant part of the restaurant.

Of me.

While Candace took to ordering food and supplies without missing a beat, Todd struggled. But as with anything, given enough time and praise, and the occasional tough love, he's become a very competent head chef. And now that we're in the slower part of the year, with the throngs of tourists long returned home, the lake sleepy and still, the locals have been more than gracious and continue to keep our reservation book full. I've been able to keep all of our staff employed, and for that I am grateful. We've made it work—without Marcus. Things have changed, but the restaurant continues to excel.

I, on the other hand, have been lost.

His absence sits with me everywhere.

In my bed. In the kitchen. In the quiet pockets of my day.

I miss snuggling up to him at night when he was so exhausted that he didn't seem to move, and I would place my hand on his chest to make sure he was still breathing.

I miss his pats on my ass when I would come behind the line to sample a new dish that he wanted to put on the menu, and his smirks when I gave him a look of annoyance, even though I was far from annoyed.

I miss talking to him on our days off, when we would hit a local market or grab a meal at one of our favorite spots and share things not related to the restaurant, like what our future held.

A future which no longer exists.

But as tired—and heartbroken—as I am, I'm grateful for the distraction of 518 and being able to throw myself into writing my memoir. These are the things that have kept me upright, along with the fact that I have managed not to run into either David or Marcus these last few months. Not sure how that has been achieved, considering how small Bolton Landing is, but someone has been looking out for me.

I send Chloe a quick text, just to let her know I'm alive and well. She replies that she'll stop by the restaurant tomorrow after work to see me. I send her a thumbs-up and then place my phone on the nightstand, hoping that sleep will overtake me.

It doesn't.

Instead, I toss and turn, like a freshly caught fish on a dock, and decide that maybe a movie will help me fall asleep.

What should I watch? An '80s movie, of course, but which one? I land on *St. Elmo's Fire*. You can't go wrong with Rob Lowe and Judd Nelson.

Of course, it opens with David Foster's "Love Theme from St. Elmo's Fire," and the tears start falling. I've avoided these '80s movies like the plague since Marcus left to work for David, but tonight, I need the comfort of something familiar, even if it punches me in the heart.

Even after all these months, I can't help but think about *why*. Why would he go to work for David? Fucking David! It's such a direct blow to my soul. If he didn't want to work at 518, he could've gone anywhere else. Anywhere. But David? I don't understand.

Did his ego make him want to work for a celebrity chef? Was it a prestige thing? A way to establish himself? There have been a few times, after one too many glasses of pinot, that I've wanted to pick up the phone, dial his number, and ask, "Why the hell did you do this?" I've refrained. It was my mistake to bring him back into my life. This is on me. And, while I want to chastise myself for not maintaining the boundaries I told myself I would keep in place when I hired him, I know that even if the boundaries had been maintained, I would still be crushed by his going to work for David.

It's late now, and I turn off the movie, not in the mood to watch post-collegiate angst anymore, even if it is with some of my favorite characters. I need to force myself to sleep. Tomorrow, I have an early call with Susan to talk about my book and its release date.

I attempt to banish Marcus from my thoughts, but he's still rambling through my head as I begin to doze off, and tears dampen my pillow.

~

"Are you ready for it? Your memoir, *The Dish on Starting Over*, releases on March first," says Susan.

"Seriously? That's just under four months from now," I say, still shocked that my publisher got this done so quickly.

"I know, I know. All the kudos go to your publishing team. They worked their butts off to make this happen. Now, Jill and the in-house marketing team have sent out press releases sharing that you will have a new book out *after all these years*," says Susan, with a chuckle. "And that it is a memoir, but there will be no advance copies distributed prior to the release date, as you instructed. Is this still what you want?"

I've flip-flopped on this the last few months, but I know that not allowing anyone to read it before the publication date is the right thing to do. It will create the biggest splash this way and save me from questions that I'm not quite ready to answer.

"Yes, no advance copies."

"You got it," replies Susan. "But I hope you're ready for the stir this is going to cause. Your life is about to be flipped upside down."

Like it wasn't almost a year ago when David announced he wanted a divorce. Or when Marcus went to work for him.

"No worries, Susan. I can handle it. I've handled a lot worse in the past year. A new book is not going to be the end of me," I say with a laugh.

"Nope, not the end, Lyndsay, only the beginning. This is going to be huge!" And with that, Susan hangs up, leaving me to wonder if she's right.

Is this book the start of something big? Something new?

God, I hope so.

Chapter Twenty-Five

Pulling into the parking lot of 518, a dusting of snow swirling under my tires, I can't help but think about how different things are from when I first came up here in February. Not weather-wise. December in the Adirondacks is much like February in the Adirondacks, just with holiday lights. Snow-laden pines bow under the weight of winter. Crisp, invigorating air bites your lungs just enough to wake you up. The partially frozen lake continues to shimmer under the winter sun. These things are a North Country constant.

What's different is *me*.

Last February, I was reeling. Raw from my husband's infidelity, stunned by the announcement that he wanted a divorce. I was bitter and spiteful, and in one of those white-hot moments that only a woman scorned can understand, I took his favorite restaurant. Initially, I only wanted to hurt him, retaliate, but then I used the restaurant as a way to prove myself, reinvent myself. There was also my writing, which was flat, lackluster, and uninspired, but I found a way to reinvigorate it by switching genres. I was lucky. Those who had supported my writing in the past didn't balk at the change. They got on board with the evolution.

I came here in desperate need of a change I didn't know I needed.

A change I have achieved.

Not always with perfection or poise.

But with diligence and determination.

The restaurant is successful despite a...setback. That's Chloe's term for Marcus. She refers to him as The Setback. I try not to refer to him at all, too many tender places, but I appreciate her euphemism.

I grab my laptop off the passenger seat and make my way into the kitchen. The kitchen is warm and alive. Todd is brining chicken. Candace is coaxing chocolate into a glossy ganache that will have our guests swooning over her new raspberry cheesecake. The rest of the crew moves seamlessly, little to no direction needed.

Todd throws a gentle nod my way, and then his eyes distinctly flick to Candace, unspoken words passing from behind the line to her prep area. I wait, knowing that Candace has something she needs to tell me.

"Um, Lynds, you have a visitor in the dining room. I asked him to wait there for you." Her voice is hesitant, as if she didn't want to tell me, but had no choice.

"Okay, want to tell me who?"

From the look on her face, she doesn't. "I think you should just go talk to him."

My heart falls to the floor, hoping, no praying, it's not David or The Setback. It would take immense balls to walk in here now—but David has never lacked audacity, even in situations where he shouldn't have it. And Marcus, well, I haven't seen him since that night. So help me God, I hope he is not on the other side of that dining room door. I don't want to see him now. I'm not ready. I don't know if I'll ever be.

I draw in a steadying breath, bracing myself for the unknown man waiting in the dining room, and walk through the swinging door.

God must be looking out for me because it's neither David nor Marcus seated at the four-top. Instead, it's Anthony, who left 518 in the great staff-poaching spree, when Blake was recruiting my staff for Montero's Meadow like he was a secret agent for the KGB.

"Um, hi, Lyndsay," he says, his voice reserved, his face repentant. "I'm sure you weren't expecting me."

"I can't say that seeing you was on my bingo card, Anthony. What can I do for you?" My tone is smooth and steady, even though my insides are churning, wondering if this is some sort of trick or sabotage that David has cooked up. Or worse, Marcus.

"I know that I did not leave on the best foot," he pauses, as if he's waiting for me to absolve him of his sins, but since I'm not a priest, I will not do that.

After a few additional moments of uncomfortable silence, he continues, "And for that, I am really sorry. David and Blake offered me more money than I'd ever seen before, money that I didn't even know was possible for someone like me."

Once again, he stops, and while I want to tell him I understand, I refrain. He came here for a reason, which I am still unsure of, so I will let him talk.

"Anyway, that's not an excuse. You and Marcus took a chance on me, and I should've known better."

I flinch at Marcus's name—small, reflexive, stupid—and hope Anthony didn't catch it.

Looking down at his feet, a sheen of sweat forming on his forehead, even though the dining room is cool from the December temperatures, Anthony says, "I quit over at Montero's Meadow, a few days ago, in fact, and I know you probably don't want me here, but I'm hoping you can forgive me. Maybe find a place for me on your staff?"

There it is. The ask. The real reason he's here. At least I hope it's the real reason, and not some ruse for David and Marcus to take more from me.

"That's a pretty big ask, Anthony, especially considering how you left." I hate that last part that slides off my tongue. I know Anthony's life has not been easy. I know I should show more grace. I still have things to work on.

"I know, and I've been given more than my fair share of second chances in this life, but I'm hoping you might be willing to give me one more. I need a job, bad."

People say you can tell when someone is lying by looking at their face, searching their eyes. The same can be said for when someone is telling the truth. Anthony is doing just that. His brown eyes reflect his honesty, and I don't have to look too deep to see it.

"Why did you leave Montero's Meadow?"

He runs his hand through his curly hair and says, "I couldn't take it anymore. The constant criticism. The yelling. The demeaning. It made me feel worse than the day I was sentenced to prison. And Marcus tries to protect us from David, but David is relentless. Nothing is ever good enough. It's not a great kitchen to work in, even with Marcus in charge. He's trying, but there's only so much he can do."

Of course. Some things never change, and David running off staff is one of those certainties, like the sun rising in the east and setting in the west. It's always going to be that way.

"I see..."

"Lyndsay, I will do any job, and I mean *any* job. I'll work my ass off. I just need one more chance. I promise. I want to be here. I won't leave again."

I thought the same thing about Marcus, that he wouldn't leave me again, but that was not the case. Yet, Anthony's sincerity is evident, and I can't help but think about the second chance that 518 Farm-to-Table has offered me. How can I say no?

"All right, this has been the year of second chances for me, so why not make it the year of second chances for you? Head back to the kitchen and see Todd. He's running the kitchen now with Candace's help. Go see what needs to be done and ask him to put you back on the schedule."

Relief floods Anthony's face. "Thank you, Lyndsay. I promise I won't let you down," He hurries back to the kitchen, where I can hear Todd and Candace welcoming him back with open arms, before handing him the unenviable task of cleaning out the fryers. A little friendly kitchen hazing that Anthony seems to take in stride.

And all I can think is: *Please don't let me down. Please don't let me down. I don't think I can take another person walking out of my life...again.*

Chapter Twenty-Six

The *Dish on Starting Over* is out today, and the buzz it is generating has been quite something. Susan and Jill started texting me at three a.m., demanding quotes for various news outlets and press releases. Not to mention the slew of remote interviews I did seemingly before the sun had risen.

There were lots of questions about David. About running a restaurant. About my breakup with Marcus (which is handled in the book with much more grace than he probably deserves), but most of the questions were about the biggest stunner I dropped.

How I was able to keep my identity as Leona Lambert a secret for the past seventeen years.

Everyone, from fans of Fiona to newscasters to reviewers, has been flabbergasted that I'm the writer behind this series. And honestly? It's been delightful making jaws drop.

I love that everyone is invested in the twist that my life took. The bestselling novels hidden behind a marriage where my name was barely mentioned. The divorce that rewrote my future. The woman who found herself again in her fifties...in a restaurant she never expected to run.

There is no greater satisfaction than sharing with the world the success you've achieved when people thought you were merely window dressing for a man obsessed with the spotlight.

I am not merely window dressing, not some decorative pair of voile curtains.

Nor have I ever been.

This evening, I celebrated with the people who are most important to me. No big launch party, just a little private fete with Chloe, my mom, and the team at 518. There were way too many bottles of champagne popped and a delicious meal and lots of hugs—and it was perfect. Or as close to perfect as it can be, only missing the one person whom I thought would be by my side for moments like this. But that was not to be.

As I walked through the kitchen to turn off the lights this evening, I wished he had been there to share a celebratory pour of Macallan with me, tell me how proud he was of me, relish in my triumphant return. But he was, most likely, at Montero's Meadow, not where I thought he would be last February when I hired him.

Now that I'm home after such a momentous day, I slide under the blankets, turn off my phone, and mentally prepare myself for another day of interviews, knowing that I will be asked a hundred times, "How did you pull this off, Lyndsay?"

To which I will smile and reply, "Women are capable of extraordinary things when the world underestimates them. Writing mattered to me. Running a successful restaurant mattered to me. This memoir is for all of the women who demonstrate that life doesn't end when things don't go your way."

As I reach for the lamp on my nightstand, ready to sink into sleep, I hear a car in my driveway, crunching on some late-season snow remnants, and headlights sweep through my windows. *Must be someone who got turned around.* Still, my senses are heightened. After all, it's March, and Lake George is still quiet, with just a few of us year-round residents basking in the quiet of the offseason.

But the vehicle doesn't leave, and I hear it come to a stop. I sit up in bed, my pulse quickening, contemplating a call to the police, or at least to Chloe, but something makes me pause. A moment later, I hear the faint sounds of "In Your Eyes" by Peter Gabriel begin to play outside, growing louder by the second, seemingly amplified by the cold night air.

I know who is outside.

There is only one person who would play this song. The person I once believed was my very own Lloyd Dobler. Only he knows how much I love this song and this scene from *Say Anything.* But am I going to be Diane and stay inside, listening to the song, not going out to see him?

That's what I want to do. I want to ignore him. Pull the covers over my head and pretend that I don't hear the soundtrack from the past echoing across the yard. But I know Marcus. He's not going to leave. He will stand there all night if he thinks it will earn him one more conversation. After all these months without seeing one another, he has arrived with a purpose. And that means I have to face him.

But how dare he? On a day so important to me? How can he think he's welcomed or wanted here?

In a flurry of anger, I grab my robe off the striped reading chair in the corner of the room, shove my arms through the sleeves, slide my feet into my Uggs, and march to the front door.

For a heartbeat, I just stare. Why is he here? And what on earth is he holding?

"Turn that off," I hiss. "You'll wake the neighbors."

We both know there are no neighbors. Not until summer.

Not until the lake wakes back up. But I need to say something that isn't *Why now? Why you? Why does my chest hurt seeing you're here?*

He reaches into his truck and turns it down, but not completely off. Peter Gabriel blends in with the sounds of the March winds moving through the trees and the hoots of a lone owl.

"Go home, Marcus. You and I have nothing to say to one another."

"That's not true." His voice—too soft, too hopeful—cuts through my armor. "Lynds, we need to talk."

The familiarity. The pleading tone. It all threatens to unravel me.

"Marcus, we don't have anything to talk about," I snap. "You made your choice months ago. And I made mine." I turn for the front door, desperate to end this scene before it begins.

He closes the distance between us, his hand grasping my arm, gentle, but firm enough to stop me.

"Please," he says. "I know you don't want to see me, but hear me out."

I say nothing and look down at where he has taken hold of my arm, my face telling him that he has crossed the boundaries that are now back in place. He releases me instantly.

"You have three minutes. Talk."

He nods—like a man stepping up to a podium to defend what remains of his dignity.

"Before Huck Monahan came to review 518, David reached out to me to ask if I would be the head chef at Montero's Meadow—which is why I disappeared the day of Huck's visit—to turn him down."

I stay silent. Composed on the outside. But inside? Inside, I'm screaming, "If you said no once, why didn't you say it a second time? Why didn't you choose me twice?"

Marcus swallows hard and continues, "After Huck's

reviews came out, David reached out to me again, asking if I wanted to be the head chef. He said that Blake wasn't cutting it, the kitchen was a mess, and that he didn't have the time needed to get the staff up to snuff with all his other restaurants. So…" he hesitates, one beat too long. "I went to meet with him."

There it is. The moment that splintered everything. I clench my hands inside the pockets of my robe to keep from shaking. And once again, I wonder why he couldn't have just said no.

"He made me an incredible offer, more money than I could ever imagine," he says, his gaze fixed on me. "And I thought really long and hard about it. Most chefs, like me, without celebrity status or an ego the size of Texas, can only dream about the amount of money he was offering."

Leave it to David to throw around cash. To use money as a weapon. It's what he does. Buy loyalty. Buy applause. Buy the one thing I wanted.

The anger simmering in my core isn't for Marcus. Not really. It's for the man who has always believed he owns everything he touches—including people. For so many years, he believed he owned me. Believed I wasn't writing. But I was stronger than him. Even if I didn't know it at the time.

I told myself I would listen, that I would let Marcus speak, but the words claw their way out. "I get it," I say, though my voice betrays me, thin with hurt, sharp with disappointment. "I'm sure the money he offered was incredible, life-changing, and working for David is a dream for most chefs, even if he is a nightmare."

I inhale, buying a moment to steady myself.

"You did what's best for you, for your career," I finish. "I understand that."

And I do. Rationally.

But rationality doesn't soften the betrayal. Rationality

doesn't mend a heart that wanted—just once—to be chosen first.

"Lynds, would you let me finish?" There's an edge to his voice, rare and raw enough to make me swallow my rebuttal and simply nod.

"I declined his offer again," he says, rubbing the back of his neck. "But David didn't accept my no. Instead, he threatened to expose you. To out you as Leona Lambert and make it look like I was the one who leaked your secret. Making it look like I violated the NDA and disclosed who you were. That I was the one who sabotaged your career. He said he had all these contacts who would make it happen, and that if I didn't want to blow up your livelihood and that of everyone working here, then I would come work for him. What was I supposed to do? The NDA is written so that everyone would lose—and not just a little. A lot. 518 needed to stay open. You have a team that depends on you for their livelihoods. For their families."

My breath catches.

That son of a bitch. Threatening to release my name and blame Marcus for it. Just to keep his empire...his reputation... intact. It's hard to fathom how deep David's cruelty runs, yet so perfectly, nauseatingly on brand. Blackmail. He resorted to blackmail to get what he wanted. While it's an escalation of the cruelty, it's one I shouldn't be surprised by.

Marcus continues, his voice low with shame. "So I went, thinking I had no choice, knowing that it would destroy you. Knowing you'd think I'd left for a bigger paycheck and a bigger kitchen. But then today...your book, you told the world you were Leona Lambert, and suddenly, you took away his leverage. David has nothing he can hold over me. I was free. So, I quit."

"You what?" I manage to squeak out.

"I quit," he repeats, firmer now. "Which left David with

nobody. I've been holding Montero's Meadow together with duct tape and dental floss these past months. It's been a revolving door of staff—both front of house and in the kitchen. David's constant yelling and berating scares people off faster than a kitchen fire during the dinner rush."

Marcus pauses, waiting for me to say something, but I have no idea what to say. There's too much crowding my chest: shock, relief, fury, disbelief. Love, buried beneath these things, bruised but not dead.

Looking at me with those blue eyes that I've so missed, Marcus says, "When I quit this morning, and David knew he had no one to help him keep things afloat, he said he was just going to close Montero's Meadow down, take his toys, and go home."

Typical David. And somehow, he'd come off looking like the king. Like this was what he had planned all along.

"But I didn't let him," Marcus says, lifting the papers just slightly. "Instead, I made him an offer."

"An offer for what?"

"To buy Montero's Meadow."

I step back. "You did what?"

"I told him I would buy it," he says simply. "And he agreed. These papers. They're the signed contract. As of tonight, David doesn't own Montero's Meadow anymore."

He lifts the stack a little higher. A white flag. A peace offering. A future?

"I do," Marcus finishes.

Marcus bought Montero's Meadow? But how does this make things better? How does this untangle anything?

As if reading my mind, Marcus says, "I had my lawyer draw up an offer, and David accepted. That's what these documents in my hand are. We both signed this evening. David is no longer the owner. I am."

I'm trying to process all this, but feel like my brain is six steps behind. Marcus no longer works for David. David no longer owns Montero's Meadow. Marcus does.

"Well, congratulations. I'm happy for you," I say, the words tasting like lies. "You'll have your very own restaurant."

He shakes his head. "But I don't want it to be *just* me, Lyndsay." His voice is subdued, as if he knows this is his final chance to get it right. "I want *us* to be the owners. I bought the restaurant for *us*. I want *us* to run it. I want *us* to be a team. Just like 518." He takes a breath, hope flickering in his eyes. "What do you think?"

I stare at him, my voice barely a whisper, and say, "You... you bought it for us?"

He steps closer to me, close enough that I can see exhaustion and longing etched in every line of his face.

"Yes, Lynds. *For us*," he says, each word a vow. "I know I screwed things up. I know I should've just come to you when David threatened to out you. But I panicked. I shut you out— just like I did in high school—and I hate that about myself." His throat tightens with emotion. "I won't blame you if you say you can't do this again, but I really want us to do this. I want to fix what I broke. I want us to build another restaurant together. You have to admit, we did good things at 518 before I screwed it all up. Now we'll have 518 *and* this new place."

As tears prick at the corners of my eyes, I can't help but think he's right. We were quite the duo, taking 518 from nothing thirteen months ago to a four-star rating from Huck Monahan last summer. We were good together. Better than good. But...can we be good again?

Can I believe again? Trust again?

"Marcus," I whisper, "based on what you've said, it sounds like David manipulated the situation to work for him. Like he always does. But you still shut me out. I don't know if I can go down this path again. I took a chance on you last February—

with my heart and my restaurant—and you didn't trust me enough to tell me what was going on."

The wind whips around us. Peter Gabriel continues to drift through the trees on repeat. He waits.

I hesitate.

"I get it, completely get it." His voice cracks. "But Lyndsay...please, give us one more chance."

His eyes are misty and pleading, and while it's late, the full moon and a sky full of stars allow me to see all of him, every vulnerable part of him. The man who left, the man who returned, the man willing to put everything on the line.

"Lynds, we are Lloyd and Diane—meant to be together, we're a team. We always have been." He pauses, as if summoning courage, and continues, "Are you in or are you out? Can you forgive me? Can we get past this? Can we try again? Because there's no one else for me but you. I need you, Lynds. I can't do this without you. I love you."

The owl has stopped hoo-hooing, as if nature is holding its breath.

And suddenly, everything clicks. My brain has processed Marcus's words.

David is the bad guy.

Marcus is here.

And he bought Montero's Meadow...for us.

As much as I want to pretend I'm stronger than my heart, I can't. I've already lived that version of my life where Marcus wasn't in it. Twice. And both times, I was left wondering... what if?

When we got that second chance this past year, it felt like destiny course-correcting. Like the love story I needed. The love story I finally believed I deserved.

There's only one thing to do.

I can give second chances a second chance.

I step forward, wrap my arms around him tight, whispering in his ear, "I'm terrified, but I'm in. All in. So don't you let me down, Marcus Bremerton. I don't think I can handle it again."

Without another word, Marcus pulls me into a kiss, one so deep and filled with promise that it feels like the stars and the moon and the owl themselves are cheering us on. His arms lock around me, and for the first time in what feels like forever, the weight of it all—David, the past—melts away.

When we finally pull apart, his forehead rests against mine, and he grins, that boyish, hopeful grin I fell in love with all those decades ago.

"We're going to make this work, Lynds. Together," he says, his voice steady and sure. "This new restaurant is just the start. We're going to build something incredible—and I don't mean professionally."

I laugh, brushing my fingers against his cheek. "I have no doubt, Marcus, no doubt whatsoever."

"Good," he says, his azure eyes sparkling. "Because like I told you a little over a year ago, you and I are kismet, Lynds, meant to be together, no matter what."

Another tourist season is commencing in Lake George. Pontoons and wave runners are on the water, zipping from Bolton Landing to the village, the sound of boat motors and laughter echoes off the lake. Cars from New Jersey, Pennsylvania, and Massachusetts cruise the streets looking for a place to park, honking when someone beats them to a coveted spot. The sidewalks are flooded with couples and families as they take in the sunshine and buy just one more T-shirt before they head home.

As I enter the kitchen, I hear Marcus giving the new staff instructions.

"Candace, can you show Elizabeth how to make biscuits? She'll be backing you up this summer," he says.

"Yes, Chef," Candace replies, while giving me a quick wave.

For 518 Farm-to-Table, it's another summer with endless reservations. We have three culinary students from the CIA working at 518. Marcus reached out to some of his instructors and asked if they could recommend any talented student chefs who wanted to gain experience in our kitchen. They sent us three incredibly hard-working young women who are renting out Marcus's house for the summer...because we're living together at my place.

Our place.

"Lynds, did you stop by the pub? Does Todd have everything he needs?" Marcus asks, without looking up from the chives he's chopping.

"Yes, he's good. His order arrived this morning," I reply, waiting for him to look up, so I can see his smile and big blue eyes.

He shows me both, which never fails to brighten my day, and continues with prep.

Close by, at L&M's Gastropub (yes, it's named after me and Marcus), people begin lining up at four thirty in hopes of getting a seat for dinner, since we don't take reservations. Yes, we did it. We successfully opened a second restaurant, this time with a bit more casual vibe, more family-friendly. Todd is at the helm there, moving over from 518. He was hesitant to leave the kitchen he started in, but we believe in him, and he hasn't let us down. The pub serves gourmet burgers and sandwiches, fish and chips, smothered fries, and mac and cheese with all sorts of decadent toppings, and craft ales that have made it a must-visit for beer connoisseurs from near and far. Occasionally, on the cooler days, Marcus's mother's stew makes an appearance on the menu, always selling out before the night is over.

In late March, Marcus added me to the deed of L&M, and I did the same for 518.

We are fifty-fifty partners in this, in all of this—and I love the life we're building.

We've found a second chance, or now that I'm in the restaurant biz, I think of it as a second course.

David used to say that the first course was the most crucial part of the meal. It was your opportunity to make an impression, to deliver the wow factor.

But what if that's not the case? What if your first course is a disaster? What if it doesn't deliver on all that it promised? What if it leaves a bad taste in your mouth?

That's why you have second courses.

You can take another stab at it.

Second courses are an opportunity for redemption. An opportunity to make things right. An opportunity to get that bad taste out of your mouth and replace it with something delicious and satisfying.

And that's just what I did.

I have a second chance at love with Marcus and at a career, but not as an author. I haven't written a word since I turned in the final draft of my memoir—and it's okay. As much as I needed to write when I was married to David, maybe because he didn't want me to, maybe because it was a means to keep important parts of myself alive, I don't feel that way now. I still do the occasional interview about my books, and, of course, people ask when they can expect to read my next novel, to which I respond, "I don't know if that will ever happen, we'll have to see." Some are disappointed in my response, but I know those who read my memoir, and really connected with it, understand. One reader said, "I read this book hoping for all sorts of juicy secrets, and it delivered. But *The Dish on Starting Over* isn't just a tell-all, it's a story about how Lyndsay Leach learned to love—love herself and discover a love for a new chapter in her life. While I am sad that I may never get to read new books from her going forward, you have to respect a woman who has found what makes her happy."

That reader was correct. I am happy. It's a simple word that, as a writer, I often tried to avoid, thinking it didn't have enough substance, didn't convey the full emotion my character was feeling at the time. But what's wrong with being happy?

Of course, if I ever decide I want to return to writing, I can. There's nothing stopping me from going back to it, but for now, I just want to enjoy this second course of my life. My life with Marcus, my life as a restaurateur, has made me extremely happy. And that feeling, that happiness, it's all I need at the moment. I am going to savor this second course life has brought me and hope that the third course is just as good.

But if it's not, I'm not worried.

There will be additional courses in life. And each course may be different. Some sweet, some bitter, some unexpected— but together, they create a meal worth celebrating. Each of them offering a chance at a new beginning.

Acknowledgments

Writing *Second Courses* has been one of the best parts of my midlife—proof that reinvention isn't just possible, it's powerful. This book began as a spark about what happens when a woman decides she's not done growing, dreaming, or choosing herself. I wrote it to celebrate women in their fifties who are still evolving.

And I never could have done it alone.

To my husband, Blaine—thank you for being the steady, grounding presence that gives me the freedom to chase big ideas. Thank you for not zoning out when I read you my favorite lines of the day or tell you the next idea I have for a book, even though the current one isn't finished. Your encouragement, patience, and humor made this book possible. I'm thrilled that we met in Lake George all those years ago and that I never said the words "apple pie."

To my sons, Caleb and Grayson, thank you for always making me laugh when I talk about the romance books I'm writing (yes, others are on the way). You've grown up watching me build chapters in my own life as we've moved around the country and around the world, and I hope you both carry that with you. Reinvention is always an option. Relevance isn't something you age out of. I'm proud of the men you are, and I love that you get to see me doing something I love.

NC Barton and Stephanie Pohnl, my romance writing girlies—you are the most amazing women! Thank you for reading more versions of *Second Courses* than any human should reasonably endure (and not banning me from the group chat with my 67 gazillion variations of this book cover). Your ideas, knowledge, and constant encouragement (along with the laughs) are the best part of this journey.

To my alpha and beta readers—Aspen Brown, Betsy Swenson, Cheri Hart, Michele, my mom (who could provide no notes—as is to be expected), Jill Robinson, Danielle M., Caro Townsend, Lee (and anyone else I may have let read in the early stages—please forgive me if I don't have you listed)—I hope you can see bits and pieces of your feedback throughout this final version. I think I took at least one thing from each of you, and I know it made this book better.

Erin McClary, you are the best developmental editor around! Thank you for seeing Lyndsay and Marcus so clearly from the beginning. Your ability to see what this story needed —even before I did—shaped this book in profound ways. You said from day one that this book wanted to be a romance. I dug my heels in (because I have a rather large stubborn streak) and insisted it was women's fiction. In the end, it turns out it's both—but romance wins. Thank you for helping me see that, even if it took me a hot minute (well, more than a hot minute —more like a couple of years) and several drafts to come around.

Kate Underwood, my copy editor and proofreader, I can't thank you enough for giving this manuscript its final shine. Your sharp eye and care elevated every page. You caught what I missed and helped this book step confidently into the world. I'm grateful for your attention, your skill, and the generosity you bring to the table. You always go above and beyond!

I also have to thank The Tastemakers because there is something so important about women helping women. This very special group, comprised of Susan Poole, Michele Eicher, Suzy England, Shannon Stannard, Annie Cathryn, Elyse Dawn, Erin Lyons, Maggie Mulloy, Linda Sienkiewicz, Kelly

Selby, and Lee Currie, graciously stepped up to help a debut author out, and I'm so grateful. Muah! Sending each of you big virtual hugs and kisses!

A huge round of applause to my ARC readers and all those who have shared about Second Courses on social media. Thank you for your care, honesty, and cheerleading.

To my family and friends, thank you for asking about my writing and liking and commenting on my social media posts when no book even existed.

To my writing community—thank you for always cheering me on. You know how hard this is. A special shoutout to Beth M., Barb K., Ann W., WFWA, and WLT members in particular!

Lake George and the Adirondacks, what can I say? I love you. You are always a place of inspiration. It is why I count down the days until I return here each summer—despite eighteen-year-old me saying that she wanted to live in a big city far, far away (been there, done that—give me the quieter life in Upstate NY!). And to the many restaurants where I worked—chefs, past coworkers, old friends (even a boyfriend or two), and the culinary world I've watched up close—thank you for giving me the behind-the-scenes details that helped breathe life into 518 Farm-to-Table.

A special thank you to the em dash—the punctuation mark that I adore so much. You're dramatic and overused, and oh-so essential. I couldn't have written this book without you.

And finally, to the readers: Thank you for picking up a story about a woman who isn't finished. Not with dreams, not with growing, not with love, and certainly not with her next chapter. Thank you for wanting stories about reinvention and romance at every age. Writing *Second Courses* reminded me that relevance isn't something you wait for—it's something you grab and hold onto for dear life. Thank you for letting me share this one with you.

Robin Blackburn is a contemporary romance and women's fiction author whose stories center on second chances, reinvention, and the beautifully complicated seasons of midlife. A native of Queensbury (in Upstate New York), she grew up surrounded by Adirondack lakes, gorgeous mountains, and all that the area has to offer—an influence that now runs through much of her writing.

She earned her BA in French Language and Culture from Penn State University and later picked up a Master's in Education from SUNY Albany. Robin spent nearly a decade in education, first teaching high school and later helping other teachers bring technology into their classrooms.

Along the way, she met her husband, Blaine, and life began

to expand in all the best ways. Together they've spent more than two decades raising their two sons, Caleb and Grayson, while moving across the U.S. and around the world. They've lived everywhere from New York, Iowa, Wisconsin, Ohio, and Texas to international stops in Kuala Lumpur, Malaysia, and Warsaw, Poland. These days, she splits her time between Houston, Texas, and her happy place on Lake Hadlock in Upstate New York. (Or, as she likes to say, "A million dollars south of Lake George.")

Long before becoming an author, Robin spent many summers working in Lake George restaurants, and, yes, dating her fair share of chefs. Those experiences stuck with her and eventually found their way into her storytelling. Somewhere between lake summers, big moves, and building a full, busy life, writing shifted from something she loved to something she couldn't ignore.

Now a writer and content marketer, Robin brings a warm, lived-in authenticity to everything she creates. Her debut novel, *Second Courses*, is set in the Lake George region and celebrates what happens when life goes off script and you decide it might just be the start of something better.

You can connect with Robin on Instagram at @robinblackburnwriter, or visit her webpage, robinblackburnwriter.com, for the latest information.